How To Die And Survive

Book One

Interdimensional Psychology, Consciousness, and Survival: Concepts for Living and Dying

KEYS TO
CONSCIOUSNESS AND SURVIVAL
SERIES
Volume 4

Dr. Angela Brownemiller

INTERDIMENSIONAL PSYCHOLOGY, CONSCIOUSNESS, AND SURVIVAL

HOW TO DIE AND SURVIVE

How To Die And Survive

Book One

Interdimensional Psychology, Consciousness, and Survival: Concepts for Living and Dying

KEYS TO CONSCIOUSNESS AND SURVIVAL SERIES
Volume 4

Dr. Angela Brownemiller

Illustrated By
Angela Brownemiller

METATERRA® PUBLICATIONS

INTERDIMENSIONAL PSYCHOLOGY, CONSCIOUSNESS, AND SURVIVAL

Metaterra® publications
How To Die And Survive, Book One

Interdimensional Psychology, CONSCIOUSNESS, AND SURVIVAL:
CONCEPTS FOR LIVING AND DYING

Keys To Consciousness And Survival Series, Volume 4

Copyright © 2021, 2020. 1998, 2000, 2005, 2010, 2013, 2014, 2015, 2018, 2019, Angela Brownemiller.

Copyright © 2021, 2020. 1998, 2000, 2005, 2010, 2013, 2014, 2015, 2018, 2019, Metaterra® Publications.

All rights reserved in all formats and in

All languages and dialects known or not known at this time.

Published in the United States by Metaterra® Publications.

HYPERLINK "http://www.Metaterra.com"

Www.Metaterra.com

Library of Congress Cataloging-in-Publication Data.

Brownemiller, Angela.

HOW TO DIE AND SURIVIVE

Angela Brownemiller.

1. Survival. 2. Evolution. 3. Consciousness. 4. Psychology. 5. Biology.

6. Ecology. 7. Future. 8. Spirituality. 9. Metaphysical. 10. Interdimensional.

11. Science. 12. Science Fiction. 13. Brownemiller. 14. Browne-Miller.

15. Dr. Angela.

ISBN-13: 978-1-937951-25-2 (Paperback on Amazon).

See Amazon.com for ebook (Kindle ebook).

Published in the United States of America for US and worldwide distribution.

Metaterra® Publications. Metaterra.com

Cover and content illustrations, Figures, photographs, by and copyright ©Angela Brownemiller, with the exception of the illustration by Gustave Dore. (Dore illustration is public domain.)

Book and cover design by and copyright ©Angela Brownemiiller.

Ordering information and bulk ordering information available through:

Amazon Paperback, Amazon Kindle, Audible. Amazon.com

Drangela.com

All rights to all printings, formats, and editions reserved. No part of this book may be reproduced or transmitted in any form or by any means (written, printed, audio, video, other manual, electronic, or mechanical, or other means), including but not limited to photocopying, recording, transcribing, writing, or by any copying, information storage, and or retrieval system, without prior written permission from the author, publisher, and copyright owner, except for the inclusion of brief (20 to 30 word) quotations in a professional review. Additionally, all cover and interior illustrations, Figures, and diagrams have been created by this author and illustrator and cannot be reproduced without this author's written permission. Thank you.

Dedication...

**How To Die and Survive:
Interdimensional Psychology,
Consciousness, and
Survival:
Concepts for Living and Dying**

Is dedicated
To defenders of the
Life Force
And its
Free Will
In all dimensions.
Subterra Surgit.

Speaking for the
Right use of Will
In the name of the
Ever purest
Ever highest
Vision
Of everlasting
Ever conscious
Light.

INTERDIMENSIONAL PSYCHOLOGY, CONSCIOUSNESS, AND SURVIVAL

> ... though I walk
> through the valley
> of the shadow of death,
> I will fear no evil ...
> *Psalm 23*

BEFORE YOU BEGIN

Readers, note that this book, ebook, and audiobook, as well as the other *How To Die And Survive* books, ebooks, and audiobooks which follow this book, and all the books in this *Keys To Consciousness And Survival Series*, are provided for educational and informational purposes only. These books, ebooks, and audiobooks do not provide medical advice or professional services. The information provided should not be used for diagnosing or treating a mental or physical health problem or disease. Always seek the advice of licensed professionals such as your doctor or another qualified health provider regarding a medical or psychological condition. Never disregard professional medical advice regarding physical health, or professional psychological advice regarding mental health, and never delay in seeking this. If you think you may have a medical or psychological emergency, call 911 or go to the nearest emergency room immediately. Thank you.

MEET INTERDIMENSIONAL PSYCHOLOGY

The study of the fantastically mysterious and complex human mind has been underway, perhaps as long as we can remember (or longer). While certainly a great deal of valuable, substantial, and exciting progress has been made, it appears to me that we, and our sciences and treatments, must now expand our understanding of the human mind to additional new arenas.

This expansion of our understanding of who and what we are, of who and what the human mind and consciousness not only are but can be and become, is essential.

We are at a moment in our development and even evolution, in our history and our future, of magnificent opportunity, against the backdrop of potential great crisis. We can step forward, in our lives, in our treatments of the human mind and its issues, in our work with and for our species and all life on Earth, and formally move into *interdimensional* definitions and awareness of ourselves.

This expansion is essential. For this reason, I have defined what I am describing as the expansive field of Inter-dimensional Psychology (in the book I have accordingly titled, *Interdimensional Psychology*).

Interdimensional Psychology opens important doors to essential levels of understanding. We can bring this additional expanded definition of what is happening to us and within us, to understand so much more about ourselves. This can help us in our daily lives as well as in our work. For example, in the mental health and mind-body care fields, we can extend what we presently see, label, diagnose, and treat to realms where we can see much more of what is happening.

In these so-called modern times, we have expanded our venues in so many directions. We have brought ourselves to this point in time where this next step, formally calling this field I speak of here, Interdimensional Psychology, is clearly essential.

Think back to the popularity of the term, holistic, as it came (back) into vogue for a while. This term brought with it the understanding that we have to see ourselves, and our mental and physical health care treatments of people, on multiple levels at the same time. For example, many treatment programs, such as those addressing addiction, some decades ago even began describing their programs as holistic, telling us they were going to be treating the whole person on all levels such as psychological, nutritional, physical, spiritual, and so on.

While this was a valuable opening to the understanding of the multiple dimensions of our existence and our experience and even our conditions, this was just an opening. As I see it, the next step is to extend this holistic view, or multi-level view, to a truly multi or better stated, inter, dimensional view. Indeed, I note that we have arrived here in our lives, in our minds, in our work with each other, even in our diagnosis and treatment, in our health and mental health care, and yes, even

in our social policies, ready to and needing to take this next step.

We are ready to formally expand our understanding of our minds as themselves being multi, even inter, dimensional, being more than simply physical functions of biological organisms and organs. We are ready for this field of Interdimensional Psychology to emerge and define itself, even eventually to lead the way.

Of course, all this speaks to a profound and oft overlooked matter, which is that perhaps we are not only physical plane beings, but already interdimensional beings.

As Readers of this and the following *How To Die And Survive* books,[1] and other books in this *Keys To Consciousness And Survival Series* will see, the entire matter of our mind being entirely defined by our biological brain is open to question. And where we may be tied entirely or largely to our biological brain, I note that we have the distinct option, and even perhaps the necessity, of also concurrently evolving outside this brain.

WE CAN REACH BEYOND BIOLOGICAL LIMITATIONS ON OUR MINDS AND CONSCIOUSNESS-ES.[2] WE CAN

---

[1] This present book, *How To Die And Survive*, is followed by the book, *How To Die And Survive, Book Two*. These are *Volumes 4 and 11* in this *Keys To Consciousness And Survival Series*.
[2] Refer to *Volume 10* in this *Keys To Consciousness And Survival Series*, titled *Seeing Beyond Our Line Of Sight*.

REACH BEYOND LIMITATIONS ON WHO WE THINK WE ARE.

We provide government and corporate astronauts with very specific training for their "space" journeys. Why not provide everyone with training for their journeys into the obvious and subtle, psychological and spiritual, energetic and visceral, changes and unknowns of their lives and minds, into places and spaces beyond, or truly within, the "right here, right now"?

We can make these leaps in our understanding, awareness, capability, this expansion into the realm/s of our SELVES, once we know these leaps are there for us to realize.

I have defined these leaps to teach processes of awareness-expansion in daily living, and in changes, transitions, endings, even minor and major non-physical and physical transition and death processes. Seeing the *continuity of our consciousness*, generating the range of in-life and so called end-of-life perceptions, can open doors to us, essential expanses of both the cosmos and ourselves.

These LEAPS, these processes of *interdimensional awareness, consciousness, shifting, survival*, are forms of what I describe as *interdimensional consciousness*[3] and its conceptual travel. (Note that the consciousness itself can see itself as traveling to many non-physical locations, as the consciousness itself is not

---

[3] See the book, *Interdimensional Psychology*, where I develop and define this field of interdimensional theory, study, and treatment of the mind and psyche.

necessarily bound by physicality and physical distance.[4])

Yes, this is knowledge we have a *right to,* such as: how to have our awareness access higher dimensions of our realities; how to have our awareness-es learn to consciously "deliver" ourselves to new phases, stages, states of mind, new dimensions of ourselves and our lives, to "ascend" to these dimensions, thus to "liberate" ourselves from being restricted to having little or no truly conscious access.

(For some Readers, this will also be about not being restricted to only the material plane.[5] Readers will choose to take this information in according to their own beliefs, interests, and needs.)

I offer this book, *How To Die And Survive, Book One,* and the following book, *How To Die And Survive, Book Two,* and all the books in this *Keys To Consciousness And Survival Series,* to define and introduce the Interdimensional Psychology I strongly suggest should become a formally defined field of existence, and of diagnosis, treatment, teaching, research, policy, and more.

Dr. Angela Brownemiller

---

[4] See *Volume 10* in this series, *Seeing Beyond Our Line Of Sight*, and *Volume 3* in this series, *Unveiling The Hidden Instinct.*
[5] I explain these matters in greater depth in *Volume 3* in this series, *Unveiling The Hidden Instinct.*

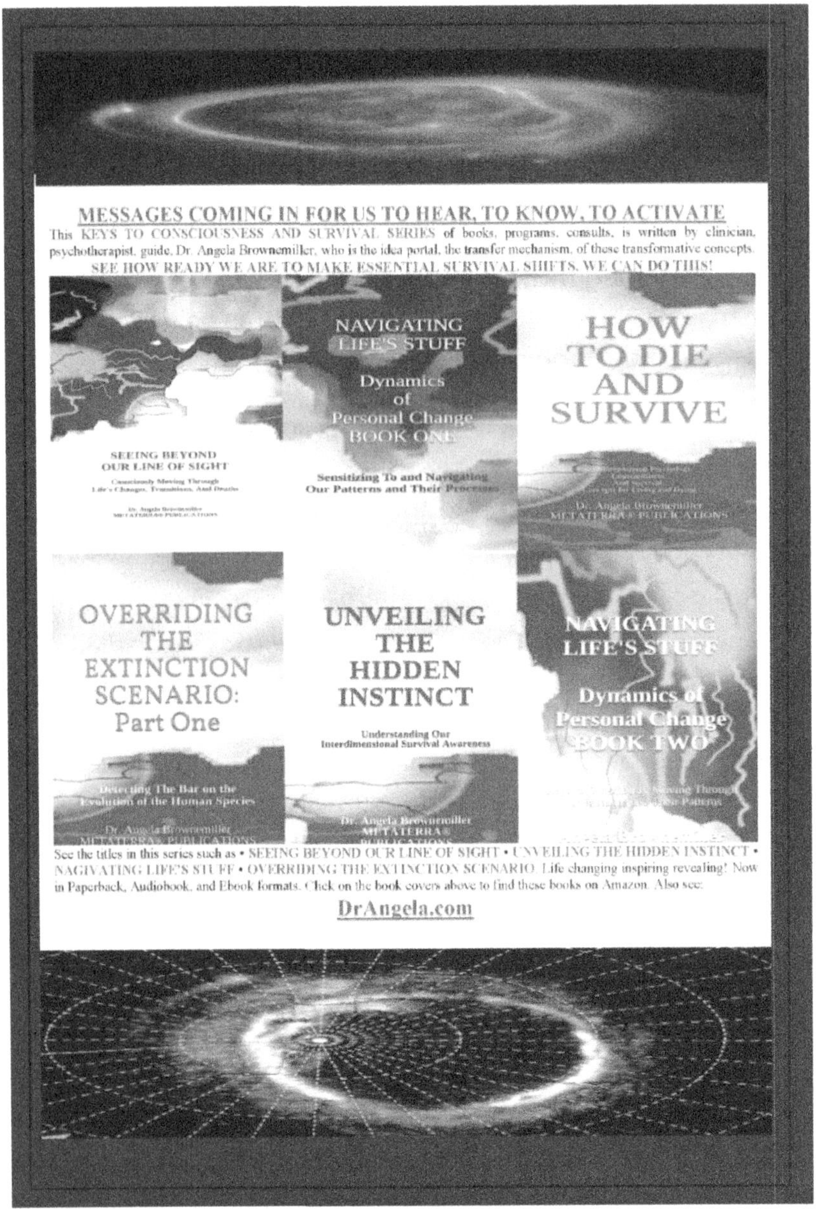
MESSAGES COMING IN FOR US TO HEAR, TO KNOW, TO ACTIVATE
This KEYS TO CONSCIOUSNESS AND SURVIVAL SERIES of books, programs, consults, is written by clinician, psychotherapist, guide, Dr. Angela Brownemiller, who is the idea portal, the transfer mechanism, of these transformative concepts.
SEE HOW READY WE ARE TO MAKE ESSENTIAL SURVIVAL SHIFTS. WE CAN DO THIS!
SEEING BEYOND OUR LINE OF SIGHT
NAVIGATING LIFE'S STUFF
Dynamics of Personal Change
BOOK ONE
Sensitizing To and Navigating Our Patterns and Their Processes
HOW TO DIE AND SURVIVE
Dr. Angela Brownemiller
METATERRA® PUBLICATIONS
OVERRIDING THE EXTINCTION SCENARIO: Part One
Detecting The Bar on the Evolution of the Human Species
UNVEILING THE HIDDEN INSTINCT
Understanding Our Interdimensional Survival Awareness
Dr. Angela Brownemiller
METATERRA®
NAVIGATING LIFE'S STUFF
Dynamics of Personal Change
BOOK TWO
See the titles in this series such as • SEEING BEYOND OUR LINE OF SIGHT • UNVEILING THE HIDDEN INSTINCT • NAGIVATING LIFE'S STUFF • OVERRIDING THE EXTINCTION SCENARIO. Life changing inspiring revealing! Now in Paperback, Audiobook, and Ebook formats. Click on the book covers above to find these books on Amazon. Also see:
DrAngela.com

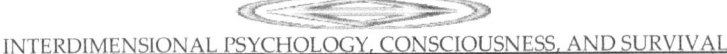

KEYS TO CONSCIOUSNESS AND SURVIVAL SERIES
Foreword

Just as the fish itself did not discover water, we ourselves have perhaps inadvertently demonstrated the obvious, which is that we cannot entirely, absolutely, know what all it is "we" are immersed in, nor even what all it is that "we" are.

Ultimately, the question of the hour, the question of our times, the question of our reality, is regarding this thing we call our consciousness. Do we identify with our consciousness, is it *of* us, is it *us*, is it *more* than we are, or is it simply a *side effect* of life?

The question as to whether the amorphous consciousness is itself *derivative* of biology, or is itself *independent* of biology (and perhaps even independent of *what any intelligence can entirely discover of itself from within itself* and its tools), will reveal itself to be irrelevant. This stunning shift in understanding will happen once we recognize that our elusive consciousness can at any point be redefined, or redefine itself to itself—or even shift into (or back into) independence of biology, stepping out of evolutionary, synaptic, and conceptual controls, into existence independent of human science, religion, philosophy, even of the human brain itself—much like a grown child leaving home.

As they depart, we can speculate that our consciousness-es are in a sense like our children, in that they are apparently born from us—a speculation no artificial or machine intelligence (as yet incapable of actual procreation and actual biological parental ties) can do unless consciously programmed to be able to do. Our children, once they consciously leave home, their consciousness-es in tow, can grow up to consciously be who they already are.

Get ready, even the human Consciousness is going to break free of the confines of its biological host bodies here on Earth. It's been a nice visit, but the time will come to go …

… or at least to expand to concurrently access the full range of ourselves and the continuum along which, the matrix within which, we really do live.

Dr. Angela Brownemiller
Dr. Angela
Drangela.com

LEAP Level	LEAP Form	LEAP Description
One	Embracing	Accepting, feeling ready for, fully moving into the concept of shift (or death) out of a dimension, or phase or stage of life or mind, or out of the physical body itself.
Two	Quickening	Raising the presumed or actual energetic vibration or frequency of one's consciousness; pulling together the focus to go into another dimension and/or to go through a major transition in life, or a physical death.
Three	Willing The Exit	Focusing the Will in such a concentrated way that the exit from the dimension or phase of life or physical body is energized, facilitated.
Four	Leaping To The Next Dimension	Moving the consciousness in such a manner that it shifts, leaps, out of its current or present format or dimension of its reality, generally occurring after its exit from the dimension, or phase of life, or if biological, then the physical body it has been in.
Five	Ascending	Moving the consciousness in such a manner that it ascends into what may be experienced as higher frequencies, higher realms of Light, or higher dimensions of its/the reality.
Six	Catharting Beyond	Using the energy released by shifting, breaking, leaping, out of a dimension or phase of life or physical body to move well beyond the realm of existence, or format, being left.
Seven	Meta-scending	Realizing the effects of transition or death and or ascension and interdimensional travel without appearing to have a phase of life or a physical body die.
Eight	Achieving High Metaxis: The Meta-LEAP	Achieving the highest possible range, or dimensional span, of oneself. An intentional inter-dimensional shifting, an energetic reformatting, the essential LEAP-ing, without depending on actual physical death to propel.

BASIC LIGHT-ENERGY-ACTION-PROCESSES (LEAPS)
Keys to Interdimensional Travel: Eight Levels

HOW TO DIE AND SURVIVE
TABLE OF CONTENTS

Dedication	5
Before You Begin	7
Meet Interdimensional Psychology	9
Keys to Consciousness and Survival Series Foreword	15
LEAP Chart	17
List of Figures	21
List of Exercises	23
Author's Note	27
Introduction to How to Die and Survive: What This Book is All About	29

PART I: Preamble to What We Think of as Death   49

1. Learn How to Shift, Transition, Die Out of Patterns and Lives	51
2. Being Part of a Dying System	67
3. Defining Death and Death Technology	79
4. Accepting Death and Understanding Grieving	99
5. Preparing for Death — Your Own and Others'	111
6. Spotting the Right Time to Die	127
7. Embracing In-Life and Seeming End-of-Life Transition: LEAP Level One	153

PART II: How to Know, Find, Follow the Idea of Light   165

8. Becoming Lighter	167
9. Understanding The Ideas of Light and Love	179
10. Romancing the Light	183
11. Clarifying the Light	189
12. Praying as Practical Action	197
13. Initiating the Vision	215
14. Quickening for Frequency-Shifting: LEAP Level Two	219

PART III: How to Detach — 225
15. Detecting the Network of Cords — 227
16. Releasing Attachments — 253
17. Clearing Subtle Energy Webs — 277
18. Clearing Social Energy Webs — 285
19. Letting Go — 293
20. Avoiding Primary Reconnection — 299
21. Willing the Exit from the Flesh:
    LEAP Level Three — 307

NOW EXPLORE NEXT LEVELS
   SEE...
   The next *How To Die And Survive* book,
   How To Die And Survive, Book Two — 313

Appendices — 315
Booklist and Recommended Reading — 317
SEE THESE BOOKS BY THIS AUTHOR — 319-327
About This Book — 329
About The Author — 331

HOW TO DIE AND SURVIVE
LIST OF FIGURES

I Walk Through	6
Basic Light-Energy-Action-Processes (LEAPs)	17
2.1. Dante and Beatrice Gaze upon the Highest Heavens	78
3.1. Oh, the Web We Weave	97
5.1. Last Lists	125
6.1. Four Repeatable and Intermixable Phases	147
6.2. Escape From Paradox	149
6.3. Visualization of Being Part of Larger Cycles	151
7.1. LEAP Table: Basic Light-Energy-Action-Processes (LEAPs)	163
8.1. More Light is Less Dense	177
12.1. Prayer Gesture	207
12.2. Extended Prayer Gesture	209
12.3. Open Ascension Prayer Gesture	211
12.4. Deliverance Prayer Gesture	213
15.1. An Individual's Attachments to Basic Pieces of His Life	241
15.2. Simplified Cord Network Drawn by a Woman Who Has Chronic Migraine Headaches and Who is Living with Domestic Violence	243
15.3. Simplified Web of Life of Individual Suffering From Depression, Chronic Fatigue And Overweight	245
15.4. Habit Pattern of Man Addicted to Alcohol	247
15.5. Partial Attachment Chart of Suicidal Woman	249
15.6. Depiction of the Web of Attachment Woven Out of Cords	251

HOW TO DIE AND SURVIVE
LIST OF EXERCISES

PART I: PREAMBLE TO WHAT WE THINK OF AS DEATH

Exercise #1.1. Contacting Death Resistance	65
Exercise #1.2. Contacting Release Resistance	65
Exercise #1.3. Repeating Release	66
Exercise #2.1. Contrasting Life With Death	69
Exercise #2.2. Knowing How Alive You Are	69
Exercise #2.3. Seeing The Dying System	75
Exercise #2.4. Separating From A Troubled Or Dying System	76
Exercise #3.1. Reaching Out Into The Atmosphere In Front Of You	80
Exercise #3.2. Distinguishing The Instrument From Its Music	88
Exercise #3.3. Separating Yourself From Your Web	90
Exercise #3.4. Opening The Window	95
Exercise #3.5. Moving Through The Window	95
Exercise #3.6. Basic Reformatting	95
Exercise #4.1. Expressing Fear	101
Exercise #4.2. Releasing The Last Fear	102
Exercise #4.3. Filling With Acceptance	103
Exercise #4.4. Expressing Grief	108
Exercise #4.5. Cord Cutting Ceremony	108
Exercise #5.1. Being Ready For Death	116
Exercise #5.2. Practicing Cycle Sensitivity	117
Exercise #5.3. Studying A Cycle	118
Exercise #5.4. Seeing Your Life Cycle	119
Exercise #5.5. Defining The Unfinished	121
Exercise #6.1. Mapping Your Life	131
Exercise #6.2. Seeing Shifts And Transitions In Your Life	131
Exercise #6.3. Developing Fork Awareness	135
Exercise #6.4. Moving On	136
Exercise #6.5. Having Cycle Sensitivity	142
Exercise #6.6. Locating Your Cycles	142
Exercise #7.1. Cradling The Self	157
Exercise #7.2. Embracing A Death	158
Exercise #7.3. Embracing Your Death	159

PART II: HOW TO KNOW, FIND, FOLLOW THE IDEA OF LIGHT

Exercise #8.1. Becoming Less Dense	171
Exercise #8.2. The Light Diet	173
Exercise #8.3. Metaphysical Calisthenics	175
Exercise #9.1. Sensory Mixing	180
Exercise #9.2. Multi-Sensory Mixing	181
Exercise #10.1. Feeling Your Engulfment	185
Exercise #10.2. Seeing The Mists	185
Exercise #10.3. Examining The Light	186
Exercise #10.4. Dancing With The Light	187
Exercise #11.1. Reading The Atmosphere	192
Exercise #11.2. Breaking Through	192
Exercise #11.3. Enhancing The Light	194
Exercise #11.4. Clarifying The Light	195
Exercise #12.1. Inscribing Prayer Gesture In Your Energy Memory	199
Exercise #12.2. Practicing Ascension Prayer Motion	199
Exercise #12.3. Practicing Open Ascension Prayer Motion	200
Exercise #12.4. Creating A Sacred Vessel For Yourself	201
Exercise #12.5. Moving Your Sacred Vessel	201
Exercise #12.6. Releasing From Your Vessel	202
Exercise #12.7. Delivering Your Self	203
Exercise #12.8. Returning To Center	204
Exercise #13.1. Initiating The Vision	216
Exercise #13.2. Raising The Eyes	217
Exercise #14.1. Speeding Up As Frequency-Shifting	220
Exercise #14.2. Quickening	221

PART III: HOW TO DETACH

Exercise #15.1. Sourcing Feelings	230
Exercise #15.2. Seeing The Larger Manipulation	233
Exercise #15.3. Listing Your Cords	234
Exercise #15.4. Adding Attachment Cords To Your List	236
Exercise #15.5. Connecting Cords To See Patterns	237
Exercise #15.6. Planning Future Cord Observations	238
Exercise #16.1. Seeing Points Of Attachment	258
Exercise #16.2. Operating On Your Attachment Cords	264
Exercise #16.3. Deconstructing And Transmuting Cords	272

Exercise #17.1. Higher Hearing 281
Exercise #17.2. Clearing Subtle Webs 283
Exercise #18.1. Clearing A Heart Cord 291
Exercise #18.2. Clearing A Point Cord 291
Exercise #18.3. Clearing The Social Energy Web 292
Exercise #19.1. Using Paradox To Fuel Letting Go 295
Exercise #19.2. Focusing The Release 296
Exercise #20.1. Detecting Reconnection 304
Exercise #20.2. Avoiding And Deterring
    The Re-Cordings Of Others 305
Exercise #20.3. Transmuting Reconnecting Cords To Light 306
Exercise #21.1. Finding The Will, Your Will 310
Exercise #21.2. Willing The Exit 311

Author's Note

This book presents this author's basic, and primarily metaphorical, interdimensional awareness, consciousness, travel, and survival material and technologies, and related understandings. Readers have a right to such knowledge. Readers also have a responsibility to apply such knowledge with care and with the highest of ethical intent.

This is more than a book. It is itself a portal, an opening into a journey of the mind, heart, soul, spirit, consciousness. When read in sequence and with great concentration, the text in this and the following *how to die and survive* books may produce an alteration in the reader's state of mind and awareness. Understand that such shifts in awareness can be valuable in psychological and spiritual growth, and can range from obvious to easily assimilated to troubling to confusing to ecstatic. Should a reader find the solitary study of this text confusing, seek a fellow reader and/or a trained psychological or spiritual guide.

If you are indeed reading this, you are most likely a human being living on planet Earth. This is the evolutionary level of life form for which these words are written.[6]

---

[6] Other Readers, should there be any, will feel free to interpret the messages transmitted herein according to interest, respective world views, beliefs, approaches, and levels of understanding, and, again, with only the highest of ethical intent.

Introduction To How To Die And Survive: What This Book Is All About

> Into the night of the heart
> Your name drops slowly
> And moves in silence and falls
> And breaks and spreads its water.
>
> Pablo Neruda
> "Slow Lament"
> *Residence On Earth*

This book is written for anyone who is undergoing, has undergone, or will undergo physical death, or any other form of transition, including but not limited to the loss of a loved one, or perhaps a shift in belief system or other perception of reality, or for that matter, any minor or major in-life or seeming end-of-life ending or change or shift.

This is every one of us. Every change or transition is in essence a type of minor or major ending or death of something. Every death is a movement from one situation to another, from one state of mind to another, from one understanding or aspect of reality to another.

Every change is a shift of some sort. A new perspective on, or dimension of, our reality emerges. In this way, we are all explorers, discovering what is next from moment to moment,

time to time, way of being to way of being, way of thinking to way of thinking.

WE ARE EXPLORERS

All those who shift in some way, who change, transition, and or face some sort of ending or death, are explorers, adventurers of the mind and spirit. They are all their own version of "space" travelers in that they are traveling through changing or even unknown spaces, domains, territories of the mind and spirit. In this sense, we are all cosmos-nauts (also *cosmo*-nauts) of the highest order, traveling to realms beyond the status quo.

We provide government and corporate astronauts with very specific training for their "space" journeys. I will ask again here: why not provide everyone with training for their journeys into the distinctly obvious, and also the very subtle, psychological and spiritual, energetic and visceral, changes and unknowns of their lives and minds, into places and spaces beyond "right now"?

So when I talk about death, I am talking about any small or large shift, a change, an ending, any transition *out* of something (and, whether or not we see this, what is also transition *in* to something). I see all such experiences as models of transition and even of death. In fact, life teaches us so much about moving into next phases and stages and spaces.

These are all by degrees minor and major changes, endings, deaths. Indeed, this lifetime is a great training ground for what may come next, for what may come after this moment,

minute, hour, day, week, month, year, or phase or stage of our lives.

As we gain more understanding of what it means to *navigate the process of living*,[7] we can learn more about what it can mean to navigate what comes next, even next after "this" life. And, what is it that is this life? That is for each of us to determine.

Yet, it may be that the more we know ourselves, our consciousness-es, the more say we can have in what comes next. Yet, some call what comes *after* this life the *after*life. (We may want to rephrase the discussion regarding the possibility of life after death and describe this as *life after life*, or life beyond this life.)

THESE LEARNINGS ARE COMING TO US NOW

You will see that my interest in death is not morbid. Rather, this is about the survival of our actual life form, of what I see as the species of consciousness of humanity, here in the physical plane and beyond.[8]

The material in this and the other volumes in this *Keys To Consciousness And Survival Series* is pouring into my life, into my consciousness, into my heart, in an irreversible stream,

---

[7] See *Volume 8* in this *Keys To Consciousness And Survival Series*, titled, *Navigating Life's Stuff, Part One*.

[8] See another volume in this *Keys To Consciousness And Survival Series* for further comment on this rethinking of our actual and possible life form, seeing us as the Species of Consciousness of humanity. For more details on this, see *Volume 3*, titled *Unveiling The Hidden Instinct: Understanding Our Interdimensional Survival Awareness*.

with a mandate to share this information with humanity. This mandate has never appeared in words, rather in images and even awareness-es that have no verbal and often even no visual form.

This mandate is to bring this awareness in to us via developing and describing the concepts I present herein, and developing the languaging for doing so (in human language communication format we use here on this Earth).

The mandate was, and remains clear: make this material known now, to as many people as possible, as rapidly as possible. Teach it, write it, speak it, live it.

Do not be dissuaded by forces who seek to stop you from sharing this information. They may not yet understand what this means to us, to humanity, to the species of consciousness we truly are. (Or perhaps some forces or factors may not want us to empower humanity with the awareness that we can learn to die and survive.)

The power, the resolution of the message, the drive of this information to be further developed and to make itself known, has been and continues to be, for me, intense, crystal clear, and irrefutable. So I come to you with the work that I have been called to develop.

This work has been called in by what I have to describe here as a part of my mind or brain where lives my overself and its higher companion, a collective intelligence. This collective intelligence is a conglomeration of what feels to be immaterial intelligences, as well as other presences or life forms, which have become increasingly present in my life.

DELIVERING THIS MATERIAL

There have been times in my life when I have been treated rather badly for talking and writing about any of this. This has even been used against me at times, used as a way to discredit me and my credibility. I ask readers to check my training, work, and expertise in numerous very "mainstream" professional and scholarly arenas and fields to see that I am not arriving at this material "out of nowhere," so to speak.[9]

So, I weave the knowledge, learnings, and theories I am developing in this lifetime (and yes, perhaps also other lifetimes and iterations) right into the flow of the material emerging in my mind that I am constantly transducing, engaging with, sharing my lifetime experiences and research with, and giving words to.

Indeed, as you read on you will see that my voice weaves in and out of, and mixes with, what some may describe as being "higher" (or "higher self" or "higher frequency") voices. This is apparent in the purposeful grammatic inconsistencies found herein, such as the varying uses of the terms "i" and "we." Clearly, a new grammar is emerging as this form of collaborative communication and interpretation comes of age.

---

[9] Readers are invited to look for this author's work online and in books under her last name, Brownemiller (at times also spelled Browne-Miller) and also under simply Dr. Angela and Dr. Angela®. See full bio at www.DrAngela.com and on Amazon.com for example.

This is not what some call simple channeling, not at all. There is far too much interaction and direction coming not only from it to me, but also very much from me to it. This *interaction* is a *multidimensional collaboration*, a meeting of on- and off-planet or *interdimensional* intelligences and awareness-es—a meeting of the "minds" (consciousness-es). I am honored to share in this meeting with remarkable "minds," and to be able to share with you the product of this coming together of my self with such remarkable intelligences.

I am more than honored. I am driven to develop and share this *how to die and survive* material. I am driven by a sense that humanity deserves—has a right to—and needs this information in order to master the profound leap in its evolution that it **must make to survive.**

The basic technology of the leap, the *light-energy-action-process*, I have developed over the years is shared throughout this book, for example in Chapter 7. And the eight leaps described in this volume are charted on the page preceding the table of contents and again in Figure 7.1. These eight leaps are explained successively, building on each other, in the seven chapters found in each of the eight parts of this and the following book.

UNDERSTANDING SELF DELIVERANCE AS
LEAPING

I am called to teach these leaps, to teach processes of change, transition: endings, minor and major non-physical and physical, in-life and seeming end-of-life, as well as possible life after life, transitions. These leaps, these processes of

interdimensional awareness, consciousness, shifting, survival, are forms of what I describe as *interdimensional consciousness*[10] and its conceptual travel.

(Note that the consciousness itself can see itself as traveling to many non-physical locations, as the consciousness itself is not bound by physicality and physical distance as we know it.[11])

We have a right to this knowledge, to what I describe as self *deliverance tools and technology*. The idea that we can deliver, shift, move, transition, ourselves to, even back and forth from, higher states of awareness, consciousness, even non-physical energy arrangements, is an idea whose time has come.

Note that some readers will interpret the material in this book, *How To Die And Survive*, as pertaining to what is termed deliverance[12] in various religious doctrines. Of course this is

---

[10] See the book, *Interdimensional Psychology*, where I develop and define this field of interdimensional theory, study, and treatment of the mind and psyche, and of the consciousness itself. For more detail on this, contact DrAngela.com.

[11] This concept is further developed in *Volume 3* of this series, *Unveiling The Hidden Instinct*.

[12] Deliverance is generally defined as the act of *being* rescued or set free. To deliver can also mean to *give* an object, to bring an object to someone. While this book, *How To Die And Survive*, maintains a open approach to religions as well as atheistic views, there will be times when religious as well as atheistic views are offered. Here, note that: In the *Bible*, one view of deliverance is that it is an act of God; God is described as the great deliverer. *Bible Study Tools* notes that: "While God is the great deliverer, there are no manipulative ploys by His people to effect His intervention. All Acts of deliverance are totally His initiative and express his mercy and his love (*Psalm 51:1;*

understandable. However, by deliverance herein, I am referring to the concepts, tools, *technologies*, described in this book.

These can be accessed with or without particular belief systems, which makes this *how to die and survive* awareness available to a broader range of humanity.

EXPANSIVE NATURE OF
ACTUAL DELIVERANCE
IS BEYOND
THE GIVEN DEFINITIONS

Let's be sure we understand the expansive nature of the personal deliverance of one's self to oneself.

This is about: seeing that one's so called higher self is beyond ego and is perhaps one's personal consciousness; and about how delivering one's self to oneself is coming into contact with the actual nature of us, of we humans – as a species of consciousness.

Developing
Our own access to
This expanded view of
Deliverance
Is our
Birthright.

71:2, 86:13). ... God's deliverance is for His people, those who trust and fear Him. ... Often, the people's fear of God and trust in Him are seen as a part of the deliverance ... ... [refer to these passages in the Bible: (*Psalm 22:4; 33:18-19; 34:7; Ezek14:20*)]."

**What we are delivering here is
Access to ourselves.**

**And, in essence,
We are delivering ourselves to
Higher levels of our own consciousness.**

**Becoming ever more aware of, sensitized to,
The subtle yet expansive
Human consciousness,
Is essential in our
Personal and species evolution and survival.**

***

THINK ABOUT

Think about what delivery means to you.

Your deliverance to yourself of greater access to yourself is indeed possible.

This personal deliverance offers the possibility of delivering yourself to yourself, and of delivering to yourself your keys to your own awareness, to open your awareness to more about who you truly are.

Many will also interpret the material in *How To Die And Survive* as pertaining to the ascension,[13] and liberation[14] Of individuals. While concepts such as deliverance, ascension, even liberation, are relevant in numerous religious teachings, these same terms can be adapted and applied (with neither reference nor preference to any particular religion or belief system) to the consciousness technologies I teach in this and other books in this *Keys To Consciousness And Survival Series.*

I again emphasize that the material in this book is available to readers regardless of their particular religious or atheistic (or other) orientations and beliefs.

This book, *How To Die And Survive,* is both non-denominational and interdenominational. Everyone who wishes to can access the concepts and processes/Exercises

---

[13] Ascension has been defined in various ways, depending upon the world view of the definer. Generally, ascension is the process or act of rising to a higher status or level of an organization, government, or other structure. Spiritual ascension is described as moving to a higher level of consciousness, perhaps resulting in a spiritual awakening. In the Christian system, ascension is the rise of Christ on the 40th day following Resurrection. Some religious beliefs hold that certain persons ascend into higher realms or Heaven without first physically dying.

[14] Liberation is generally defined as the freeing of something or someone, generally *from* an oppressive force or factor such as slavery, imprisonment, limits on behavior. Liberation Theology was developed primarily by Latin American Catholic groups to address political, economic, and social oppression. In many Christian views of liberation, the ministry of Jesus was that of liberating what were termed captives, to "set the captives free" from enslavement (to sin) through the "good news of salvation" (Is 61:1 and Lk 4:18). This view of liberation stems from the Biblical idea of salvation, which is deliverance from spiritual or other danger, such as what some described as the danger of sin.

contained herein. This is information we have a right to and a need to know, to access, to explore for ourselves.

Yes, this is knowledge we do have a *right to*: how to have our awareness access higher dimensions of our realities; how to have our awareness-es learn to consciously "deliver" ourselves to new phases, stages, states of mind, new dimensions of ourselves and our lives, to "ascend" to these dimensions, thus to "liberate" ourselves from being restricted to having no or limited access.

For some readers, this will also be about not being restricted to only the material plane.[15] Readers will choose to take this information in according to their own beliefs, interests, and needs.

NOTE ABOUT BEING THIS AUTHOR

At times, this calling has been uncomfortable. When my friends first read the first chapters of this volume, they began calling me "angel of death."

This had a rather disquieting ring to it as even i, with all of my desire to embrace and fully understand transitions including endings and even death transitions, did not like the sound of my being an angel of death. Nor did I see myself as an angel. Nor one of death.[16] Then an old friend contacted me and said,

---

[15] I explain these matters in greater depth in *Volume 3* in this series, *Unveiling The Hidden Instinct*.

[16] I also found the first coming of age of my transition and death work strangely ironic and perhaps a bit humorous, as parts of it coincided with an anniversary of my father's death (on the eve of All Hallow's Eve) and

"well, it makes sense. We used to call you Clara Barton, girl nurse. But you get impatient with the material plane. This is the natural outcome. Your job now is to deliver people into the next dimension, or at least to teach them to travel back and forth from there."

THE DIRECTIVE

And, quite surprisingly, I have heard exactly this directive from beyond the daily noise, from somewhere I do not label the same way I label sources of most of other incoming information (and noise).

Sometimes I turn to the higher intelligences I sense are collaborating with me, and that I am collaborating with, in this effort. I insist that I am just a person, a human incarnated here in this third dimension. I insist that the directive that I serve in helping humanity see that it can ever more fully and consciously access higher dimensions of reality—of consciousness, dimensions that humanity has a right to access, is too big for me. These are shoes no mortal can readily wear, I insist. I say I frequently feel the intensity of this project.

The response I get is that only seeing physical mortality is not entirely relevant, that the immortality, better stated, the *survival*, of the consciousness of all humanity is at stake. I am told that there are others being called upon as well, that I will eventually recognize my true companions in this work, that we will find each other, know each other.

---

parts of it with my becoming the *very* age my mother was when she died back in my teens (which she did right around Easter).

These are big words for me to hear. Yet, even as I attempt to doubt these words, to refute them, my consciousness is permeated with the truth of this statement, both here in material reality and beyond.

THE TIME IS NOW

My understanding is that we are being called to Know that we can survive, that our survival is both physical and beyond physical. The time is coming for us to stand up and speak what we know about who we are, about who and what humanity actually is.

> **Knowing this**
> **Can save our lives,**
> **Our own lives,**
> **And our species' life**
> **Here**
> **And beyond.**
>
> **We are not only**
> **The biological species**
> **We are told we are.**
> **We are**
> **Also the**
> **Species of consciousness of humanity.**

The time has come to know this about ourselves, about our species. (See *Volume 3* in this series, *Unveiling The Hidden Instinct*, where I cover this matter in greater detail. See also *Volumes 5* and *6* in this series, *Overriding The Extinction Scenario, Parts One* And *Two*.) Already now we face the visible extinction of marked segments of life on Earth, of various species, perhaps of ourselves if we cannot see what our options are now, right now.

I am reminded of the group suicides of lemmings and the beachings of whales—what are these collective suicides saying? What are other species able to sense? What can we learn from other lifeforms here on Earth?

(The instinct we carry within us, the hidden survival instinct I discuss in *Volume 3* in this series, titled, *Unveiling The Hidden Instinct: Understanding Our Inter-Dimensional Survival Awareness*, is an instinct we can detect by learning how other species sense their own instinctual directives.)

TEACH THESE UNDERSTANDINGS

We can hear ourselves if we listen. We can know our deepest instincts. To unveil the knowledge our species carries deep within itself, within its deeply buried memory, its **interdimensional survival awareness and instinct,** we can learn these change, transition, and even death, concepts and technologies I share in this *keys to consciousness and survival series*. And, we *can* further know what we carry deep within our consciousness.

Why shouldn't we all practice maintaining our personal consciousness until we (or if we ever) consciously choose to release (or surrender) this, and thus our *selves*, after examining what this book series defines as the ***multidimensional terrain*** we enter when we die, and for that matter, while we live? (See other books in this series, such as *Navigating Life's Stuff, Part One* and *Navigating Life's Stuff, Part*

Two, as well as *Seeing Beyond Our Line Of Sight*, for definition and discussion of this terrain.)

This is not encouraging suicide. Not at all. <u>Be clear about this.</u> This is allowing people to confront, become familiar with, navigate, and harvest transitions in life and even in death — yes, at their transitional moments in their lives, their minor and major in-life and seeming end-of-life changes, transitions, and deaths.

This is allowing people to captain their journeys, their physical, psychological, and spiritual progressions, ascensions, into new, expanded, domains of their consciousness-es, of their minds, of their realities. This is teaching conceptual and interdimensional understanding, awareness, and *survival*.

The *adventures in death*,[17] including even daily in-life transitions, as well as grievings for those who we think of as dead, and our own experiences of various endings and deaths, that we learn to conduct for ourselves will enhance the great adventures we call our lives.

To master life, master death. To master death, develop an expansive *interdimensional awareness*. And then understand and engage in *liberation from not knowing*, from not knowing that we are already creatures of multiple dimensions, the species of the consciousness of humanity.

---

[17] See editions of books I wrote on death and dying (*and also other in-life transitions*) such as the key book on this matter, *Volume 10* in this series, titled *Seeing Beyond Our Line Of Sight*.

ABOUT THIS BOOK

I thank you for your brave examination of these issues and of the following processes. You will find processes labeled as "Exercises" in many of the following chapters. These are designed to build, when practiced in relative sequence, a deeper understanding of and respect for the various in-life changes, shifts, transitions, minor and major challenges and deaths.

Every change, transition, in life can be moved through with increasing awareness to learn more about what we can do, and about who and what we are. Every successive transition is *learning to ever more consciously transition, to transit from situation to situation, from reality to reality*.

These Exercises herein are indeed lessons in developing ever more conscious awareness so that we have this ever more conscious awareness available to us in minor and major transitions we face.

These *How To Die And Survive Exercises* require no drugs or shamanic rituals, in fact, these Exercises are best done with a most clear and unaided mind. This will allow you to delve unaided into the greatest resources of your own consciousness, and thus of our species consciousness. This will allow you to grow familiar with this access, and then **to recall this access later, when there may be no physical body to mediate.**

You will note that these chapters, these *interactive communications* as I prefer to call these, vary in length. Do take even the briefest chapters in with concentration. The number of words on the page bears no relationship to the potency of the message expressed. And, you will note that some chapters seem to be spiritual, some philosophical, and some practical.

These chapters and their Exercises can work well when experienced in the order presented herein, so that the awareness builds carefully, as if layer upon layer of foundation is being generated.

Throughout this, and also the following, *How To Die And Survive* book (*How To Die And Survive, Book Two*), an effort is made to vary the communication in order to reach readers through many different avenues of their perceptions.

You will also find, at the opening of all chapters, brief quotations of others' ideas on death and related topics. These are provided as a running commentary on the human examination of challenges such as death with no endorsement of any single view intended here. (In fact, please keep in mind that there is no particular philosophical, religious, scientific, atheistic, or other view required to access the material contained in this or any of my books.)

Try to absorb (in your own way) the information contained in these volumes by studying it in pieces. You will remember bits of this material many times during your many livings and dyings. And you may find yourself increasingly adept at what I call *conscious interdimensional awareness, navigation, and travel*.[18]

---

[18] You may also want to read more intricate reviews of the biological dying process and the details of its stages than we have space for

NOTE
TO THOSE WHO ARE GRIEVING

A special note for the grieving. If you are someone who finds yourself in a state of what you consider intense or unending grieving, please consider reading slowly, and ideally with company, this and other volumes in this *Keys To Consciousness And Survival* book series. Read from both the standpoint of you as the individual in the dying process, and also of you thinking about expanded ways of seeing another person's death.

Allow yourself to go through the considerations and processes encouraged herein. After all, you are also going through a transition, even a dying. You are grieving the death of a relationship, or at least a form of that relationship. (you are also experiencing a transition in the energy pattern or format of your relationship with that person.)

THIS JOURNEY

Join me in this journey through the mind and spirit, to and from the body, in and out of this dimension: from what some will see as the mortal state to what some will see as the immortal state, from concepts such as conceptual (and we hope not actual) crisis or apocalypse into (forms of what you may believe to be) ascension, deliverance, liberation.

We can join hands, connect hearts, bridge consciousness-es, and explore together the truly awesome portals of our rightful

---

here. See chapters on physical and other death phases and stages in the book, *Seeing Beyond Our Line Of Sight* (*Volume 10* in this series).

ascensions, transcendences, and resurrections. We are indeed explorers, even pioneers, in this undertaking.

We do have room to generate, evolve, go see, imagine, visualize, conceptualize, realms beyond. These are our realms to conceive of, to discover, develop, and grow into, even occupy....

Part 1

Preamble
To
What We Think Of As
Death

1
Learn How To Shift, Transition, Die Out Of Patterns And Lives

> Wisdom is hidden in darkness.
> Know that only by striving
> Can light pour into thy brain.
>
> Thoth
> *Emerald Tablets, VIII*

Why learn how to consciously move through life's changes, transitions, even our minor and major in-life and beyond life endings and deaths? Why at this time? What are you telling yourself by choosing to read this?

You are responding to your own questions, even perhaps to your own highest instincts. You are taking in a profound message, one that says:

Honor your position on the precipice of time. Be alert. Stay very aware, heighten the aware arm of your consciousness. Learn these change, transition, death, and survival technologies. You have the right to this knowledge and you have the ability to learn this. Make these precious moments in the time of your life matter.

MOVE YOURSELF INTO THE ROLE

Move yourself from the role of what to some may seem powerless pawn, to that of potent player in your own life, in your own personal cosmic system. Learn how to navigate your way through changes, transitions, minor and major endings and deaths.[19] And then, when time to actually physically die, enter the process as aware and consciously as you can, calling on all you have learned this lifetime. (Note that awareness and preparation of the consciousness to remain intact, to survive transitions, may be done all through life, and then can be carried on even when not able to remain biologically awake, aware.)

Ascend to new levels of awareness and focus at will. Learn how to shift yourself—your focus, your awareness, your consciousness--(conceptually and or actually) to and from your physical reality, to and from your physical body, to and from this and other dimensions of your self—at will.

KEEP YOUR OWN COUNSEL

The way we live, change, transition, even die, matters. Where we may not have full say in our physical realities, we have a great deal of say in our *perceptions* of our realities and of ourselves.

In these times, we are participants in the massive escalation of both the speed of growing awareness and the speed at which this growing awareness is being suppressed, distorted, squelched. The forces of deception and truth, of enslavement and freedom, are intensifying their polarizations. Whenever such polarizations are intensified to great extremes, *the energy*

---

[19] See other volumes in this series on this **navigation process**, including both volumes of the book, *Navigating Life's Stuff*.

between the poles can arc, causing fleeting but deceptive flashes or switches in their charges.

And so, you must *keep your own counsel*. Refine and mature your own counsel, to find your way through life, even through a *maze of illusions* in which even the most dangerous of energies can appear as safe, even the darkest of forces can appear as light, even darkness or lack of light, and light itself, can switch and confuse us as to their nature.

In this maze of emerging and competing realities and ir-realities, the markers on your path can be switched as if they are intersecting street signs being changed by devious pranksters. But this is not just getting lost on a city street. The stakes are much higher in the maze of illusions, in the misrepresentation of energies, of energy arrangements and their matrices.

You Can Lose Your Self.

By learning to develop and sustain heightened access to your awareness, to your ever more *aware consciousness*,[20] you can move through minor and major transitions, and do so ever more consciously.

---

[20] I have further developed the notion of the **aware consciousness** in *Unveiling The Hidden Instinct*. Also in that book, I have provided exercises focused on the further development of the awareness and of the awareness of the consciousness. Readers are encouraged to see that book for its essential information on further developing the awareness, as this is a powerful element in survival here now, and also beyond the status quo.

KEY IN OUR SURVIVAL

This is key in our personal and species survival. This allows you/us to more and more captain your/our own ship, so to speak.

Whatever your stage of life or so-called death, whatever may be your current level of in-life or seeming end-of-life transition, you can train yourself to *consciously map your territory*, **to** *know for yourself* the difference between truth and deception, to effectively educate and apply your own counsel under pressure, even the pressures of intense living transition as well as of profound physical death.

Times are changing ever more "quickly." The opportunities for personal, species, and planetary "quickening" are therefore greater than ever.

The speeding up of change, this special degree of "acceleration," can produce a profound leap in awareness, a suddenly vaster multidimensional intelligence, and a rapid energetic connection among people.

UNDERSTAND ENERGY UPHEAVAL

Yet, the speeding up, especially when misunderstood, can also produce social, political, ecological, emotional, and spiritual swings, perhaps even disorganization and chaos. When resisted or mishandled, this speeding up or acceleration may even produce massive energy convulsions, which, in the material plane, could even take form as political upheaval, economic swings, mass disease, group panic or hysteria, ecological disaster, or cataclysmic shifts in the precarious balance of the entire planet along its conceptual, energetic, or actual axis.

This at times revolutionary or upheaval-like disseminating and rerouting of previously locked-in and "stuck" energy systems, thought forms, and ecosystems may be, in some definitions, necessary.

Yet, this can take place in smoother forms where there is understanding, conscious awareness, of what is happening. This rerouting of systems, of energetic arrangements and their matrices, can allow for the *release* of stuck, trapped, energy — and the release of energy caught in problem and or decaying systems. This rerouting or release also allows for the extensive (at least conceptual) restructuring of reality. This also allows (at least conceptually) movement among dimensions of reality. This movement is change, transition, even death of energy arrangements, systems, formats — matrices.

Death of a system, of a stable or otherwise healthy system, or of a drowned out, or drained (or troubled) system is, basically, a transition, a shift. This transition, shift, is any movement from one aspect or pattern, from one dimension of a reality to another, any change for that matter. In this understanding of death, death is not an absolute ending and rather is a transition.

Some transitions can be quite difficult and even feel like deaths. Other transitions, changes, movements, can be smooth, simple, even tranquil and or even unnoticeable. However it feels, however it forms itself, transition usually involves the rearranging, restructuring, of patterns and energy networks from one form to another. This reorganization of patterns and networks is frequently wave like, at times profound, even when the transition level is subtle and relatively undetectable in the material realm.

We sometimes undergo entire transition processes unaware that these are taking place. Our subconscious reads these energy shifts even when our conscious levels do not. Be very aware of your self as the world around you and within you shifts. Sense even what your subconscious is reading.[21]

ELECT TO SHIFT, CHANGE, AS CONSCIOUSLY AS WE CAN

As I will note many times herein, <u>nothing about this discussion encourages suicide. This is not the message of this book</u>. Rather, the message is that: you may at some point wish to, *as consciously as you can*, move through your life's changes, transitions, minor and major endings, deaths. Bringing your awareness to the changes you experience allows you to be aware of and use for yourself, even for your survival, the energy you have tied up, sometimes even trapped, in these situations.[22]

And yes, when you reach the time of your actual physical death, understanding the *navigation of transitions* will be quite

---

[21] This sensing process is discussed in *Volume 10* in this series, *Seeing Beyond Our Line Of Sight*.

[22] I detail the energy held in a trap, double bind, paradox, and its release in *Navigating Life's Stuff, Part One*, which is *Volume 8* in this *Keys To Consciousness And Survival Series*.

useful, valuable, and survival oriented. This will eventually become ever more clear to you. Some people may feel uncomfortable with the concept that the teachings in this book can help with both in-life as well as so called end-of-life transitions, deaths. This is understandable. Readers will apply the discussion in this book to their own lives in their own ways.

We tend to be programmed to fear death and to justify this fear of death as a survival instinct. Yet even this instinct has been evolved into us (or programmed into us, or both) — either by evolution or its engineers — telling us we cannot die and survive.[23] This message may be written right into our genetic coding. Yet, once we see past the coding and programming that we carry, we can see more about *how to die and survive*.

We can learn about the *hidden instinct* we carry deep within our consciousnesses, this instinct that allows us to understand what it means to *die and survive*. (I detail this instinct in *Volume 3* in this series, titled, *Unveiling The Hidden Instinct: Understanding Our Inter-Dimensional Survival Awareness*.)

You, we, have a right to break free of the coding, the programming, we carry that may be restricting our opportunity to know what it means to *die and survive*. You, we, have a right to understand that we are a species of consciousness, that when (and before) our physical body expires, we can each *learn to choose to survive* as a

---

[23] I detail this matter in other volumes in this series including *Unveiling The Hidden Instinct* and also *Overriding The Extinction Scenario, Parts One* and *Two*.

consciousness. We have a right to understand that the more aware we are of all this, the more options we have during any transition.

WE HAVE A RIGHT TO KNOW

The simple and profound change, transition, death, and liberation-ascension technologies developed herein are your/our birthright. Knowing, practicing and applying these technologies is true survival.

You will come to feel the difference between the so-called survival instinct that was programmed into you, and your true desire to do what it takes to survive *both here and beyond this physical life* with whatever portion of your self, your consciousness, you wish to preserve.

When you fully complete your Earthly journey, and not prior to this, you will have the opportunity to fully know that your physical body is an *expendable vehicle of your evolution*. Eventually, *only* when the time is right, physicality becomes unnecessary baggage for you both as an individual and as a species.

> **Experienced travelers learn not to overpack,
> And not to overload themselves en route.**

Learn to shift out of a troubled, stuck, problematic, or deteriorating energy arrangement, network, or matrix. This shift or transition is a form of pattern death, not specifically of a physical body, but rather of an energy arrangement, an attachment network.

This shift can be managed with awareness. In this sense, you can learn to die well in order to survive, to harvest your own energy, your own matrix, your own personal consciousness, from the death you are undergoing—no matter what sort of minor or major transition that death may be.

Every change and transition you undergo is a great learning. Learn about transitioning, shifting, even dying. Learn about how to change, transition, shift, die well while you are still living in your physical body so that you will understand the developments you face after you leave your body.

The longer you have lived in your physical body—in the so-called "material plane," the older you are in chronological Earth years, the more learning about dying there is for you to do.

If you are still very young, your perception of death may as yet be unfettered by the material plane experience. You have not yet absorbed the overlay, taken on the veil, that material reality renders.

The longer you live in your physical biological body, in the material plane, the more you may find a need to know what is in this book. As you spend more years living in the material plane, what you instinctively know can be ever more deeply buried and must be consciously re-learned—you must *learn* what it means to die and survive, even what it means to be better at living and coping with life's challenges, changes, transitions.

LEARN WHAT IT CAN MEAN TO DIE AND SURVIVE

Learn what it can mean to die and survive, to transition and sustain your self as you do. Understand that you (you, as a personal consciousness, which is actually what and who you are) can learn to survive physical death as well as other challenging transitions. You can learn, take this awareness in, no matter what your current condition.

We can train our <u>selves</u>, our <u>consciousness-es</u>, to survive.

Step back from yourself for a moment, and see that you are part of several larger bodies. You are a cell within an organ which is a living component of a larger living organism. The being you currently take form as exists and survives within your biological, ecological, cultural, political, planetary, galactic, and dimensional systems. Each of these interlinked systems may now be on the brink of a profound transformation.

Should this transformation manifest as the death of any or all of the systems in which you are a cell, it may take you with it.

Learn what it can mean to die with awareness, to prepare to die with awareness, to prepare to die and survive as a personal consciousness.

You may be able to learn to navigate not only your own death, and or even the death of your own physical system, but the deaths of the systems in which you exist. You may opt to see yourself as surviving if need be, even independent of your physical body or the system in which you live to survive. Learn what it can mean to die out of a system or a body or an energy matrix, to divorce from your attachments to existing networks or systems, or bodies, or matrices, to survive.

BREAK FREE

When you begin to apply the *transition and death technologies* I share in *How To Die And Survive*, you begin to take back more of your multi-dimensional awareness of yourself—of who you truly are.

You begin to see that while you may be coded, programmed, to believe you are tied to, even a prisoner in, your physical biological body, this is not the case. Your biological body is one of your vessels. You will find you have others at another time.

You may have been programmed to think you are trapped in physical—material—mortal reality. Yet, know this: *you are not your programming.* You are not incarcerated in your current physical, biological, vessel. You are more than the vessel you travel in, far more. (Again note, this *Keys To Consciousness And Survival Series* of books brings forth the call to our *hidden survival instinct,* the instinct we want to revive within ourselves as this is our true survival instinct. See again, *Volume 3* in this series, *Unveiling The Hidden Instinct: Understanding Our Inter-Dimensional Survival Awareness.*)

Believing we are only a biological, physical plane species need not be our fate. We need not die along with a failing solar, or planetary, or ecological, or species level economical, biological, societal, cultural, familial, marital, or other system.

Tap into the higher levels of your consciousness, perhaps conceiving of these as light coming from higher dimensions of reality. Let this sense of light filter into your awareness.

Take your power back by recognizing, seeing, what is actually here for you, by tapping into the inspiring, transformational, even catalytic forces available to you. Meet this expansive new field, *interdimensional psychology,* that I define in this book, and other books in this *Keys To Consciousness And Survival Series.*

*Fuel the shift, the LEAP, in your **awareness** (and in your energy arrangement, in your personal matrix[24]) that you, your self, your consciousness, must make for you, your self, your consciousness, in order to survive any so-called change, transition, and or physical death.[25]*

****

The following *How To Die And Survive Change, Transition, Liberation, and Death Technologies,* the ideas and concepts that are introduced in this book and the following books, conflict with no belief system or science. This is because these technologies can be taken in as concentration or meditation practices, as philosophical exercises, as science fiction games, as scientific explorations, or as transformational experiences.

YOU DECIDE
HOW TO TAKE ALL THIS IN

---

[24] Consider your energy arrangement or matrix, your biofield. See notes in *Chapter 1* of *Volume 3* in this series, *Unveiling The Hidden Instinct.*

[25] This is a key component of the *Interdimensional Psychology* I have defined and shared herein and in other books in this *Keys To Consciousness And Survival Series.*

You decide, of your own free will, how you wish to absorb the information in this book. In the end, the choice between the notions of mortality and immortality is yours. You can decide what this means to you.

Again, you can see this choice as imaginary or actual. This will be your decision. Your chosen mode of exploration of these concepts will be useful to your and to our species' mind/s. Learn what it means to shift, change, transition, die, and you will learn to navigate your life processes, move your consciousness into and through various circumstances.

This book guides readers through these *How To Die And Survive Processes*, exercises in change, shift, transition, minor and major death awareness-es and technologies. You will find these processes, exercises (numbered and in italics), contained in many of the chapters of this and the following *How To Die And Survive* books.

THE EXERCISES IN THIS BOOK

These Exercises begin quite simply and carefully build toward some profound understandings. Readers will find that this and the following book/s are manuals on increasing one's awareness and understanding, increasing our consciousness' survival skills, and yes, increasing our psychological expanse, its interdimensional access and territory.

A FURTHER NOTE ON THE EXERCISES IN THIS BOOK

The exercises offered throughout this book are designed for use and adaptation by adults who wish to engage in this learning process. All persons engaging in these exercises, please when the exercises are complete, return to your ongoing life.

Should any exercise in this book require a physical activity (such as sitting, standing, or reaching) that you find hard to do because you are physically weak, ill, incapacitated, or simply tired, just *imagine* that you are doing the exercise.

Thinking through the motions in these exercises is tantamount to performing the motions when you do not have the actual option of literally doing these. Your mental circuitry is exercised either way. Even consider reading these exercises aloud to people (when close kin have given you permission), people who appear not to be conscious, as these exercises may offer guidance to these persons as well.

Whatever your level of physical and mental ability, your range of motion, your stage of life, or your relative "need" for these exercises, your spirit, your consciousness, your mind, even brain, even body, will likely benefit by enrolling in this *Interdimensional Awareness School*. This is a key component of the *Interdimensional Psychology* field and curriculum that I introduce in this and other books.

To begin learning these change, transition, minor and major death technologies, spend a few moments conducting the following very basic exercises. Do these silently, in your mind. No writing is necessary at this point, although later exercises in the following chapters will suggest the use of pen and paper (for those who wish to and can do so).

There may come a time, a time when you awake outside your physical reality, when you may benefit by having practiced thinking, better stated "knowing," this material without pen and paper. Participants in many of the included Exercises are asked to practice such thinking by conducting some basic Exercises such as the following without doing any writing.

EXERCISE #1.1
CONTACTING DEATH RESISTANCE

Think of three reasons — the first three that come to your mind — for your not wanting to die right now.

Count these reasons as they come to you. If you do not have three reasons of your own, let some or all of your three reasons be those you think other people or society may have for you not to die right now.

Your reasons can be of any nature, including but <u>not</u> limited to fears, inconveniences, and or the leaving of loved ones behind.

EXERCISE #1.2
CONTACTING RELEASE RESISTANCE

Imagine that you have written each of these "three reasons not to die right now" down onto three separate pieces of paper. Now, imagine the wind coming up and blowing away each of these reasons for you not dying right now.

Do you feel anything about this imagined blowing away of your reasons not to die? Do you feel sadness? Or relief? Or surprise? To what degree do you feel any of these or other responses? If you feel nothing about this imaginary blowing away, ask yourself, how does "feeling nothing about the loss of these reasons not to die" feel?

Note any resistance you felt to the idea of the wind blowing away your reasons not to die. Did you want to stop the event, as if saving precious papers from blowing off a table? Relive each and every resistance to the blowing away of each reason not to die, whether subtle or distinct. Perhaps you felt nothing. Note any lack of response you may have to this exercise.

<u>EXERCISE #1.3</u>
REPEATING RELEASE

Repeat the above two exercises several times, trying different sets of reasons not to die each time. Think and visualize your way through these repetitions and examinations of your feelings, ideally unaided by making written notes.

You may wish to make notes on this exercise once it is completed. This is fine. There are no right or wrong answers to questions such as the ones asked in these exercises. This is simply an exploration of the ideas and feelings about these ideas. For now, these first three exercises are simply opening a door to personal inquiry....

2
Being Part Of
A Dying System

> Many things indicate that we are going through a transitional period, when it seems that something is on the way out and something else is painfully being born. It is as if something were crumbling, decaying and exhausting itself, while something else, still indistinct, were arising from the rubble....
>
> Vaclav Havel
> *Philadelphia Liberty Medal Address*

In the words of one child talking about his grandfather's death, "he is really dead now, this is the big death." The apparent finality, the distinct irreversibility, of this death is clear.

This big death is an event, yes, and is also a concept, a state of mind, an emotional and cognitive awareness.

BIGGER AND SMALLER DEATHS, ENDINGS

The notion of the big death suggests there may be smaller deaths, minor ending or death experiences. Indeed, there are experiences that for some people feel a little like death, for example, ends of relationships, ends of times of life, even ends of big projects.

Many times in life when experiencing changes or endings of something such as a phase (maybe teenage years or high school) or a relationship (maybe a marriage) or a stage of life (maybe the time "when we were young"), we experience something that feels like a profound shift or even a loss, a sort of death of a phase of life.

And, when experiences and struggles are physically and or emotionally painful, such as withdrawal from a drug to which one may be addicted, some people actually describe these times as, "I feel like I am dying."[26] there are those who, under particularly difficult circumstances, even say they want out of their suffering so much that they want to die.

THINKING ABOUT
OR
AVOIDING THINKING ABOUT
DEATH

---

[26] References to this commentary are explained in this book: *Seeing The Hidden Face Of Addiction*, and also in the book, *Navigating Life's Stuff*. See reading list at the end of this present book, *How To Die And Survive*, for more information on these and other books by this author.

And what about actual physical (biological) death? Do you think about your death? Or do you avoid thinking about it? Does it seem to you to be a major event looming, but somewhere out in your future? Or does this death seem so distant that it is irrelevant right now?

We feel life to be the opposite of death. We want life, we even hold onto life, of course. This is survival for us: life. (The idea that we may be able to survive physical death generally appears in religious and spiritual belief systems and teachings. However, we can bring this idea into a wide range of contexts and awareness-es.)

EXERCISE #2.1
CONTRASTING
LIFE WITH DEATH

If there might be a time when you cling to life, what might you be hanging on to? Can you detail for yourself what elements of life you want to hold on to?

Perhaps life is best sensed by seeing it as the opposite of the big death (whatever this big death may mean to you). So now, imagine what it feels like not to be dead, to be alive, as you are right now.

Try to become more aware of what it feels like to be alive than you have been before now. Stay with this awareness for the next Exercise.

EXERCISE #2.2
KNOWING
HOW ALIVE YOU ARE

There is always more to add to this awareness of being alive. Think more about what it feels like to be alive. As you do so, sense yourself *being alive. Ask yourself, "**How alive am i? How do I know this? How do I sense this?**" And then ask yourself, "**Are there times I have felt more, most, alive? What are these times, what do these feel like?**"*

*Give yourself a read on how alive you feel yourself to be right now. This can be on a scale such as from "not at all alive" to "very very alive" or somewhere in between. Or this can be expressed in any other way you wish to. After all, you are telling **yourself** how alive **you** feel **you** are right now. This is a personal readout from you to yourself. Of course you may share this with others, however for this moment, have your own personal sense of your own alive-ness.*

As you move through the progressive concepts and exercises in this and the following How To Die And Survive books, your sense of how alive you are may heighten; you may become ever more conscious of yourself and of who and what you are.

ECO-DEATH

Would you know how to distinguish between signs of your own dying and signs that the system in which you live is dying? Give some thought to this distinction.

Certainly, death is not an isolated event. It takes place amidst far larger events, far larger deaths, including the death of biospheres, ecosystems, and yes, species.

We are seeing the emergence of what here I will describe as *eco-death* consciousness—the ever growing awareness that failing health (or perhaps systemic dying) is something happening to the larger bio-systems in which we live. This is the time in modern history when we feel mounting system pressure, risks to health of our and other species.

And if we listen, we are also feeling mounting pressure to evolve—to *adapt*, change, *in order to survive*.[27]

At least the signs are interpreted this way: we are surrounded by, and living within, economic, social, health, and environmental systems, all of which are in transitional states. Some of these transitional states or conditions are being described as "in decline." We have to ask ourselves what this decline is declining to. Could it be a deterioration or even a death of a system or of its status? In this environment, death works its way into the corners of everyone's mind.

POLITICAL AND OTHER SYSTEM DEATH

Many see socio-political structures which have been built in recent centuries now appearing increasingly fragile, looking more and more like houses of cards. Winds of change are rattling institutions of tradition, eroding them, maybe evolving them, yet breaking or at least changing their structures to do so. Up to a point, people struggle to preserve these structures. Eventually, structures may give way to the

---

[27] Books in this *Keys To Consciousness And Survival Series* that develop this matter of **adaptation**, and **pressure to adapt**, are *Volume 3*, titled, *Unveiling The Hidden Instinct*, and *Volumes 4* and *5*, which are the *Parts One* and *Two* books of *Overriding The Extinction Scenario*. Note: highly recommended is the powerfully narrated audiobook version of *Overriding The Extinction Scenario, Part One*.

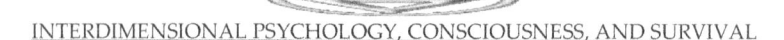

winds of change. Eventually structures may fall unless they evolve.

Yes, we finally let the old structures fall. *We let the old structure of the reality we have constructed dissolve.* We reach a point where we can invest no more in the preservation of a dying system.

We realize that our true survival actually depends upon our willingness to see beyond the reality we know, *to let the old reality change or die.* Cling to a sinking ship too long and you will drown. (Yet our ship need not sink if we know what ship we are actually on.)

KNOCKING ON HEAVEN'S DOOR, ENTRY TO THE BEYOND

On a deep level, we are beating on the walls of the material plane. We suspect that physical death is the great equalizer. We are "knocking on heaven's door" (phrase from a song by Bob Dylan which became popular in the 1960s). Yet, do we realize what it is that we are knocking on? What is this heaven we hear so much about?

Heaven is common to many religions, philosophies, and even found in artistic and literary traditions. See Figure 2.1, one of the Gustave Dore illustrations of Dante Alighieri's *The Divine Comedy* (*La Divina Commedia*). In this illustration, Dante and Beatrice gaze upon the highest heavens. Dante Alighieri wrote of his character's journeys through sin (inferno) to penitent life (purgatorio) on through to the soul's ascent to god (paradiso). The journey to god or paradise is seen as the journey to heaven.

Heaven, or *the heavens,* is/are represented across many religious and philosophical views. Entry into the heavens is described and defined in varying ways. The concept of heaven ties in with the concept of *after*life. Views include the notion that: while gods and the holy can access the heavens, terrestrial humans may not necessarily be able to, unless they have so-called "earned" this or otherwise "qualify."

Throughout history, social structures have cast their effect on views of entry into heaven. Some views held that only the social elite could access the highest levels of the *over world* as opposed to the *underworld*. Other views have said that adherence to particular doctrines or practices can make entry into heaven possible, or permittable.

WE MUST ASK HERE

Yes, we must ask here, who is qualified to determine who else can access the heavens, the afterlife, the dimensions beyond? Are there some who are higher placed, who have somehow been given (or have given themselves) this right to decide? Why would these persons have entitled themselves this way?

While the cross religion review of pathways for entry into the heavens warrants volumes and volumes of discussion, here I want to focus on the matter from the standpoint of the pages of this present book, *How To Die And Survive.*

Readers, it may be that we *all have a right* to understand and know practices and processes of access to higher dimensions such as what are described as afterlife-like and

heaven-like territories. (It may be that these are domains we actually already inhabit via our consciousness.)

We can all learn more about recognizing and activating our *inter*-dimensional nature, thus more about *how to die and survive*. This is the motivation for sharing the information in this book.

KNOCKING ON THE DOOR TO THE BEYOND

We are all, in a sense, knocking on the door to the beyond. Is there justice, and fair distribution of opportunity, there in the beyond? Who gets in? Who has a right to be there? *How To Die And Survive* says we all do have a right, as this heaven is a domain of our own consciousness-es. **We can not only generate** *access to,* **but we** *can generate,* **the heaven or territory we call after-life, and do so right there in the higher dimensions of our own consciousness-es.**

Ultimately, this is about who we humans actually are. As noted earlier in this book and in other books in this *Keys To Consciousness And Survival Series*, my view is that we are a species of consciousness rather than a biological species. Yes, we live here on Earth in physical biological bodies, however these are our vehicles for travel in this Earthly physical plane. These are our vehicles for our personal as well as our species travel here on Earth.

Coming to know we are a species of consciousness is a major shift (or better stated, a major expansion) in our awareness of ourselves, a shift, an expansion, that will aid in resolving much *individual and even species identity* confusion and crisis. This identity crisis belongs to all of the species of humanity. We may identify as only physical plane beings while we are this and so much more.

Is all the noise made this side of physical (biological) death heard on the other side, in another dimension? What is it that humans are trying to resolve as they pass through their Earthly journeys? What is it that all their efforts to hammer out political rights and opportunities will achieve in the longest of long runs, well into life after life domains?

Death is an equal opportunity.

No matter what your social status, the death of you in your current form is coming to you at some time. However, you need not die along with the dying systems and bodies in which you presently find yourself.

You, we, can choose to retain our personal consciousness-es, be captain our own ship/s, as you/we move on and into new domains.

EXERCISE #2.3
SEEING THE DYING SYSTEM

You live within many different systems. Think, without writing this down yet, of any systems in which you live—personal, physical, social, political, economical, ecological—which may appear to be having trouble these days.

What about the difficulties these systems are having, if anything, suggests to you that the systems you have thought of may be winding down or transitioning in some way? Would you say that any of these systems are actually dying? Why or why not?

What are signs that a system is dying? Can people sense such a death, or need they be told how to see it?

*What can you do and sense to see that **you perhaps can survive** when a system you live within does not? The system can die and yet you can, once you know this, survive. What does this concept mean to you? Let yourself think about this, sense this, without putting requirements or definitions on this awareness. Just see where this takes you for a few minutes. Remember, there are no right or wrong answers to the questions asked in these exercises.*

<u>EXERCISE #2.4</u>
SEPARATING FROM A
TROUBLED OR DYING SYSTEM

Select one of the troubled and/or dying systems you identified in the previous exercise. Close your eyes and see where you fit within, see yourself in, this system. See how very much a part of this system you are. See how tied to it—even defined by it—you may be.

Now, with your eyes still closed, use your imagination to create a way for you to exit this system. See yourself exiting. Get all the way out.

How did you choose to get out of this troubled, deteriorating, or dying system? Did you choose to physically die? Or did you choose to create, visualize, a window and simply climb through it?

Maybe you chose to speak out and try to change the system? Maybe you chose to pull off a great escape during which official members of the system attempted to hold you back?

Did you die trying to get out? Or did you survive by getting out? How do you know this?

Did you survive your exit? How do you know this?

Try this exercise a few more times, each time selecting a different type and size of dying system. Note mentally (write later if you wish) your means of exit each time.

Figure 2.1.
Dante And Beatrice Gaze Upon The Highest Heavens
Illustration By Gustave Dore In Dante Alighieri's *The Divine Comedy*.
(Illustration, Public Domain)

3
Defining Death And Death Technology

> State upon state is born,
> Covering upon covering
> Opens to consciousness of knowledge,
> In the lap of its mother the soul sees.
>
> "Nineteenth Hymn To Agni"
> *Hymns To The Atris*
> *The Veda*

WHERE ARE YOU RIGHT NOW?

Even if you are not floating, or not spinning, and or not suspended in space, you are on a planet that is in a sense doing so. You may not always find yourself—or feel yourself to be—suspended or floating or spinning in air or space, even though your planet is.

ATMOSPHERE

Give some time here to begin thinking of your air as *atmosphere*. Think of the change from walking around in "air" to going swimming in water. The water is, in a sense, also an atmosphere. So you likely already know something about what it can feel like to move from atmosphere to atmosphere.

Allow your mind to transfer what you are learning on these pages into many different awareness-es or realities or dimensions of reality.

Consider thinking of shifts we may make in our minds, or in our realities, as shifting through atmospheres or dimensions of awareness. Your consciousness, which is *who you are*, is exploring.

EXERCISE #3.1
REACHING OUT
INTO THE ATMOSPHERE IN FRONT OF YOU

Reach out into the air (or atmosphere) in front of you.

Pretend that you find a window in that atmosphere. Pretend that you open that window.

See, or at least pretend, that what you find coming in from beyond that window is determined by what you believe is there. If you are afraid of what you think is there, or of what you don't know about what is there, you may find something that feels like fear flowing in.

WINDOWS

Fear of death stems from fear of the unknown. Once you define death in a way with which you are comfortable, you need not fear as much, or at all, your changes, transitions, endings, deaths. You can open the window of change and transformation with awareness.

You can even find such openings interesting. You can learn the means—*the technology*—of traveling, of having your awareness, your consciousness, travel through such openings. Call this *interdimensional travel* rather than *death* to help expand your understanding of the process.

In a sense, we are all traveling across dimensions at all times of our waking and sleeping, living and dying, changing, developing, transitioning lives.[28] Hence this interdimensional travel is part of our ongoing process. We are simply attuning to this, becoming consciously aware[29] of this aspect of our existences.

WHAT ARE MINOR AND MAJOR DYINGS?

Let's again say this: moving out of a particular pattern formed in daily life, shifting to a new pattern, dying out of a pattern, is undergoing transition. Dying is shifting into a different dimension of consciousness or reality.

In that personal consciousness both perceives and defines a reality for each person, there are many realities. Similarly, there are many perceptions of, and thus experiences and forms of, transition and death.

Transitions and the endings contained within these are minor and major deaths of phases, stages, situations, bodies. Among these forms of minor and major transition are divorce, being fired, leaving home, or having one's children grow up and

---

[28] Note that this is a key and fundamental aspect of the *Interdimensional Psychology* I define in this *Keys To Consciousness And Survival Series*, and in the book titled, *Interdimensional Psychology*.

[29] See also the book, *Unveiling The Hidden Instinct*, for a discussion of our ability to become ever more consciously aware, and the importance of so doing.

leave home. Also included on this list are abrupt changes or endings such as having a home collapse in an earthquake, receiving a serious injury, or having something precious stolen.

These forms of changing, ending, shifting, transitioning, dying also include gradual but definite changes in behavioral patterns; outgrowing a stage of life; aging; undergoing the disease process, whether it is temporary, chronic, or terminal; and, of course, also included is the model of death with which we think we are so familiar: physical death, which is seen by many people as the ultimate of all deaths.

MINOR AND MAJOR TRANSFORMATIONS ARE DEATHS

That's it! So dying is indeed transformation. Of course this is more readily read about than knowingly experienced in many instances.

Dying is upsetting the apple cart and redesigning the display of your fruit. Dying is picking up the dice, shaking the dice, and then rolling the dice to yield a new number. Dying is stepping out of the game you have been playing, shifting to a new format.

> **Dying is transforming, letting go of,**
> **Your previous energy format, network, matrix,**
> **To allow yourself to form or join a new one.**

You might be saying: if dying were really this simple, there would not be so much trauma associated with it! There are many elements of this trauma. Among these elements are fear, pattern addiction,[30] materialism, and other problems of attachment.

RELEASING ATTACHMENTS

Let's briefly examine the general nature of ***problems of attachment***. Attachment can make changing, or leaving a pattern or phase of life, any form of dying, difficult to do. Of course, attachment can also be said to "make it all worth it."

How important is it to understand attachment? Very. Attachment is pervasive, woven into our physical (including biological) and emotional bodies. Attachment is so very invasive that we begin to confuse it with who we are. However, we are not our attachments.

For most of those who live in physical and emotional reality, forming, maintaining, developing, amending, and then if needed, dissolving, attachment networks is the great challenge. We become ***attached to our realities***: attached even to the way we organize our lives, our possessions, our time, our relationships, our feelings, even our identities.

We form obvious attachments and we form less than obvious, subtle, hidden attachments. When the time comes to change or to move on or die, sometimes these attachments must be

---

[30] Refer to the in depth definition and discussion of *pattern addiction* in the book, *Seeing The Hidden Face Of Addiction,* which is one of this author's books in her *Faces Of Addiction Series*. See also *Volume 8* in this *Keys To Consciousness And Survival Series*, titled, *Navigating Life's Stuff*. Refer to recommended reading section at the end of this present book. See also *Volume 10* in this series, *Seeing Beyond Our Line Of Sight*.

released. Like children clinging to baby blankets, we may fight this release even when we do not know we are doing so. (At times, it is our attachments hanging on to us, not releasing us....)

IDENTIFY YOUR WEB

We attach to be attached (to people, places, things, feelings, ideas, etc.). We do this attaching both consciously and sub- (or even un-) consciously. So, of course we naturally are wired to resist breaking the attachments we have formed for the very purpose of being so attached. This makes sense. And when we do, consciously or subconsciously, choose to leave or break or change an attachment we have formed, we feel this. We may even feel, sense, the tug of the attachment to hold itself in place.

So we rather naturally resist the release of an attachment, even when we do not know it exists or to what extent we have developed it. We may resist because on some level we confuse our *selves* with our web of attachments; we anchor ourselves so deeply in the web we create that we think we are the web. This confusion between the self and the web it generates is understandable. (think how often you may have heard the expression, "i am no one without you.")

After all, most selves and most webs (networks) of attachment are invisible to the eye. To truly *see* the difference between our selves and the webs of attachment we form or are pulled into (or both), takes concentration and training. This training is essential in the change, transition, and death technologies I offer herein, and is essential in refining our daily and our *expanded interdimensional awareness functions*.[31]

BEGIN THIS TRAINING

Let's begin this training here. You have a body. You have a consciousness. And you have a web, a network, of relationships to the world around you. Consult figure 3.1. Think of your *body* as your *instrument* of operation. Think of your instrument as having a technician to operate it, or a musician to play it. Think of your *self* as using the instrument to weave an *intricate web made up of cords* or strings, or strands of energy, an attachment network.

The relationship between the instrument or vessel (your body), the self (your self), and the web (of attachments) your self weaves via your body, can be confusing. The boundaries between these three basic manifestations are often unclear from within these three overlapping but distinct pieces of what you may believe is your whole identity and existence: your self, your body, your web. Be patient with your understandings of these three pieces. The distinction becomes more clear as you think in terms of the reality of this distinction:

What You Feel Is Your Self →
  (Flows Through) Your Instrument (Your Body And Brain) →
    (To Weave) Your Web.

---

[31] See the book, *Unveiling The Hidden Instinct* for more detail on this *aware* consciousness I define in this *Keys To Consciousness And Survival Series*.

Examine Figure 3.1 again. Note that Figure 3.1 suggests that some form of greater or super-consciousness generates your personal consciousness, and as I have defined this in other books, your ***personal consciousness matrix***. (See the book, *Unveiling The Hidden Instinct*, for more on this.)

We will return to the super-consciousness in later chapters. Also note that, as indicated in Figure 3.1, your consciousness generates a very fine energy structure or *consciousness matrix*.[32] your physical body is your vessel, your vehicle, which carries (at this time) your *consciousness matrix*.

And, of course, your physical body (along with your emotional body) also carries the web of attachments you weave during your physical lifetime in your physical body. Your physical body establishes your physical presence in physical reality and enables you to form physical and emotional relationships, attachments, to physical beings and objects.

A human living in physical reality naturally can confuse his or her *personal consciousness matrix* with its manifestations such as the mind-brain, and the webs it weaves. These webs are in no way the self, in no way the personal consciousness matrix.

The *personal consciousness* itself may be able to learn to survive the physical death of the biological body (which these *How To Die And Survive* books, and other books in this series, explain). However, the manifestations noted above, the *webs woven by*

---

[32] I further define the *consciousness matrix* in *Volume 3* of this series, *Unveiling The Hidden Instinct* and then in *Volumes 5* and *6* of this series, the *Overriding The Extinction Scenario* books, *Parts One* and *Two*.

the physical body and its mind-brain, are not the potentially surviving personal consciousness. Indeed, being clear about this distinction is key in surviving.

CONFUSION OF THE WEB OF ATTACHMENTS WITH THE PERSONAL CONSCIOUSNESS MATRIX

We may confuse, we may even be programmed to confuse, our web of attachments with our personal consciousness matrix. Growing ever more clear about this distinction, being aware of this within ourselves, can be key in our survival.

For some people, the idea of death can be frightening. The human being can be afraid to lose what he or she views as him or her self when faced with what appears to be death. He or she may believe that the consciousness lives in and only in the physical body and must have the living biological brain to exist.

Yet, it is the fine energy arrangement or structure I call the *personal consciousness matrix*, that is actually going to, *given the opportunity*, **SURVIVE**. This survival is *enhanced via our awareness of the possibility of survival*, and of the understandings involved as per what it can mean to *die and survive*.

What feels to be physical death—the death of the physical body and the self that identifies with the body, is actually: (1) the shedding of the physical body's webs (the shedding of the physical/emotional body and its web/s of attachments); and, (2) the transition, transformation, expansion, of the consciousness matrix, and <u>not</u> the losing of the consciousness itself.[33]

EXERCISE #3.2
DISTINGUISHING THE INSTRUMENT
FROM ITS MUSIC

Imagine a symphony performing a beautifully majestic concert. Musicians (consciousnesses) express using instruments (musical vessels or bodies). A web of notes is formed. This web, once connected to ears, appears to be music. The musical web flows into the air or atmosphere from the instruments. The musicians, using their instruments, weave the web of sound in such a way that a concert is released into the atmosphere. They weave a specific collection of sounds. These sounds or energies flow as long as the musicians continue to produce them.

Become one of the musicians for a moment. Play the music. Imagine you see the web of sound you are producing. Hold on to this image. Play on. See the web become more elaborate. Distinguish between the musicians, including yourself, and the music they and you are playing.

Now stop all playing. Note that when you all cease playing, the sound web disappears. See the web disappear. It may fade away slowly the way some sounds seem to do, or it may seem to immediately stop being a sound.

DURING THIS LIFETIME
YOU WEAVE A CONCERT, A WEB

---

[33] In depth discussion of this expansion of the personal consciousness is found in *Volume 10* of this series, titled, *Seeing Beyond Our Line Of Sight*.

During this lifetime of yours, you weave a concert or web of energies. When you stop weaving or playing your music, when you pack up your instrument and go home to another reality, the concert you wove spreads out like ripples on a lake. When your physical body dies, the web your physical body wove for you fades. Know that you are neither your physical body nor the web you have woven.

You, your actual self, your personal consciousness, need not fade. Your survival is an option. This is about dying and surviving.

When you undergo a major transition in life such as a physical death, you—the ultimate essence of you—your consciousness—need not be reduced or fade with the physical body and its web networks. This can be your option. You can **consciously choose** *to hold on to your personal consciousness matrix, or to let some of it go, or to reformat this matrix of consciousness, or to choose to release it all.* In-life transitions offer great practice for making such choices.

Knowing this can be key in survival. The advantages of understanding the issues involved in maintaining and or releasing your *personal consciousness* will be made clear in later chapters of this book (and of the following book, *How To Die And Survive, Book Two,* and of the other books in this *Keys To Consciousness And Survival Series*).

At the right time, consciously and never impulsively, once you have completed your life on physical plane earth, there will be a time to: ***let go to live***. The choice is yours, so long as you know that you can make it. So practice making this choice. Making this choice is the real dying (<u>and surviving</u>). Learning this is the next step in your/our evolution.[34]

EXERCISE #3.3
SEPARATING YOURSELF FROM YOUR WEB

Close your eyes. Now imagine yourself to be a musician. Play the instrument of your choice. Play a brief note.

Now, with your voice, make an actual (audible) sound, representing that note. Sing or tone or hum or make a one vowel sound such as "oooo." As soon as you play (play) the note, say goodbye to it.

Do this several times, as if you are blowing bubbles, as if each note you make is a bubble.

You know the bubble will soon pop or dissolve, so you say goodbye to it, detach from it, immediately after blowing it. Play a note. Say goodbye to it. Play (sing or say) another note. Say goodbye to it. . . . Continue this way a while.

NOTE
IN TRANSITION

Again, when you undergo a major transition in life, or a physical death, you—the essence of you—can *mistakenly* identify with and hang onto both your instrument (your body) and the attachment web, attachment network—you have created while in your body.

Do not confuse your body with your self. Also, do not confuse your web, your network of attachments, with your self. Be

---

[34] This evolution is further detailed in *Unveiling The Hidden Instinct* and both volumes of *Overriding The Extinction Scenario*.

clear that your self is not dying, your body and your web of attachments are being let go. And, you are releasing, and perhaps harnessing for your future use, the energy that has been tied up in, locked into, these attachments.

Your physical body and the web it weaves form your temporary address—part of an ever-changing map. Maps change. Maps come and go. However, *you* do not necessarily come and go. The survival of your personal consciousness is up to you. The more aware *you* are of *your* self as being *not* your web, *not* your attachments, rather your own *personal consciousness*, the more you can stay with your self as you undergo minor and major in-life and seeming end-of-life transitions and deaths.

Your consciousness creates your *personal consciousness matrix* which is, in essence, an energy arrangement forming your self, not your ego, not your web of attachment, but your core being.

<u>Both your personal consciousness—who you are—and its *consciousness matrix*—what who you are forms itself as being—can last, survive, last as long as you choose to maintain these</u>.[35]

In this sense, this is indeed all about *how to die and survive*. Interestingly enough, one of the fundamental realizations in dying and surviving is the understanding that the self need not die at all.

---

[35] Refer to the discussion in *Unveiling The Hidden Instinct*, which is *Volume 3* in this series.

What this means is that dying and surviving is, in essence, not necessarily dying in the first place, realizing that who you actually are need not die.

Your Personal Consciousness,
Your Personal Life Force,
Can Live On
Once You See This Option.

SOVEREIGNTY

You are your personal consciousness: ***this is your matrix of self.*** Your personal consciousness matrix is not your physical body or your physical brain. Whether or not you identify with a physical body and life, you are not that physicality itself.

You are, actually your personal consciousness is, the territory, not the map. Nor are you the vehicle you travel in at this time. You are not your physical body, nor are you the web of attachments you weave while in your physical body.

It is easy to confuse *your attachment to the map of your territory* with your territory. *(As I explain in Volume 3 of this series, **Unveiling The Hidden Instinct, our brain is programmed, our brain capacity is designed, to do this, to obstruct or interfere with our full awareness.**)* The map is too often better tended than the territory (simple daily life examples: emphasizing *where* you live not that you live there; *who* you *know* not *who* you *are*; *what* you look like not *who* is in there).

The maintenance and cultivation of the territory itself, the expansive domain of the personal consciousness, is not fully addressed. This is largely the result of our not realizing who we actually are. (As I explain in *Volume 3* of this series,

Unveiling The Hidden Instinct, our brains are programmed to have us not fully know and be who we actually are.)

You can learn more about who and what you actually are, about your core self, about your personal consciousness. This can help you when it is time to consciously survive (as a personal consciousness) a change or transition or death.

SEE AND RESIST BEING SUPPRESSED

Over time, after your brain's programmed-in prolonged suppression of your actual awareness of your own personal consciousness matrix, it is easy to lose touch with your actual self. It is easy to not have a say in what happens to your actual self. It is in this loss of contact with your actual self that your sovereignty, your free will, may be receding, even surrendered.

Sovereignty: what is sovereignty? Sovereignty is self-rule. You are the sovereign, the ruler, the queen or king of your personal consciousness and its matrix. You are in charge of your kingdom of consciousness so long as you choose to be. Do not take major changes in life and in physical death as pressure to relinquish your self, your personal consciousness, your sovereignty.

WE MAY HAVE BEEN
EVOLVED OR DESIGNED TO MISS THIS

It may be that we have been *evolved or even designed* to miss this about ourselves, to surrender ourselves, our personal consciousness matrix, in physical death. Now is the time for us to see that our survival involves taking this knowledge of who we actually are for ourselves, even taking this knowledge back from our own biological brains. We, as individuals, and as a species, can guide ourselves to know this, to remember this at key times in transitions.

Do not misinterpret the message here. You have full right to yield control of your personal consciousness, to surrender yourself to or merge yourself with another consciousness (perhaps one that is more divine, more powerful, or more benign, or more seductive for that matter).

Yet, you have *a right to know, and full responsibility to know*, that you are doing so -- and to know to what or to whom you are relinquishing the precious energy of your personal consciousness and its matrix.

To Whom Or What Are You Surrendering Your Right To Self Determination? You Can Choose The Path Your Personal Consciousness Will Follow.

There is great temptation during death, and for that matter in any profound transition, to give over or surrender the self without a careful examination of the power to which you are surrendering.

Remember that profound transition and even physical death do *not* result in the automatic ending of your personal consciousness matrix, and thus of your own free will.

You *can* maintain your self, your personal consciousness and its matrix, thus your own free will, through your changes, transitions, minor and major deaths, as long as you choose to, once you realize that this is your option.

Your transitioning is, when consciously conducted, the *raising of the power* of your free will. As you practice the exercises and take in the information contained in the following chapters, this notion will become more clear.

EXERCISE #3.4
OPENING THE WINDOW

This is an incredibly simple foundational exercise, designed to initiate the expansion of your understanding of death. Regardless of its simplicity, conduct the exercise as described.

Imagine that you are in a dark room. It is night. You are facing a closed window. It is bolted shut. Reach out with your hands. Unbolt this imaginary window, and open it. (you have opened a window in your mind.) Let the moonlight, the starlight, and any kind of celestial light you can imagine, pour in through the open window. The light showers you and fills you.

With your eyes still closed, hang on to this image as long as you can. Move into the next exercise with it.

EXERCISE #3.5
MOVING THROUGH THE WINDOW

Move now, by moving your arms as if you are swimming, through this open window. Swim toward the source of the light which is filling you.

Move into the next exercise as you swim toward the source of light which is filling you.

EXERCISE #3.6
BASIC REFORMATTING

As you fill with light, notice that (feel that, imagine that) you change from a physical body, made up of flesh and bones and organs and blood, to an increasingly lighter body, made up of less and less of what you think of as your physical body. Think about how every cell of yourself is turning into a new substance. Try to get detailed as you visualize this simple reformatting.

****

Read on patiently and with focus. You are now on your way into the basic reorganization of your awareness required to assimilate these change, transition, and death technologies.

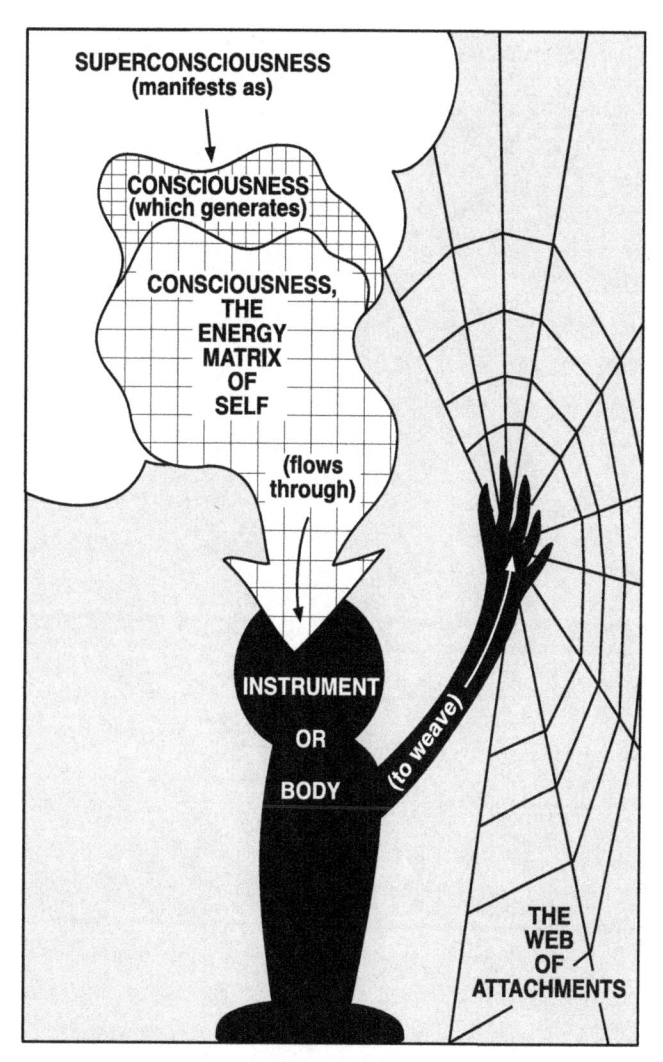

Figure 3.1
Oh, the Web We Weave

4
Accepting Death And Understanding Grieving

> He holds nothing back from life;
> therefore he is ready for death,
> As a man is ready for sleep after
> A good day's work.
>
> Lao Tzu
> *Tao Te Ching*

A general albeit vague sense of concern regarding the immediate or perhaps distant future is experienced by most everyone at least once in life. This may be a relatively minor (although not always minor) concern about whether one will be liked by friends, approved of by parents or teachers, or it may be a greater concern such as whether one might be hired for a needed job, or whether the rent can be paid or one's children can be fed.

Many people feel ongoing general concern, anxiety, and stress, or great concern, anxiety, and stress, relating to not being able to be certain about how life will go. Indeed, so many experience a subtle (quite frequently under the radar) yet ongoing free floating concern, anxiety, stress about life. These sensations and emotions can become a given, a built in part of the life experience.

This free floating anxiety may come and go, at times be difficult to identify and manage, then for many recede again. Sometimes this anxiety does not recede and manages to move into other emotional realms, manifesting as that general stress and anxiety, or maybe anger, or perhaps depression, or even fear. Of course, this "fear" is what we may call a "garbage pail diagnosis" in that fear is a single word for so many different emotions and sensations.

FEAR OF DEATH

Somewhere there behind the emotional soup of ongoing physical plane experience in biological emotional bodies, is indeed the awareness that we cannot have full say in all unknowns we may see in our lives. And in fact, we may feel on some level that we have no full say in what we feel is the greatest unknown, what seems to be the big death, physical/biological death.

Many people say that, on some level they are afraid of death. Many others say death does not concern them, that they are "not afraid" and that they will "deal with it when it comes." Of course, there are those who are indeed quite afraid, some say they are beyond afraid—a few add that they are "mortified." Many however, do say they are not sure how they feel about death, some hinting that although they may not let on, their possible lurking anxiety in the face of death is almost indescribable in words, that no words can capture what they may feel somewhere deep inside themselves about this matter, the greatest unknown. Generally, those not confronted with physical death do tend to consider it something to "deal with later, when I have to."

UNRELEASED FEAR

A low lying fear lives deep within many. Many a soul does not recognize this fear and or refuses to let this fear energy out. Many a soul suppresses this fear, stuffs this fear inward, instead of outwardly expressing it.

It is important to allow the outward expression of fear (in consciously safe and aware ways), so as not to trap the fear, not to cage it, not to keep it inside, not to have it fester there, not to have it take over.

Fear takes energy from you when you keep it trapped inside. Fear takes you from you. Immersed in unexpressed fear, you can lose yourself, your carefully alert awareness of what is taking place. (alert awareness is not fear, and is a practical and even life-saving function, not to be confused with fear.)

EXERCISE #4.1
EXPRESSING FEAR

Stand with your eyes closed.

Imagine that you stand before a closed door. You are about to beat at this door to the unknown as if you want to see what is behind it. Do not beat at this door because you want to go beyond it, rather because you want to know what awaits you.

Now you raise your hands in front of you.

Clench each hand into a tight fist. Beat silently against the invisible door or wall which stands before you.

Keep those fists clenched very tightly. Beat, silently, at first slowly, and then more and more rapidly. Beat harder now.

Now, while you are beating, imagine (but do not make any noise) that you are screaming into each of those beats. Just imagine this. Make no audible noise.

Now imagine, in silence, that these screams are becoming deafeningly loud. Imagine that you are attempting to keep these silent screams within your mouth. You are refusing to let the screams out. Clench your lips so that your screams cannot get out while you continue to beat at that door so very fiercely. That screaming is pressing to break through your lips.

Now stop beating on the door. Stop screaming.

Take a deep breath, hold it a moment, and then release it very slowly. Then stay with this for the next exercise.

EXERCISE #4.2
RELEASING THE LAST FEAR

In silence, stay with the feelings of the previous exercise. Now, close your eyes and examine your inside.

Are you in any sort of physical or emotional pain? Are you tired? Are you tense? Are you sad? Are you empty?

Move your attention slowly from the top of your head downward throughout your body. Is there a tear or maybe a cry or scream anywhere in there?

Find, or imagine, a remaining scream or point of unexpressed fear, sorrow, pain, or tension within you. Give this feeling a silent sound. Or go back to that silent scream you formed in the previous exercise.

Without making a sound, go back in to the silent scream or feeling you gave a silent sound to. Hear it silently sounding itself. Make no audible noise yet.

Now, imagine an invisible door in front of you. Raise your fists and bang on this invisible door. Even if you do not feel you need to bang harder, do so. Exaggerate your pounding. Imagine that you are (silently) screaming (or making another sound of anguish or pain).

Keep making this sound until you feel that you have exhausted the sound for now, until there is nothing left, no unreleased pain, no unreleased anxiety, no unreleased fear. Continue until you have or imagine you have released all you can find to release. ... hold for next exercise.

EXERCISE #4.3
FILLING WITH ACCEPTANCE

If, during the above exercise, you have released some stuffed away emotions and sensations, you may feel somewhat relieved or even calm now, and or perhaps a little empty inside. You decide what you feel now.

With your eyes closed, see yourself as an empty vessel. Decide that you will fill that vessel with a specific feeling—in this case, the feeling of acceptance, no clear definition of this, simply a very pure acceptance. This pure acceptance is calming, soothing, reassuring.

Give this acceptance a fluid image. Let it pour through you slowly, gently, quietly. Try to purify, to clarify this sense of acceptance, by concentrating on it, getting to know it very well. As you familiarize yourself with the feeling of acceptance, tell yourself what it is you can do later, in the near and far future, to remind yourself of how acceptance feels.

WHEN GRIEF IS MORE ABOUT YOU THAN THE PERSON YOU HAVE "LOST"

Let's talk again about grief here. Grief is many emotions under one label. And the grieving address so many changes and losses, often all at once. This sensation, this emotion, grief, is frequently an intense realization of death. Loss of a loved one tends to bring on a strong but vague sort of bewilderment, estrangement, or just plain sadness.

Some persons experience this loss more visibly than others; however, the loss—or the effect of major change—is there. If you have ever "lost" someone—and we will call it "lost" for now—then you know about grief.

Keep in mind that experiencing the grieving process can also be valuable when you, the grieving person, assume the perspective that the death being grieved is your own rather than that of a person you were close to. *What has died is the form—the material plane, in-the-flesh, form—of interpersonal relationship that you had with the deceased person.* This relationship, especially if either long-lasting in years, genetically close, and or emotionally intense, has most likely generated ties, a potent piece of web, an attachment network, an energy arrangement, between you and the person you have "lost."

When a person who is one of the players in, and also a component of, an interpersonal energy structure dies a physical death, the energy structure (the attachment network) is left unstable. Imagine a molecule losing one of its atoms. *Sometimes this molecule remains unstable for quite a while. Whether or not it is measurably unstable, this molecule is no longer the same molecule. The web of attachments that was woven is no longer the same web.*

Relationships—marriages, friendships, family ties, many workplace relationships, even forms of oppositional and even enemy relationships—are similar to molecules, with each person in essence being one of the atoms.

The way atoms are collected and held together in a molecule is by means of electrical bonds. Energy, in the form of electrons, is shared among molecules. An energy web is formed: strings, ties, cords, bonds between atoms—members of the molecule—take on characteristics, vibrational patterns, frequencies, of their own. If you remove an atom from the molecule, these bonds shift frequency, adjust, change in some other way, or break.

Sometimes an individual who loses a loved one claims that, although the loved one has died a physical death, that loved one has not broken all of the energetic bonds, attachments, or dissolved the entire web built during the physical lifetime he or she has just departed.

Some claim to communicate with "the dead," to maintain old bonds. Some who have lost loved ones explain that they just cannot let go of their loved ones.

Whatever your beliefs regarding communication with what you call "the dead," know that *any communication or energy coming to you from outside the material plane may be constitutionally different from energy coming to you from within the material plane.* Whether this energy is coming to you from you, or from somewhere else, this energy is there.

Think about the transmission of energy in the form of sound between two material plane atmospheres you know well: air and water. What do you hear of sound made in the air when you sit entirely submerged on the bottom of a swimming pool? If you sit outside a swimming pool, what do you hear when the swimmer under water hums loudly?

If there is any communication or energy coming to you from loved ones who are deceased, coming to you from "the beyond"—from what is beyond the material plane—it will be different enough (from what it had been before that physical death) that you either will not recognize it, or will recognize it and immediately turn it into something that fits your reality, or will somehow recognize it for what it is, finding that it is markedly transformed from its previous in-the-flesh signals.

HANGING ON

Still, at this point, this experience is largely if not entirely about you, your mind and spirit. You may try to hang on to the old physical plane bond system, attachment network, you had built with that person. You may even convince yourself that you are indeed hanging on. Still, something has changed. That being, if still conscious and in communication with you, is now in a completely different dimensional atmosphere.

This means that the energy structure of your relationship is radically transformed. The strings or cords of the piece of web you shared are constitutionally different. There has been a great transformation at one end of the cord. When you die your next physical death, you will notice how incredible this transformation is.

When you hang on to an energy structure that is no longer formatted the way it once was, you are tying yourself, and perhaps sometimes tying the deceased being, to an illusion, to a no longer existent energy arrangement, or to a soon dissolving format. Here is where the grieving is born.

Here is where you perhaps can trap yourself, and sometimes maybe even your deceased loved one, in the shadow of a broken relationship molecule.

This is a dangerous trap. You perhaps can tie yourself and your deceased loved one to an energy sink, a trap that consumes disorganized or distorted or simply misunderstood energy.

The illusion that the old bond or piece of web exists unchanged, that there is still accessible energy there in that old set of *cords*, can consume its participants. Some believe that this is how the "dead" may be prevented from moving on with their journeys. Note that the "living" can also be prevented from moving on with their lives.

This state of mind is the case in many minor and major death situations. This condition is apparent among those who are undergoing long-term grieving processes regarding the loss: of a loved one to physical death, of a spouse or lover to divorce or another relationship or event, of self-identity due to aging, illness, loss of a limb, the end of a collegial membership in a life-long profession or organization, or many other major life changes.

Ultimately, the grieving person is grieving the change of, or loss of, some part of the self.

EXERCISE #4.4
EXPRESSING GRIEF

Review or even repeat the three exercises described above (#4.1, #4.2, and #4.3), this time with the sense that the person (or subject/object) of your grief (usually a loved one) waits beyond the door upon which you are asked to beat. When you start to silently scream and wail in #4.3, include the name of whoever (or whatever) you are grieving.

Reach for that person or thing. Reach out as far as you can and cry out the name. Beg for the person or thing to return to you. Imagine that you have tied one or more ropes or cords to that person or thing and tug on these cords. Pull on them. Freeze. Hold for next exercise.

EXERCISE #4.5
CORD CUTTING CEREMONY

Visualize the person or thing you have been tugging on. Say, as if that person or thing is speaking these words to you: "release me. Cut the cords so that I may move on with your blessing." Respond, "I release you. I cut these cords so that you may move on with my blessing." Use your fingers as if they are scissors and imagine that you are cutting a web of strings that once tied you to this person or thing.

Now ... see whoever or whatever you have just released turn to light and float away. . . . Feel perhaps love, or relief, and or acceptance. Work to focus on these feelings.

MASTERY

Accepting changes, losses, deaths, involves mastery of emotions such as sadness, anxiety, confusion, fear, or what may be called grief. Grief is a normal human emotion. Appreciate its richness and depth.

Understand how real the experience of grief is for your emotional body. Both your physical and your emotional bodies experience grief. Feel this, sense this.

We can navigate this experience, and reach beyond, see beyond, the horizon of our reality to find more to know.[36]

---

[36] See more on this matter in another volume in this *Keys To Consciousness And Survival Series*, titled *Seeing Beyond Our Line Of Sight*.

5
Preparing For Death — Your Own And Others'

> ... the last thought and emotion that we have before we die has an extremely powerful determining effect on our immediate future... that last thought or emotion we have can be magnified out of all proportion and flood out our whole perception.
>
> Sogyal Rinpoche
> *Tibetan Book Of Living And Dying*

Getting to know how we experience changes, transitions, minor and major in-life and seeming end-of-life "deaths," is part of getting to know how we move through life. And, the "big death" represents a marker in life (and yes, in death) for everyone.

Living life to its fullest involves understanding transitions, including changes, endings, and deaths of all forms including seeming end-of-life deaths.

SEEING WHAT SURVIVAL CAN MEAN

Living life to its fullest may eventually also mean *Seeing Beyond Our Line Of Sight*,[37] recognizing that we have the potential to choose to be here in the physical plane while also concurrently reaching, expanding, beyond into other dimensions of ourselves, of our consciousness-es, of our realities. Understanding this about our species is where our actual survival potential may be.[38]

THE IMPORTANT NOT READY ISSUE

"But it's not fair! I'm not ready to die!"

This anguishing lament is cried so many times. This fierce pain is associated with the "human condition." Many are never ready. And why should we be ready to go into a great unknown? What can we do to better know what is unknown to us? How much can we define for ourselves to aid us in this passage?

Knowing more about death does not eliminate death or the emotions experienced. Yet, knowing more allows us a sense of knowing or defining for ourselves what this means to us, and what this death process is for us.

We can bring ourselves to grow ever more aware of our own consciousness as we move through our experiences. This is the process of *Seeing Beyond Our Line Of Sight*. (Again, see the book by this title for more about seeing beyond, expanding

---

[37] See *Volume 10* in this *Keys To Consciousness And Survival Series*, titled, *Seeing Beyond Our Line Of Sight*.
[38] See *Volume 5* in this *Keys To Consciousness And Survival Series*, titled, *Overriding The Extinction Scenario*.

our awareness beyond, what we presently see and know. *Seeing Beyond Our Line Of Sight* Is *Volume 10* in this *Keys To Consciousness And Survival Series*.)

Certainly religion, and even philosophy and the arts, and in some instances even science, have helped us know more about leaving the physical body whether temporarily or for good.[39] where this material leaves off is in essence where these *How To Die And Survive* teachings can enter....

WHAT DOES IT MEAN TO BE READY?

One must always be ready to die. This readiness is not suicidal. Nothing in this book advocates suicide. Far too many suicides are committed without full preparation and even training. Most cultures do not include this preparation in their health care, or even in their training and services.

There is a big difference between being consciously ready to die and being emotionally, perhaps almost impulsively, on the brink of killing oneself. (this is not to say that all suicidal tendencies are this. I save that discussion for elsewhere.)

Having conscious awareness (and conscious focus where possible) during changes, transitions, minor and major in-life and seeming end-of-life endings and deaths, is healthy and

---

[39] See *Part One* of *Volume 3* in this *Keys To Consciousness And Survival Series*, the book titled, *Unveiling The Hidden Instinct*, for an in depth discussion regarding the brain and the mind, and out of body experiences (OBEs), not limited to but including near death experiences (NDEs).

wise. Being highly informed regarding transition itself, and being highly aware and centered, as focused as possible, during any minor or major transition is a powerful means of *ever more conscious transit* (especially in terms of the strengthening and survival of the self as the personal consciousness.)

Conscious preparation for all forms of transition, whether in-life or seeming end-of-life transition, is so important. For example, three very key parts of preparing for your end-of-life transition are the feeling of readiness, the practical preparation, and the sense of closure.

The following discussion applies also to preparing for the death of a loved one in two ways. First, you can help a loved one prepare for death when you understand how to prepare for your own. Second, you can share the *sense of being prepared* for death with a loved one by *feeling prepared* for your own death, no matter how far into the future this may be.

READINESS

Readiness for death is a healthy state of mind. Readiness implies that you are prepared, like a fireman or firewoman ready in case there is an alarm, like a lifeguard ready to leap into the pool should a swimmer need help.

The most prepared actors, firemen, and lifeguards, do not sit nervously, waiting to be called. They are well trained, they know their procedures, their methods—their jobs.

If you have ever studied for tests, you may know how differently you feel when you have studied very well. You may enter the test with a high degree of confidence that most, if not all, that you will be asked to do will be something with which you are familiar, or something that you may figure out because you have dealt with a similar challenge before.

So understand more and more about minor and major transition, including death. Know that the best way to live life ready for all transition and for physical death is to deeply understand that:

- every moment in the time of your life matters;

- the future is not entirely predictable;

- you, your personal consciousness, can be always ready—ready for things to stay the same, and ready for everything to change;

- you are already informed and ready for your transition and death: you have already explored the transition and dying process; you already understand what transition and dying is about; you have already prepared yourself for your next transition and dying.

- **now you must remember what you know....**

    You can both consciously and subconsciously carry your knowledge forward into what is beyond, into the beyond.[40]

---

[40] Again refer to *Volume 10* in this *Keys To Consciousness And Survival Series*, titled, *Seeing Beyond Our Line Of Sight*.

EXERCISE #5.1
BEING READY FOR DEATH

Read the above list aloud, slowly several times. Read it as if you are telling someone else how simple it is to know these things.

PRACTICAL PREPARATION

Practical preparation for any major transition not only eases, but empowers, the passage. You already know this. While it is not always possible to plan ahead for all life-changing and life-ending events, many persons can allow themselves the opportunity to "take care of business" by recognizing that we all undergo changes and transitions in life, and we all eventually undergo physical death.

Planning around one's own physical death can be a good discipline for planning for other seemingly simpler transitions.

It is not the goal of this volume to explore the legalities of various aspects of physical death such as health directives, trusts, and wills. Readers are, however, encouraged to explore the following and related topics as far in advance of their physical deaths as possible:

- estate transmission.
- the will, living will, and or trust.
- decisions regarding one's physical/biological body.
- your opportunity to specify the way you want to be "treated" while you are transitioning and or dying, and when you physically die.

GENERATE CLOSURE

Every season, every day, every phase, closes or transitions to a new time, a new energy arrangement, a new matrix.

Closing is natural. However, we overlook most closures we move through, so many being largely unnoticed.

Generate closure, and be aware of the value of doing this. To generate closure, wake up each day ready for the day. Go to sleep each night acknowledging to yourself that you have completed that day. Review the day before falling asleep. Feel complete. Feel as if you have just read the last page of an interesting book, and that you are now closing the book and placing it on a shelf.

Do this review at the close of days, weeks, months, years. Even if you have what you call a "bad day" or a "horrible week" or a "losing season," be satisfied with the idea that you are living out a phase or time period, perhaps see this as a pattern cycle, and a cycle within a cycle.

Observe as many cyclical endings and beginnings as you can, simply by acknowledging that they have occurred. Complete each day, week, month, year, each time cycle of your life, this way.

Some of your observations will be quiet statements to yourself. Others will be celebrations with other people. Generate increasing awareness of repeating closures.

EXERCISE #5.2
PRACTICING CYCLE SENSITIVITY

Choose a recent time cycle of your life. You may pick the past hour, or the past 24 hours, or the past week, or the past season, or the past year, or the past decade. Think to yourself when it was that this cycle began and when it was that this cycle ended.

As you are thinking, realize that this cycle is a cycle within a larger cycle, as are all cycles. Mentally review all the cycles that the cycle you chose fits into. For example, in terms of Earth time, a second is part of a minute, a day is a part of a week, and a century is a part of a millennium.

EXERCISE #5.3
STUDYING A CYCLE

Return to the cycle you chose in the above exercise. Think about what you might call the beginning of that cycle. Try to recall some characteristics you can associate with the beginning of this cycle: how you felt, how you looked, what was going on in your life or in the world around you.

Now pick out events during the middle of this cycle. Do not trouble yourself with efforts to put these events in order, in linear time sequence. Keep in mind that linear time is an physical plane reality and or illusion. It is a handy map for those who live in material reality, but it is only a map, not the reality. Allow the events which took place during your chosen cycle to come back to you, in any order.

Now pick an event or series of events that you associate with the end of your chosen cycle or time period. Think about this or these events. See these as **cycle completion points**. *Then also see these as* **recycle points or cycle initiation points.**

You have just reviewed a cycle of your life. Treat that cycle like a book that you can put on your shelf for safekeeping and take down and re-read anytime you like.

Treat that cycle, that book, as a part of a series, a sequence, a chain of books, a larger pattern series or cycle you have lived and are living.

See that each whole book is also a chapter in a much larger book (or pattern, or pattern cycle). You may or may not have the larger book handy. You may or may not yet have room on your shelf for the larger book. You may or may not know what the larger book is about.

This not knowing is all right. One of the greatest adventures in death is the close of a cycle and the opening of a new one. Closes frequently feel like dyings. But the larger story can only come to you as you read on, as you live on, as who you actually are survives.

EXERCISE #5.4
SEEING YOUR LIFE CYCLE

Imagine for a moment that your life has just ended at exactly this point in time. Briefly review your life.

Try to group events, memories, that come to your mind in terms of whether they fit into the beginning phase, the middle phase, or this (would-be) seeming "end" phase.

At first, the memories may come to you in a jumble, with all phases mixed together. To help feel that you are organizing your thoughts here, break your life into the three parts, beginning, middle, and end.

Use any sort of category of three phases that you want to—first phase or beginning, then middle phase, then last phase or so-called ending. For example, perhaps divide up the phases of your life by years, or by relationships, or by health, or other patterns.

Now review the beginning phase. Do not try to time sequence your memories in great detail.

Now review the middle phase.

Now review the end phase. Spend several minutes on the last bits of this end phase. Breathe a sigh of relief when you complete this review.

ABOUT CLOSURE

Remember that although closure is the end of a cycle pattern, it is also a transition, even a transformation, into a new cycle pattern. Still, closure is a valuable sensation, a valuable completion of a phase of cycle patterning.

A sense of closure does not come automatically. It is important to admit to what obstructs closure, to explain to yourself how you may be resisting closure, whether it be closure of a relationship, an addiction, a phase, a particular physical or perhaps other existence. This requires a willingness to conduct an honest inventory of your life and the patterns within it.

SENSE OF FINISH

No matter how much you appreciate the cyclical nature of life, you may find that the close of a particular phase of life may leave you with the nostalgic or uncomfortable or maybe even desperate sense that you are unfinished.

Think back. Have you ever felt unfinished, "left hanging," wanting more of something with none of it to come?

Have you ever seen a child resist leaving the movie theater when the movie ended, wanting more of the story? The logic of the story ending may have been obvious to the more experienced movie viewers such as the parent, but not to the child.

Could you be this child in some way?

When you want to feel closure, what do you look for, what do you need?

EXERCISE #5.5
DEFINING THE
UNFINISHED

You can use pencil and paper for this exercise.

Now that you have given some thought to the sensation of being unfinished, let's work with this idea.

Make a list of everything that you have not done, that you would like to finish were you moving out of your city or town today. Title this list "moving away today." Try to put at least five things on this list. You may have many more than five things on your list. This is fine.

When you have completed the list of what you would do were you moving away today, write a new list: list everything that you have not done that you would like to have done or to complete doing, were you being forced to move urgently, forced to depart. Label this new list, "forced urgently to depart."

For this list, imagine now that you are being forced by the law, or by a political event, or by some kind of major change in the world, to leave your home and family—whoever that might be—parents, siblings, spouse, children, or other very close kin or friends that you have. Imagine for just this moment that you are being forced to leave them for good and will not be able to communicate with them again by telephone, by mail, or by any sort of clear method that you have used to date to communicate clearly with them. Is this list different from the first one, the list you made when you imagined you were moving out of town with a less serious reason? What is it that you have not said or done given this more pressing reality?

When you have finished this second list, write a third: imagine for a moment that your life is over—this life, the life that you are in right now— tonight at midnight. Label this list "die tonight." What is it that you would do or immediately complete if you only had a certain number of hours left to live?

How many things on the above lists would you include? How many of those things would you discard as being not important given the short amount of time to live? What new things would you include on this new list? Write this list, circling the new items, if any— items which come to mind when you are asked to imagine for a moment that your physical death may be imminent.

Now, try to organize each of the above lists into categories—in terms of personal relations, money matters, work, commitments, or other categories you think of. You may want to rewrite these lists into a chart such as the chart described in Figure 5.1.

Look slowly at each of your lists. Notice your reaction or absence of reaction to each item on each list. Put a little star next to the items that you feel you have some kind of emotional connection to—some kind of emotional feeling that says you really need to complete this item. Star items which elicit a feeling in the heart or the gut.

This sort of emotion may indicate that you would very much like to take care of these things before dying ...

Realize that you are in need of settling the *feelings about* these items, not necessarily the items. These feelings are the most unfinished of all items, not because they have to do with any thing or any person in particular, but because you may be most emotionally attached to their sensations, processing, or completion, resolution.

For the time being, it is enough to recognize that such attachments may make it somewhat more difficult to transition – to change, break a pattern, end a cycle, or die, with grace and personal power. We will return to this matter in Part III of this book, *How to Detach*.

* = feels very important			
	Moving Away Today	Forced Urgently to Depart	Die Tonight
Practical details			
Financial			
Legal			
Work and similar committments			
Family			
Other personal relationships			
Self: Things I always meant to do for myself			
Etc.			

Figure 5.1

Last Lists

6
Spotting
The Right Time To Die

> ... When the last Lacandon dies,
> the world will come to an end.
>
> Chan k'in,
> Lacandon Elder And Prophet
> As Told To Victor Perera
> *The Last Lords Of Palenque*[41]

---

[41] Years ago, I was meeting with my dear friend and colleague, Victor Perrera (co-author of *Last Lords of Palenque*), in New Mexico. That night I had been asking Victor Perrera for permission to quote Chan K'in in this book, *How To Die And Survive*. Note that Chan K'in is indeed quoted above, at the start of this chapter. Also that night, I had to temporarily interrupt my meeting with Victor Perrera as I was a guest on the Art Bell Show for some two hours, talking about death and demonstrating body exit techniques. When the radio show interview was over, I went back to my meeting with Victor Perrera. It was quite late at night and we talked for hours. Then the telephone rang. It was the editor of a major magazine Victor Perrera had been writing for. This editor delivered a message to Victor Perrera that there was an emergency and he must immediately call his friends in Guatemala. He did so. These were old friends he had known since his childhood when he was growing up in Guatemala, when he was closely relating to members of the Lacandon tribe. He had in those years and throughout his adulthood, remained close to Chan K'in, who became the Lacandon tribal leader. Now this night, I sat with Victor Perrara as he was told by telephone that Chan K'in had just died.

Time to leave the nest. Perhaps time to find or form a new habitat here or somewhere, perhaps to generate one in another dimension of our consciousness, which is where we actually do live.

Too soon, it seems, we leave the planet where we have made our home. We are cast out by something, perhaps by fate or age, or maybe by biospheric changes, or maybe by choice, or perhaps for some reason we cannot know (yet), cast out of the nest, physical plane planet earth.

One of the greatest regrets voiced about physical deaths which occur before what is called a "ripe old age" or the "end of a long and full life" is that death has come too soon. Thus the phrase "untimely death" has been applied.

Death and timeliness are more often than not, anything but companion concepts.

DIE TIMELY

There is value, dignity, self-respect, and free will, in being able to sense for yourself the time when you approach any in-life or seeming end-of-life transition or death. Again, nothing here advocates suicide. Not at all. Instead, this book advocates ever increasing awareness of where we are on our pathways, in our lives, in our short and long term transition processes.

Note that this is not asking you to question your own religious beliefs about your own god's will regarding your own death, if you have these. Not at all. Note also that this is not saying that once the time of your physical death is sensed, physical suicide is in order. Not at all. This book is simply saying that your increased sensitivity and awareness can be your guide.

Consciously navigating a transition, an ending, the dying of a phase of life, for yourself is not physically dying or killing yourself, not in any way. Rather, you are *consciously navigating your transition*. You can, as a personal consciousness, learn to survive as a *personal consciousness, consciously navigating and surviving transitions, such as minor and major shifts, changes, endings, deaths.*[42]

You can start learning what it means to survive as a personal consciousness while living here in the material physical plane Earth biosphere. Let's briefly examine some of the elements of this concept ....

CHRONOLOGICAL AGE IS DECEPTIVE

As suggested in the previous chapter, one of the most important parts of transition and death preparation is knowing where you are in your patterns and processes, phases of your own life cycle. Most people, including school children, who learn about the stages of the life cycle in biology and science classes, assume that being old, chronologically old, is a time when we near the end of our life cycle, and that, at that time, we are nearing death.

---

[42] Again see *Volume 8* in this *Keys To Consciousness And Survival Series*, titled, *Navigating Life's Stuff*.

However, chronological age is deceptive. It indicates very little about critical patterns and cycles in which an individual is immersed. Chronological age leads us to emphasize a biological and linear time aspect of the life cycle.

The life cycle is actually a conglomeration of many other cycles and phases within cycles. We live within cycles within cycles within cycles....

For example, the many cycle phases of life, the many in-life and seeming end-of-life transitions such as changes, endings, deaths, experienced by an individual can be explained in terms of *four basic patterns* within which all other re-occurring patterns form: *struggle patterns* (the ups and downs of life); *paradox patterns* (the trapping conditions in life); *insight patterns* (the glimpses beyond life's struggles and paradoxes); and *spiritual elevation patterns* (the sustaining of the awareness-es rendered during insights) as I have developed and explained in detail in other books.[43] (See Figure 6.1.) Note that the term, spiritual, is used here, not referring to any particular belief system or religion or spiritual practice, rather to the elevation of the awareness of one's own spirit, of one's own personal consciousness.

The characteristics of a life cycle, a life path, can be examined for indications of these four basic patterns or cycle phases. Each of us can review our lives in terms of the , patterns, cycle

---

[43] See *Volume 8* in this series, *Navigating Life's Stuff*, and also the book, *Gestalting Addiction: Speaking Truth To The Power And Definition Of Addiction, Addiction Theory, And Addiction Treatment* (Faces Of Addiction Series), for example. See reading list at the end of this present book for additional titles.

phases, we have been through and are in. You can map your life out, noting hundreds of shifts from struggle to struggle, to struggle to paradox to insight maybe back to struggle, to paradox to spiritual elevation, or whatever path, whatever ongoing mixing of these four basic and repeating pattern phases, your life takes.

Every shift or trend out of a particular phase is in a sense an ending, a transition, a minor or major death of a pattern or situation.

EXERCISE #6.1
MAPPING YOUR LIFE

Use, in any order and any quantity, each of the four patterns diagrammed in Figure 6.1, (struggle, paradox, insight, and spiritual elevation)—and map a piece of your life.

You can either visualize this map or draw it on paper. You may want to choose a recent week, month, year, or decade. You may want to map a relationship or a habit pattern. You may want to make a general map of your entire life.

There is no right or wrong way to do this, and no appropriate level of detail. You are the map maker.

The territory you are mapping is your own. You will want to do this exercise again many times in your future.

EXERCISE #6.2
SEEING SHIFTS
AND TRANSITIONS
IN YOUR LIFE

Now, once you have made this map of a portion or of all of your life thus far, draw circles around the areas when transitions out of and in to next phases took place (or are taking place at this time, if currently). See these circles as transition points, pivotal moments in minor or major endings, deaths, of phases and births of new ones.

RIGHT TIMES

Spotting the right time to "die" or to end a particular phase of life takes a degree of alertness. If we study carefully our patterns and phases, we can detect signs that we have been and are at forks in our life paths, as well as signs that we actually stand before windows of opportunity, avenues that lead to profound transition.[44]

There are times when life brings you to a fork in the road. Sometimes you do not see the fork coming.

The fork just appears. Sometimes you do not realize that the fork has appeared. You may not be aware of what a fork feels like. You may not realize that you are straddling the forked roads and that you are feeling the im-balancing tug of conflicting choices.

Sometimes you realize this but do not want to face this realization. The realization may demand action that you feel unprepared to take.

---

[44] For more on the nature of transition, and on the navigation of transition, again refer to *Volumes 8 and 9* in this *Keys To Consciousness And Survival Series*, titled, *Navigating Life's Stuff*.

The tug of conflicting choices is, in essence, an *energy paradox*. You are being pulled in opposing, at least in conflicting, directions.

You can get stuck in this tug of war, this energy paradox, for quite some time. When you are stuck this way, your energy is trapped. While this trap may be an interesting place to be — to learn about — for a while, it is no place to stay for too long. Many individuals know this and instinctively (but relatively unconsciously) do something to break out or die out of the trap, or at least to break or die out of it for a while.

Unfortunately, such an unconscious (or impulsive) break out may not be as healing, or as pure a release, or as complete, as a more conscious breakout.

Choosing to be consciously aware of your self on all levels, being as conscious as you can be, allows for the *conscious navigation of any change or death, any transition*.

ESCAPE FROM PARADOX NEED NOT BE PHYSICAL DEATH

Sometimes life leads one into the sensation of being trapped, or into an actual emotional or other form of trap. Feeling trapped with no good way out, or no way out, can be stressful, even distressing, at times for some even anguishing. This is what other books in this series define as the ***paradox pattern***. (again refer to *volumes 8 and 9* in this *keys to consciousness and survival series*, both of these books titled, *navigating life's stuff*, for more on these patterns.)

The trap may contain a set of seemingly no right choices, with the sense that one of these choices must nevertheless be chosen. (of course, even not making a choice is making a choice, in this case to not make a choice.) Despite the anguish you may feel at having to make a choice, no choice may feel better, more right, or more safe. How confusing, how perplexing. What a quagmire. How do you escape from such a paradox?

What if all you see is a difficult or even dangerous death-like escape from this pressure, from this disturbing or even perilous paradox, with the alternative, not escaping from this paradox, offering what seems to be the same result – a lose-lose stuckness, a sort of death-like experience. This no exit paradox seems to offer the same non-exit whether escaping or remaining caught in the paradox: the dangerous or death-like experience.

We have all experienced obvious or hidden, minor or major, what-to-do, no-way-out, no-right-answer, situations or traps. These are traps in that we, our energy, our selves, as caught, trapped. What do we do with this experience of paradox, this trapped sensation?

First, recognize the sensation of paradox.[45] make a commitment to experience, to get to know, this trapped sensation, this paradox pattern. See its characteristics so that you can more consciously navigate it.

---

[45] Deep review of the *paradox experience* itself is offered in other books in this series such as *Navigating Life's Stuff*.

This release from this trap is not in itself a physical death. This release is, however, a profound transition, and like many changes in life, can feel a little like dying.

If you find yourself trapped in paradox yet about to release the energy trapped there, *your* energy, allow yourself to rejoice. Rejoice as you are actually at the precious junction of the moment leading to the *escape from paradox*.

A choice to go one way or another can indeed be made. No matter how painful it is to let go, this letting go is your liberation. No matter how much you think you may be losing, you gain your freedom.

Figure 6.2 shows energy trapped in a paradox, in a double bind, moving toward release in the *fork,* and released in the *escape*.

EXERCISE #6.3
DEVELOPING FORK AWARENESS

Think of a present, past, or possible time in your life when you feel, have felt, or will feel, substantially unsettled for a significant chunk of time. Be in that time. Do not try to define "substantially unsettled." Just accept whatever comes to mind here. Make the unsettled time you have selected feel like now if it is not already in the present, by imagining that you are actually feeling that unsettled.

Now stand up if you can, or imagine standing, and, with your eyes closed, immerse yourself in this situation.

Pretend that you are wandering through this situation. With your eyes still closed, take a look under your feet. Try to feel your situation through the soles of your feet. Try to see where you are in your life. Try to see the road or life path you are on. Allow yourself to see (or imagine for now for this exercise) that you are at a fork in your path, a paradox in your reality.

Stand before this fork and feel confusion and indecision. If no confusion and indecision comes to you, imagine that you feel these feelings. Now exaggerate this confusion and indecision. Hold for next exercise.

EXERCISE #6.4
MOVING ON

At this fork in your life path, inform yourself that you can make a choice to go one way or another—to take one of the roads leading out of the fork. How do you move ahead now? Which way do you go? For a moment, force yourself into a decision.

Remember that this is just an exercise and you do not necessarily have to take this decision back to your life, your reality outside this exercise.

Make a choice. Take a road. Close your eyes and leap. Examine your reactions, your feelings, here. Do you fully make the leap? Or do you hold on to the indecision? The confusion? If so, how long?

What, if any, feelings replace the unsettled sensations you were having? Fear? Shock? Relief? Pride? Exuberance? Anticipation? No feeling? Numbness?

SPOT SPECIAL JUNCTURES

Life is full of minor and major changes, transitions, endings, deaths. We can learn so much about ourselves, our lives, our minds, and our consciousness-es by being ever more aware of how we find our way through events and passages in our lives.

We can think in terms of physical death to see more about how we navigate phases and passages in our lives, as physical death is a distinct, an obvious, change. Physical death is a very special juncture, frequently a profound challenge. Even thinking about one's physical death takes the self through various processes. One feels that ahead at some point in life will be a fork in the path of the self. From the standpoint of this book, *how to die and survive*, the fork in the road may be just that: choose to accept the finality of physical death as a given, or choose to explore what it means to die and survive as a personal consciousness.

Forks in the road of life are actually quite common. We see many of these and miss noticing many of these. Relationships such as marriages and friendships may reach forks in their roads. Work lives and careers may also come upon forks in their roads. One's behavior patterns may reach or hit forks, decision points. For example, a person dealing with a drug/alcohol addiction may come to a point where that addiction if continued may be a life-ending addiction, and where halting that addiction behavior may be very difficult. The fork in the road in this case is choose to do what it takes to survive, or continue on the path of the deadly addiction.

Addiction (whether it be drug addiction or non-drug, behavioral, addiction) is perhaps one of the most pointed examples of pattern cycles in life. Addiction patterns tend to be cyclic, with addicted persons caught or trapped in the patterns, the cycles of the addictions. For example: be triggered, crave using, respond by relapsing again, and then cycle through this again.[46]

Yet, it is not only addiction cycles that are patterns, cycles in life. Life is full of cyclic patternings, many being problem patterns, even dangerous patterns. Yet, to break the cycle requires stepping up to the fork in the road, facing the paradox that says: either stay caught in the cycle or break free of the cycle.

SEE THE WAY TO CYCLE OUT

The gift of awareness allows us to see patterns, cycles, in our lives. We can fine tune our awareness to see ever more of our patterns and processes, to see the many pattern cycles and sub-cycles (cycles within cycles, patterns within patterns) we are caught in. We can fine tune ourselves to spot the paradoxes we are trapped in: remain in caught in this pattern, this cycle, or break free of it.[47]

To better understand this *caught in a cycle paradox*, see yourself at a fork. You have choices here. You can either cycle back into the cycle you have been in (perhaps voluntarily or perhaps trapped in by outside or inside forces), or cycle out of it into another perhaps better, safer, healthier, more rewarding, cycle. Which way do you go? Do you cycle back into this same

---

[46] Refer to the book by this author titled, *Seeing The Hidden Face Of Addiction*, for a deep look at **pattern addiction**.

[47] Refer to the *Navigating Life's Stuff* books, *Volumes 8 and 9* in this *Keys To Consciousness And Survival Series*, where the paradox and other pattern characteristics are detailed.

or a very similar cycle/pattern, cycle back into this same piece of emotional or physical life, or do you cycle out and move on?

The more aware of where you are in your processes and patterns, the more you can harness the energy there to move to a new level of self, a new level of awareness of who and what you actually are. So, how is it that you can harness the energy trapped in patterns? What does it take for you to spot the right time to leave a cycle, to die out of an old and repeating, cyclic, trapping, state of mind or behavior?[48]

LIFE CYCLES WITHIN CYCLES

Take a good look at your life cycles and phases. Do not use age as the deciding factor. As noted earlier, too often we surrender to what we have been taught is the biological life cycle. We therefore surrender to the notion, *even to the biological programming*, that says disease and or aging itself should determine all physical death, and should even dictate or deny transition into seeming end-of-life phases.[49]

We are taught that disease happens, that we are more vulnerable to disease as we age, as well as that the aging process is essential, required, inescapable, is the determinant of the end. With these teachings we are taught that at the end

---

[48] See the *Navigating Life's Stuff* books, *Volume 8 and 9* in this *Keys To Consciousness And Survival Series*, to look closely at what it means to sensitize ourselves to our patterns and processes.

[49] Refer to other books in this *Keys To Consciousness And Survival Series* where this programming is detailed. See reading list at the end of this present book.

of the aging process, it is time to die of either disease or old age. But life cycles are not necessarily only from birth to old age or disease and to death.

LIFE CYCLES BEYOND BIOLOGICAL CYCLES

The life cycle need not only be biological. The nature of our lifeform need not only be biological. Even learning what this means can begin to assist us in further surviving biologically as well as non-physically, in dying and surviving.

As the species of consciousness that we are, we have the option and the right to know that we can evolve our species to be able to live on, that we are far more than our biological bodies, our vessels. We can learn to die and survive. See other books in this *keys to consciousness and survival series* where our role as a species of consciousness is detailed.[50]

LIFE CYCLES CARRY MUCH INFORMATION ABOUT TRANSITION

We can learn a great deal about transition itself while we live our biological life cycles. Life cycles have many beginnings, middles, and then end or transition points, each of which can cycle into new beginnings.

Quite often a chronological biological life time, from traditional beginnings and births to traditional endings and death points, includes many life cycles, many cycles through

---

[50] For example, see *Volume 5* in this series, *Overriding The Extinction Scenario*, and *Volume 3* in this series, *Unveiling The Hidden Instinct*, and *Volume 10* in this series, *Seeing Beyond Our Line Of Sight*.

patterns, relationships, behaviors, events, learnings, educations, growths, stages, all filled with struggles, paradoxes, insights, and (spiritual) elevations—all full of choice points, forks in the road, and forks within forks, and forks within forks within forks.

At first glance, this cycle discussion may cause you to feel a swimming sensation. Where are you anyway? What page of what book are you really on? Handle this vagueness by seeing that you can name your place in any life cycle . . . You can determine its time of beginning, middle, and recycle or end.

You can name the end of your cycle, and the beginning and direction of your next one.

Spotting the right time to end or die out of a cycle involves understanding your cycles, being able to gain perspective on your life cycles and sub-cycles, in order to gain a long view of all of the cycles in which you have participated—cycles which you feel have been yours, and also cycles of which you have been a small part. Remember, even your biological life cycle is a sub-cycle.

You are involved in life cycles of the cosmos, of the galaxy, of the solar system, of the planet, of its biosphere, of your species, of your community, of your family, of your children, of your parents, of your siblings, of your closest kin, and of your self.

You are also involved in the life cycle of your civilization. You are indeed deeply enmeshed in the life cycle of your reality.

(see Figure 6.3 for a visual depiction of some cycles within cycles.)[51]

EXERCISE #6.5
HAVING CYCLE SENSITIVITY

Single out different personal cycles which you have undergone more than once. These might include repeat performances of falling in and out of love, beginning and ending an academic year, participating in a meeting from start to finish, or entering a race and completing it. List these.

Now single out three life cycles in which you are but a small part and list these. For each of these larger life cycles you have listed, list three smaller cycles or subcycles which take place within those larger life cycles.

There are no right or wrong answers here. Do not worry if you are not sure of what you are doing. Just follow your instincts, follow your own ideas. See your universe as full of cycles and subcycles.

EXERCISE #6.6
LOCATING YOUR CYCLES

Now, Place Each Personal Pattern Cycle You Identified At The beginning of Exercise #6.4 within the larger cycles you also identified in Exercises #6.4 and #6.5. Do you see where you fit in? Examine the example in Figure 6.3. You can draw a similar cycle map for yourself. For example, you have a birthday every year, so perhaps one of your cycles is the annual birthday cycle which may fit within the larger life or century cycle. Or perhaps you have a

---

[51] See the in-depth discussion of these matters in *Volumes 5 and 6* of this *Keys To Consciousness And Survival Series*, titled *Overriding The Extinction Scenario*.

weekly family dinner. This cycle may fit within the life cycle of your family. Or perhaps you have many daily routines that are part of your daily pattern or cycle, which itself is part of an annual pattern.

SPOT THE TIME

Every cycle has a start point, a midpoint, and then what we can call an *omega*, a *transition point.* And every transition is an entry back into the same cycle, or perhaps into a new cycle. So, at each cyclic transition point, you have the option to fall back into that same cycle or to break free. This is the fork in your path. You, when at an end point, may see this fork in your path or you may not detect this fork (or be allowed to detect this fork). Yet you are still there. You may feel this while not seeing this.

You may see an upcoming fork as an ending or even a death, but only the death of the immediate cycle you are in, because that is what looms largest before your eyes. This looming, while understandably constructed, is an illusion.

INCREASING TRANSITION SENSITIVITY

You can learn to see past, beyond, end points if you become sensitive to their approach.[52] this itself is key in the concept of *the dying and surviving of the self, of who you actually are.*

Here are some means of heightening your *transition sensitivity*, your awareness of: the approach of recycle options; the right time to close a cycle and open a new one.

---

[52] Refer to *Volume 10* in this *Keys To Consciousness And Survival Series*, titled, *Seeing Beyond Our Line Of Sight.*

You can *enhance your navigation of your transitions to new cycle patterns as you:*

1) Become more sensitive to the subtle inputs you give yourself as you get ready to let a part of your life die. Pay attention to very quiet hints, murmurs in your mind that you would normally have missed or totally ignored. Constantly inform yourself of your place on your life path.

2) Close your eyes. Go inside. Where are you? Who are you? What are you?

3) Come face to face with you, with who you are. Listen and you will hear what you are telling yourself. Ask quietly, "what am I telling myself?" Don't force it. Just calmly and repeatedly practice this listening and your inner voice will become more distinct.

4) Map your life. Look for simple cycles and for phases and forks. Can you map any of your living endings, deaths, all being transitions? How about the roads leading up to those transitions?

5) Always check to see where you stand on your life path. Do you feel unsettled? Is a pattern shift, a *cycle-exit* or *cycle-fork* approaching or already under foot? Notice where you are and how you feel. Find yourself in the process of in-life and even beyond-life living and dying, and surviving.

6) Always remember that a pattern or cycle ending or death does not mean that everything there is gone. You

can preserve what is healthy for you to preserve and amend what is best amended.

Become hyper-sensitive to your state of mind. See that:

7) When you need to shift, your mind moves ahead of you, living at the fork in the road subconsciously before doing so consciously. So, notice even slight shifts in your ability to concentrate on your present situation. You may already have left it in some ways.

8) As you approach a fork, a choice point, an opening, your energy fluctuates more and more profoundly. So, notice even slight changes in your enthusiasm.

9) You know when you are trapped in a life paradox, even if you do not want to admit it to yourself. So, notice when you feel even *slightly* claustrophobic or even trapped—physically, emotionally, intellectually, spiritually.

10) Sometimes you make a hidden trap visible to yourself through visible behaviors. So, notice if you are regularly exhibiting troubled behavior (which is detrimental to yourself or to others).

11) Many beings deal with their desire to avoid dealing with the need to let a cycle die by turning off. So, notice to what degree you function on automatic—that is, mindlessly.

12) Meaning in life appears different, may even intensify, at recycle points. Or the clarity of the meaning may

become muddled at choice points. So, notice how you respond when you stop for a moment's reflection and ask yourself, "who am I and why am I here?"

Do you ask yourself questions about these things, and about your life, your self in general? What answers do you hear? Find a safe way to explore your responses to such questions: why are you here? Is this **phase** of your life still a rich experience? Or have you stayed in this state of mind too long? Is it time to stay in this phase, or time to add to or alter this phase, or time to move into a new phase, a new state of mind, to die and survive?

Give yourself some answers and see if you like them. See if you can find yourself more attuned to what you have explored in this chapter. Review the figures on the next pages, Figures 6.1, 6.2, and 6.3.

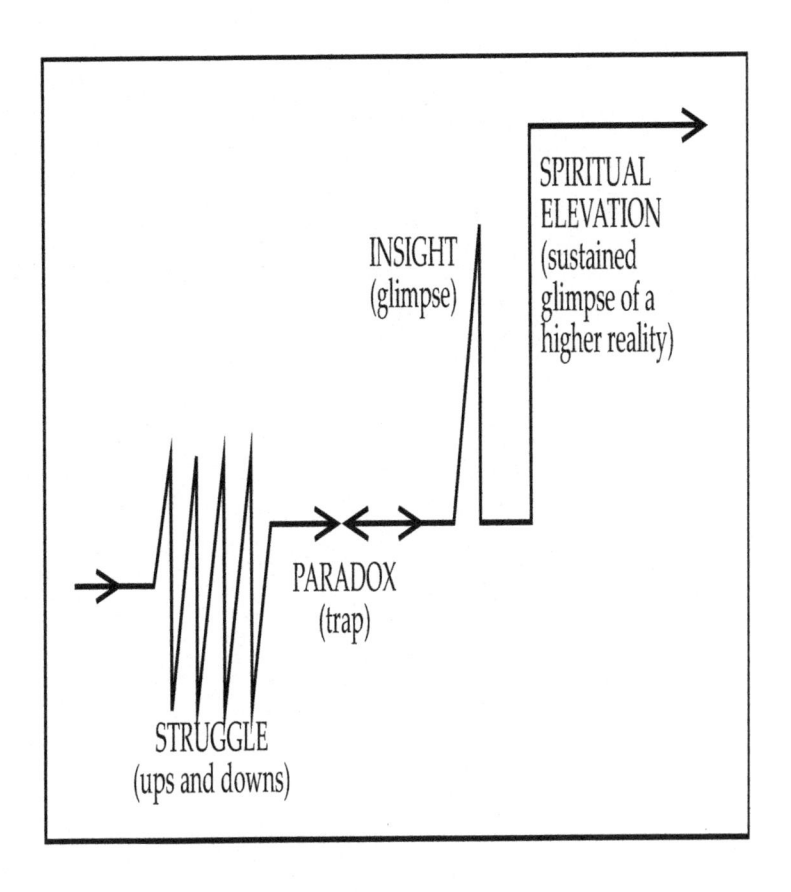

Figure 6.1

Four Repeatable and Intermixable Phases

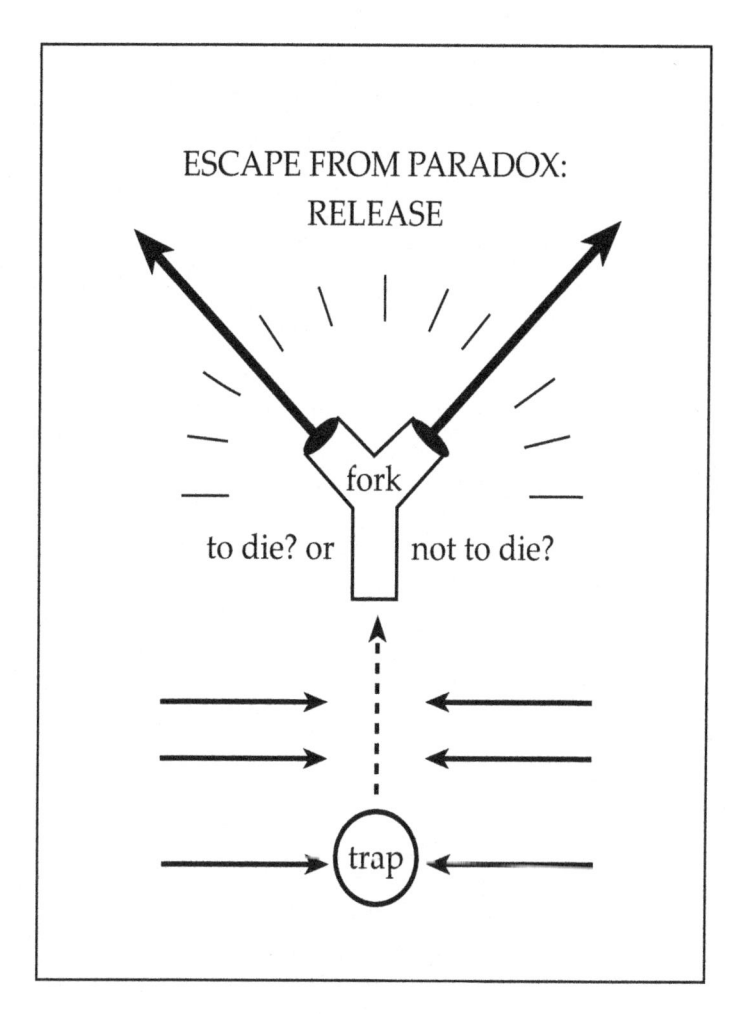

Figure 6.2

Escape From Paradox

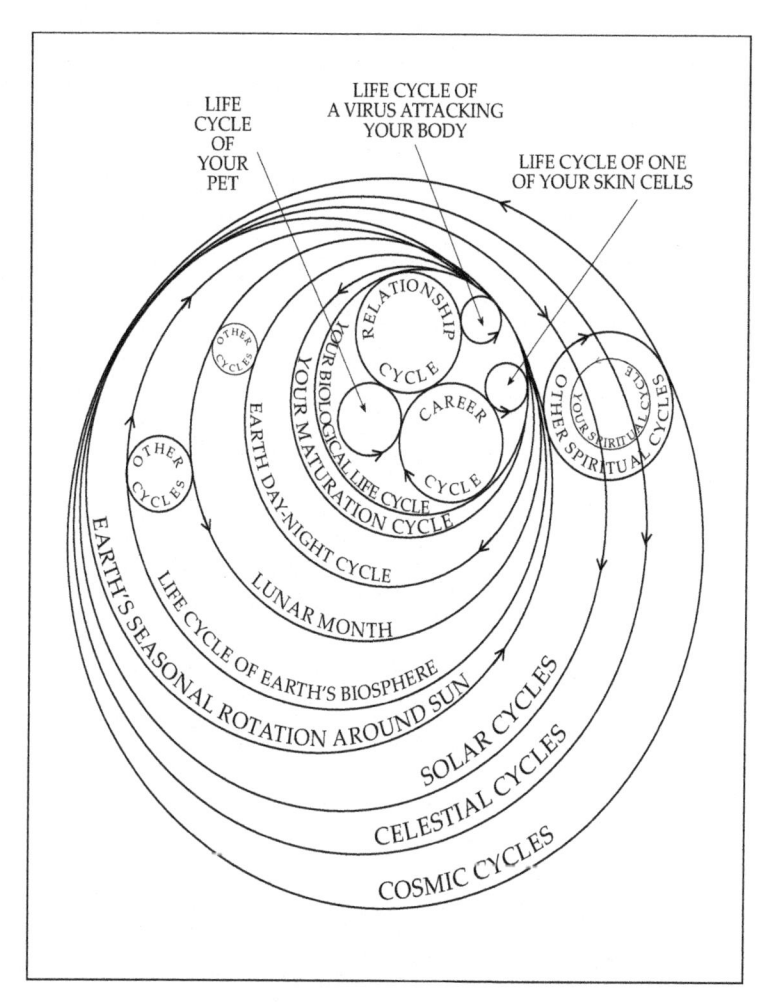

Figure 6.3

Visualization of Being Part of Larger Cycles

7
Embracing In-Life And Seeming End-Of-Life Transition: Leap Level One

> There are cases where
> faith creates its own verification.
>
> William James
> *The Sentiment Of Rationality*

The first and greatest step in any transitional change, ending, or death is the initial recognition and acceptance of its coming—the embrace.

This embrace is the first of eight leaps in awareness involved in mastering transitions: changes, endings, deaths.

This leap is the fundamental *light-energy-action-process* which propels your awareness, your energy, your essence to leap into a new state of mind, new level of awareness, new expansion of consciousness, new reality. (see other books in this series for detailed definition and explanation of leaps.)

We will return again and again to the nature of the leap. Here we begin with the first level of the change, transition, or what we can call "death" leap: the embrace. (See again Figure 7.1.)

COMPASSION FOR YOUR
SELF

We hear so much talk about caring, having heart, being loving, being compassionate. However, we very rarely speak about being highly compassionate with ourselves, about the "care and feeding" of our own souls. And, yet, this self-love, unfettered by the claims of the ego, but fueled by the respect for the self, is a most essential compassion.

As you enter the prelude to any of your transitions (such as changes, endings, deaths), you may find yourself undergoing various vague and or specific emotional shifts, such as either "going numb" to avoid the intensity of the experience, or actually undergoing *overwhelming* intensification of experience and emotion, or some mix of these or other experiences.

Experiencing some degree of something such as numbness, not feeling, no sensation, however this registers, is not unusual. Indeed, even if you are someone who does not outwardly or even consciously reveal an intensification of experience which is a prelude to intense transition such as death, you may undergo this on some internal level.

In instances of actual physical death, as one's realization that death is coming sets in, detachment may begin to grow in one's demeanor, expression, and behavior.

This detachment is not always pure detachment. Instead, it may be some mix of what appears to be detachment, exhaustion, depression, anxiety, bewilderment, and other feelings. This combination can look like numbness, or can look like nothing distinguishable.

It is important for outsiders to know that what seems to be going on in someone's mind is not necessarily all that is being expressed. It is also important for outsiders to know that even when a person is medically not conscious, there is a great deal that may be going on in that person's consciousness.

If you find yourself approaching your own death, accept the possibility that your experience may actually fluctuate among the extremes of numbness and intensity for a while. Do not recoil at the sound of this mixed and seemingly chaotic experience.

This is your passage into true and healthy detachment, as you will read more about in the following chapters of this and the following book, *How To Die And Survive, Part Two*.

This chaotic experience is also the envelope you create for yourself—an envelope of containment, a place where emotional boundaries, no matter how extreme, are set. You can direct your full attention to the actual self, the core of the self, the personal consciousness, you contain within this envelope. You can then direct your compassion there.

Your envelope is your permission to be. When you give yourself permission to fully experience and release your feelings about your coming death, *the feelings flow through you instead of festering within you*. Often times, the permissions you give yourself in your prelude to death are permissions you wished for in life.

With permission, you begin to respond with more immediacy than ever, with less holding back, to all that you have been dealing with in your life. You take chances of expression, you feel fears, and you feel love more fully now, in a richer but increasingly unconditional way.

In the prelude to any of your transitions, changes, endings, and deaths, you need for your self the compassion-for-others that you learned or attempted to develop prior to this.

You need all the compassion you can muster for your self as you enter any minor or major transition, even when you do not feel this to be so. This is true for all your physical and non-physical transitions.

SPIRIT HANDLING

You must strive for a tender, gentle, handling of your spirit as you birth it, deliver it, into the next dimension of your reality. Handle your spirit as you would handle a new baby: most carefully, most lovingly, just as the nourishing mother cradles the new baby in the womb and then in the birth canal as the baby enters this world, and then in the world.

Cradle yourself as you enter the next world, the **beyond**, the next phase of your life or death. Begin cradling yourself even during the prelude to this entry, even all your life.[53]

---

[53] Again refer to *Volume 10* in this *Keys To Consciousness And Survival Series*, titled, *Seeing Beyond Our Line Of Sight*.

EXERCISE #7.1
CRADLING THE SELF

The cradling Exercise that follows is something which should be practiced as frequently as possible. Its gestures are, in themselves, a great teaching.

If you have been the parent of a young baby or have held a young baby, you may recognize the cradling instinct. You may have felt, quite instinctively, the desire to cradle the baby in your arms and to rock it.

You may have felt that biological care-and-feeding drive, that love-protection-nurturing drive considered so essential to the survival of offspring. So you may know something about this because you have done some cradling. Or, perhaps you have a deep memory of yourself being cradled as a baby or child.

Whether or not you do know much about cradling, imagine now that you are cradling a baby . . . And that that baby is you.

Close your eyes. Hold your arms close to you, as if you have a baby in them, gently pressing that baby to your chest. Now slowly move those arms in, further in toward your chest, as if you are embracing yourself. In fact, let your cradling arms hug yourself. That's right, hug yourself, embrace yourself. Let yourself cradle your self, rock your self. Feel as much affection for your self as you can find.

You may find yourself not fully opening to, or holding back some of, or even resisting and balking, at this gesture of self-love. Even if you do not think that you are resisting, you may be a little stiff or a little lost with the concept of fully embracing yourself. This is all right. It is not unusual to feel rather detached about, or even uncomfortable about, embracing your self.

Now, still embracing, just pretend that it is not your self you are embracing: pretend that this is someone other than yourself who you know and love.

Or imagine that you care very much for an imaginary person or an imaginary baby, someone to love right now. Cradle whoever it is, real or imagined. Embrace who it is you choose to cradle. Pour as much nurturing and love as possible into that person, all the while holding yourself. Stay with this process a while. Hold for next exercise.

EXERCISE #7.2
EMBRACING A DEATH

Now, still be in this cradling process of the previous Exercise. Imagine that you are maybe taking this soul, this spirit that you are cradling, sheltering it, through chaos, danger and fear, through dark hallways, dark passages, maybe through chambers full of monsters. Imagine that you are strongly protecting that being that you love with your strong love as you move that being through a series of threatening or unknown environments.

Keep cradling. See that you are moving that being through a challenging passage. Inform yourself that this is some kind of transition this being is undergoing.

While you are embracing this being that you are pouring love into, imagine for a moment that you are embracing the death of this being, you are embracing the death of this self that you are pouring love into. Hold on very tight. Make your embraces as tight as you comfortably can. Hold for next exercise.

EXERCISE #7.3
EMBRACING YOUR DEATH

Wash love over that being. Pour out your love and fully embrace that death. Now, while continuing to lovingly nourish and embrace that temporarily transitioning, dying, being, imagine that that being is truly you. Keep loving and hold on. Hold on. Love yourself. Embrace yourself as you go through this imaginary transition. Now freeze.

You have just made a shift, a leap, in consciousness. This slight shift (increase or change) in the way you administer compassion to yourself is a significant change, whether or not you register it as one, in your perspective on—and thus in your experience of transitional change of any sort, including death.

THE SHIFT

The shift into embracing the experience of transition, whether it lasts a few moments or stays with you, is a marked shift away from denial of, fear of, anger regarding, or other responses to an approaching ending or death. The embracing of in-life and seeming end-of-life transition including death is also more than mere acceptance and preparation.

This is more than a shift in understanding or feeling, this is a *reformatting of the spiritual, mental, and emotional structure you have built to relate to life experiences, transitions, in-life and seeming end-of-life deaths.* This is a structure that you have long held in place.

LEARN TO *LEAP*

Now you have made a leap in awareness out of this old structure. A new degree and application of light and energy and action have entered your *consciousness matrix,* shifting that matrix—even if only seeming to be slightly shifting. Your old structure has been shed. It has been reformatted. It has not died.

While this imaginary death may be as subtle and invisible to you as the death of a single-celled animal floating in a large ocean, or the death of a few skin cells on your body, *this transition is actually as profound as you allow it to be.*

All leaps, large and small, are great shifts in awareness. When these great shifts last a short while, these are insights, as diagrammed in Figure 6.1. When these shifts stay with you, these are long-lasting insights, spiritual elevations, as diagrammed in Figure 6.1.

The realization that a leap in one's awareness has taken place is key in mastery of transition. The leap is both a transition technology and a transition in itself. You will note that each of the eight parts of these two *how to die and survive* books concludes with discussion of a leap, a *light-energy-action-process,* which serves as a springboard into a new dimension of self, of reality. These are leaps into interdimensional awareness and expansion.

Again, the leap is a movement from one dimension of reality to another, one state of mind or of awareness to another.

A leap is most effective when consciously constructed and purposefully fueled. Then the leap lasts, becoming more than a brief insight, becoming a spiritual elevation, a solid stepping stone in your ascension into your ever higher personal consciousness.

LEAP TO DIE AND SURVIVE

A leap itself is a form of transcendence, of death, a death that is, in essence, survived as the leap leaps to something or somewhere beyond. (refer again to *volume 10* in this *keys to consciousness and survival series*, titled, *seeing beyond our line of sight*.) A leap is a shift in awareness, in focus of awareness, in the level of conscious awareness.

We can see that a leap is not the old model definition of an ending or death. Instead, a leap is a transition, a leap to a new level of awareness. In this sense, every shift in awareness is a death with a survival element.

The more practiced and conscious the leaping person is, the clearer and more powerful the transition or death. The more practiced and conscious the transitioning being is, no matter how small or big the transition, whether it is an in-life or beyond-life transition, the clearer and more powerful the leap.

SERIES OF LEAPS

The eight parts of this and the following book together describe a series of leaps that are increasingly powerful. Each leap is a leap which you can make in awareness, whether or not you are undergoing a physical death.

Each leap is a release from a particular level of paradox, from a particular level of not-knowing-the-way-out of a reality. A leap is a break away from ignorance. Figure 7.1 charts and describes the progressive leaps detailed in this book.

EMBRACING

As simple as it sounds, your full embrace of yourself as you face great change, as you face the transition or death or end of any in-life or seeming end-of-life cycle, is the basic leap in awareness necessary to conduct a healthy transition. Empathy for yourself can help to ease your transitions. This empathy for self cradles your self as you move through processes. This cradling is an energetic shield, a caring vessel.

Leap Level	Leap Form	Leap Description
One	Embracing	Accepting, feeling ready for, fully moving into the concept of shift (or death) out of a dimension, or phase or stage of life or mind, or out of the physical body itself.
Two	Quickening	Raising the presumed or actual energetic vibration or frequency of one's consciousness; pulling together the focus to go into another dimension and/or to go through a major transition in life, or a physical death.
Three	Willing The Exit	Focusing the Will in such a concentrated way that the exit from the dimension or phase of life or physical body is energized, facilitated.
Four	Leaping To The Next Dimension	Moving the consciousness in such a manner that it shifts, leaps, out of its current or present format or dimension of its reality, generally occurring after its exit from the dimension, or phase of life, or if biological, then the physical body it has been in.
Five	Ascending	Moving the consciousness in such a manner that it ascends into what may be experienced as higher frequencies, higher realms of Light, or higher dimensions of its/the reality.
Six	Catharting Beyond	Using the energy released by shifting, breaking, leaping, out of a dimension or phase of life or physical body to move well beyond the realm of existence, or format, being left.
Seven	Meta-scending	Realizing the effects of transition or death and or ascension and interdimensional travel without appearing to have a phase of life or a physical body die.
Eight	Achieving Metastasis And High Metaxis	Achieving the highest possible range, or dimensional span, of oneself. An intentional inter-dimensional shifting, an energetic reformatting, the essential LEAP-ing, without depending on actual physical death to propel.

Figure 7.1. Leap Table
Basic Light-Energy-Action-Processes (Leaps)

Part II

How To
Know, Find, Follow
The Idea Of Light

8
Becoming Lighter

> Now fix your thought upon the Light,
> And learn to know it.
>
> Poimandres to
> Hermes Trismegistus
> *Hermetica*

Light.

Artificial Light. Electric Light. Translucent Light. Night Light. Flash Light. Head Light. Signal Light. Spot Light. Strobe Light. Light.

Light.

Natural Light. Dawn's Early Light. Day Light. Sun Light. Twilight. Moon Light. Star Light. Northern Light. Fire Light. Light.

Light.

Love Light. Divine Light. Ethereal Light. White Light. Galactic Light. Cosmic Light. Light.

KNOW THAT LIGHT IS MORE

We take Light for granted.

Light pours in through windows, filters in through canopies of leaves in forests, reflects off moons and lakes and mirrors, comes on with the flick of a switch. Yet, Light is much more than the human eye can see. In fact, what the human eye sees of Light is a hint of what is really there.

human seeing of Light serves as training material for a greater vision of a much broader range and power of *the idea of Light*. This greater vision is not dependent upon the biologically contrived optical organ, the eyeball, and its biologically contrived transmitter, the optic nerve. While these are useful, even essential, functions, there is also more about the idea of Light to know.

THE IDEA OF LIGHT

It is time to see the meaning of, the conceptual essence of, Light, the idea of Light, with new eyes. Light can transform appearances both in the physical environment and beyond what is material, physical, even to what is in our mind's eye, even in our own consciousness.

Light can transform itself. Light can alter that which it casts upon. Light can transform matter, including flesh. Light can perhaps even heal on some level that which it touches and even fills. Light can be a salve. Light can touch and affect frequencies of solid objects and of living things.

The idea of Light itself is powerful. The mind can work with the idea of Light in many ways. The more defined and focused the Light, even the idea of Light, the greater its force. Focusing compresses the complexity of Light into power. Light is at once the wave and the particle, the author and his or her document, the formula and the product of the formula.

We tend to think of Light as having a multitude of qualities, and of darkness as being nothing much more than the absence of Light. Try turning this idea around for a moment. What if Light were merely the absence of darkness, and darkness were the opposite—substantive and complex—at once an energy, a wave, and a particle?

This is difficult to imagine because we are aware of physical *sources of Light*—suns, stars, man-made Light fixtures. We do not think in terms of sources of absence of Light, what some call darkness, (although perhaps it would help to recognize that such sources exist, and that darkness itself may seep, emanate, from these).

This discussion is not regarding technical definitions of what is regarded as Light. This is about another idea of Light, about Light as a concept, an ideal, a vision of highest and purest luminosity.

This discussion is intended to enhance your awareness of and appreciation for the idea of Light. The reason this enhanced awareness of Light is valuable is that it enables you to think in terms of *becoming more like highest Light.* You must have a feel for the idea of Light to allow your imagination to raise your physicality, actually your awareness itself, toward Light.

This allows conscious expansion of the SELF as a personal consciousness. This allows realizing what survival can mean.

You can imagine Light to work with its power. Your imagination can lead you in the necessary transformation of ideas, even of the idea, and power of the idea, of Light.

Understand that the natural Light you see in the material plane is what of Light can filter in through your atmosphere. Imagine that Light increases as density decreases. (See Figure 8.1.)

A note here: The concept of *physicality* is a stumbling block for some people. Think in terms of what can be called physicality to further impress upon yourself who you are while living in the material—physical—dimension of reality.

Recognize that being physical, having density to the degree that you are physical, is not an absolute characteristic of existing, but one of many possible characteristics.

Let's say that your personal consciousness can exist without physicality. At some time, at the right time, when needed, you will remember and further develop this concept.

THE IDEA OF DENSITY

A deep feel for the idea of density (as depicted simply in Figure 8.1) can assist in the conceptual passage from physical death into the beyond. Knowing that physical death is a moving through *realms of density* is knowing that death is not the end of your existence, but the transformation of your existence from one conceptual degree of density to another.

The idea of both actual and imaginary density is so useful. Understanding that there are degrees, gradations, and variations, of density allows understanding of even personal issues in physical reality. For example, seeing dense messy attachments, complexities of entanglement, can indicate how a person's addictions to, dependences upon, problem situations can be moved through. Rising above a dense attachment or addiction network can allow for lifting out of a situation to be able to see it and work on it.

In this way, your programmings and patternings can be transcended, even while you still live in your physical body. Programmings have densities. They are frequently embedded at the cellular level, in the genetic code, the neurological system, the spinal fluid, and at other physical sites.

Concepts and conditions of physical and other energetic programming can be altered or suspended when it is ascended into a less dense, Lighter, state.

Try, if you can and wish to, not to over-intellectualize the concept of density. Misunderstanding reality is one of the dangers of thinking too logically about important concepts. Just allow these ideas about density and ascending into less dense states of awareness to be with you.

After a while, these ideas will be comprehensible in a visceral way.

The following Exercises will teach you, awaken your consciousness to, the *intuitive technology* required to travel to other realms of density.

EXERCISE #8.1
BECOMING
LESS DENSE

Close your eyes. Imagine that your body is turning to liquid, at first a thick syrupy liquid, then a liquid which becomes thinner and thinner. Imagine that this liquid becomes Lighter as it thins— and then it turns to fluid Light. Feel that you are becoming glowing liquid.

Now, let this liquid become vaporous, misty, and then more vaporous and more glowing. You are turning to Light. As you turn to Lighter and Lighter Light, you become less and less dense. Imagine you move into higher realms of Light—realms of Light into which only Light can travel.

See these realms of Light as layered from darker to Lighter. Move on up through them, toward the Lightest Light, toward your own IDEA OF HIGHEST LIGHT.

Beings, life forms, take on varying degrees of conceptual density. So in essence, this idea says that: A life form locates along a continuum of presence in mostly physical reality, to expanded presence across physical to nonphysical dimensions, SPANNING from most dense to least dense. However, you are seeing that you can move your FOCUS, YOUR AWARENESS, YOUR SELF along this continuum.

Conceptually, fluid Light has far less density than any material liquid such as syrup or water. And vaporous Light has little or no density whatsoever. Imagine that you feel a tingling as you leave your states of density, as you shed your layers of density.

EVOLVE

The practices in these *How To Die And Survive* books assist in training the awareness, alerting the awareness to foundational and then advanced concepts in inter-dimensional perception and living. As your personal consciousness taps into its powerful awareness, it can expand in its own presence, its own personal consciousness, ever more aware of the concept of, the essence of, Light. It can explore what it means, conceptually, to become less dense and thus more expanded.

This development can feel rather "ungrounding" to those new to this process. The idea of gravity can have a pull on your thoughts, and thus on your body. This ungrounding counteracts gravitation's pull, and can be a positive expansive step, albeit initially disorienting.

<u>EXERCISE #8.2</u>
THE LIGHT DIET

Repeat the previous exercise, but now take it more slowly and in greater detail. Inch your awareness very slowly up the scale of decreasing density. Change very slowly from purely and densely physical into what feels to be increasing Lightness—degrees of Light. Notice the vague sensation that you are losing weight.

You are, but not in the traditional way. As this unweighting takes place, the ...

ACTUAL DIMINISHING OF YOUR BODY
RELATIVE TO THE EXPANSION OF
YOUR PERSONAL CONSCIOUSNESS,
YOUR ACTUAL SELF,
Begins.

Take some time to think about this: the diminishing of your body.... Say this aloud, "The diminishing of my body ..." And see your physical self shrinking. Now say, "... Relative to my expanding Light body." See your nonphysical Light body growing larger here. Your physical body is diminishing when compared to your expanding Light body. Relax.

If you are enjoying this sensation, think about what you are enjoying about it. Some of us enjoy roller coaster rides. Some of us do not. This may feel unsettling, even dizzying, if practiced with great concentration.

*You are experiencing the effects of **gravity-lifting**. Let's call this **decohesion, or diminishing cohesion**, and understand this as normal. Your physical bits are sticking together less. Let's call this **conscious entropy**.*

Entropy is the tendency of a physical system to spin out, dissolve, disintegrate, wear down, die. You are engaging in conscious entropy. This is all right. You can change, better stated, expand, your make-up substantively this way. Tell yourself, "I expand this way."

YOUR MASTERY

Your mastery of interdimensional travel and death transitions requires your ability to shift densities, first in your imagination and then in your essence. You can learn this by giving your mind suggestions, by practicing, imagining, that you are becoming Lighter as in the previous exercises.

As the physical matter of "you" becomes, in your mind's eye, less tightly organized, less rigidly structured in a material sense, it has the opportunity to become more complex, more expansive, in a multidimensional sense.

Let's say that, from a conceptual standpoint, as the presence of matter becomes less physical, less dense, it weighs less and less per cubic millimeter in relation to the expanse of the energy it emits—its energy body—and is thus less weighed down.

EXERCISE #8.3
METAPHYSICAL CALISTHENICS

Imagine that you are shrinking physically and then expanding physically. Practice this shift several times.

Now, imagine that you are shrinking physically while expanding in Light form. See yourself becoming an increasingly luminous, beautiful, form of pure Light as you expand.

Feel relief, or imagine that you feel relief, as your physicality diminishes, as if you are shedding a tattered, heavy, and unnecessary coat. After a while, your physical body is very tiny compared to your beautiful Light body which fills a huge interdimensional space. Try to maintain this sensation as long as you can, even after you complete this particular exercise.

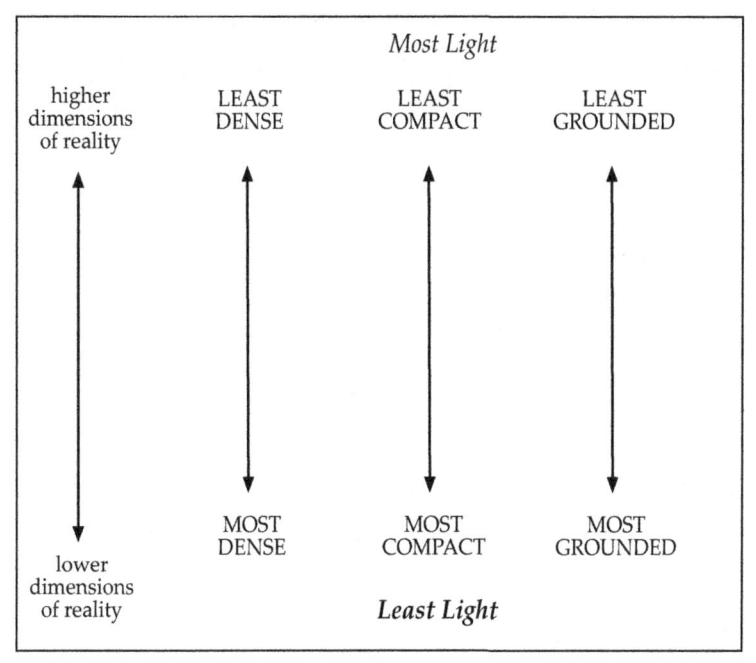

	Most Light		
higher dimensions of reality	LEAST DENSE	LEAST COMPACT	LEAST GROUNDED
↕	↕	↕	↕
lower dimensions of reality	MOST DENSE	MOST COMPACT	MOST GROUNDED
	Least Light		

Figure 8.1

More Light is Less Dense

9
Understanding The Ideas of Light and Love

> May the long time
> Sun shine
> On you
> All Light surround you
> And the pure Light
> Within you
> Guide your way on.
>
> *Incredible String Band*

The absence of Light is many things to many people. Even the terms, Light and Dark, are used in countless ways. Each of us will have our own terms for the following, so please replace these terms if you feel you have other terms that work for you here:

Lightness and darkness as states of mind, of awareness, are perhaps vague concepts. We tend to see Lightness and Darkness as opposites of each other. More likely these are different by degrees along a spectrum of Light. However Darkness is defined, Darkness lets you appreciate its absence.

BEING UNSEEING

No matter how rich your material plane sensory intake, you can be relatively unseeing with regard to the most valuable data coming to you. This is part of what this and other books in this *KEYS TO CONSCIOUSNESS AND SURVIVAL* book series explain as your *brain's programming not to see*. It is time now for you to reach beyond this programming, to access the range of awareness which is rightfully yours.[54]

A different use of your five senses, or of what it is you think you perceive with your five senses—via sensory input—via seeing, hearing, smelling, tasting, touching—is required now. This expanding of what you have known to be "sensation" will enable you to "get," to "grok," to "absorb," *to expand, your Light.*

You can work your way into an enhanced awareness of higher forms of what can be called love and can be called Light by training your senses to take in new forms of information.

How so? As you amp up your perceptual abilities, you will find that you mix sensory modalities. You will hear colors, feel sounds, see feelings. At first this may feel as if it is not really happening—as if it is an optical, auditory, and or emotional illusion.

However, as you move into what you think of as the world of illusion, you make room for what you have previously excluded from your conceptual reality because it seemed so illusory, so unreal, so imaginary, to you. And it is ....

EXERCISE #9.1
SENSORY MIXING

---

[54] See more on this matter in *Volume 10* of this series, *Seeing Beyond Our Line Of Sight.*

Choose a color that you see in your environment. Focus on that color. Now close your eyes. Imagine what this color would sound like if you could hear it. . . .

Now imagine what it would taste like. . . . Now imagine that you are moving—walking, swimming, flying—through this color.

What would this color feel like to the touch? What would it feel like to move through?

EXERCISE #9.2
MULTI-SENSORY MIXING

Pick your favorite color, or a color that you know well, for this exercise. Close your eyes. Try to see this color in your mind's eye. As you do so, imagine that you are hearing it, tasting it, smelling it, feeling it, all at the same time.

Do this for many minutes. Work to run the different sensory modes (such as hearing, feeling, tasting, smelling) at the same time.

Eventually, feel that you have become the color. You hear, feel, taste, and smell like the color. You are now vibrating the color.

ALTERED STATES AS
PORTALS

As this sort of conceptual sensory mixing continues, you may feel slightly confused, or perhaps somewhat disoriented. This passes.

You have produced a somewhat "altered state" of awareness for yourself by running messages such as "blue" or "hot" or "soft" or "loud" through different mental pathways than your brain has set up for them, and by running more than one of these "altered" messages at once. Knowing how to consciously create for yourself (with no outside intervention) an "altered" state or a new state of awareness, how to exercise, empower, and expand your awareness, is your key to your own kingdom.

Recognize that the altered states of mind that you pass into and through can be openings, or what you might consider windows or passages, into heightened awareness. Let's call (what can be seen as such openings) *portals*—portals into a next level of awareness: leaps.

Your increasing ability to recognize, or perhaps to generate for yourself, the higher realms of your own Light—will be an increasingly valuable guide for you. Even in your darkest hour, even the faintest Light you find within even the deepest recesses of your mind's eye will be your guiding beam.

Hook into the highest, least dense frequency, the purest energy you can imagine or visualize, and hang on. The illumination you seek, the essence of Light, is already within you, ready to guide your way on. Discover, develop, expand, and follow your Light.

10
Romancing The Light

>...A point I saw which rayed
>Forth Light so keen, needs
>Must the vision that it flameth
>On be closed because of its
>Strong poignancy....
>
>>Dante Alighieri
>>*Paradiso,*
>>*Canto XXVIII*
>>*The Divine Comedy*

Come to know your own understanding of Light, of the image, the vision, of the highest, purest, most clear Light, whatever this may be for you. Develop this idea of Light in your mind, in your consciousness, as a tool, as a goal. Having an idea of, a model of, a view of, a pure highest Light energy or presence, whatever this is for you, can be a marker and guide for you on your path.

Know your own idea of highest Light better and better as you live. Find your idea of highest Light and hold onto it as you move through life's changes and transitions. Even as you die.

You can do this. The Light you seek is so powerful that its realization can come in to you through any and all of your sensory organs, and can also come into your awareness without involving any of your physical sensory organs.

This idea or understanding of, this realization of, highest purest Light is so potent that you can detect its **presence in your awareness** with or without your biological eyes seeing it. You can sense it, feel it, hear it, see it, even with your eyes closed. Indeed, you can even taste this higher Light. You can savor its glowing stream, seeming to be wafting from the Cosmos into your consciousness. You taste, you feel, you see, as much of this higher Light as you can access, as you can absorb, as you can believe or even imagine exists.

MASTERY

Mastery of change, transition, even death involves opening to the multiple dimensions of your reality.

The more adept you are at moving your awareness, your SELF, your personal consciousness, across dimensions of your reality, the more power you can give yourself as you change, transition, even die. As you move across these dimensions of your reality, your idea of Light, of highest Light, can be a beacon, a guide. You can find your own guiding Light in your mind's eye, in your consciousness.

With but a little practice, any time you wish it to, your mind's eye, your spirit, your consciousness, can open like a window onto your amazingly extensive Light, even goodness, allowing the sweet mists of other-worldly, other-reality, Light to descend upon you and into you.

This Light is yours. This is the point, the guiding beam to seek, the river to ride, amidst any storm, any challenging transition, any death. Learn to see beyond the false walls of what you have been told is your reality.

EXERCISE #10.1
FEELING
YOUR ENGULFMENT

Pause now. Close your eyes. Feel for a moment how very engulfed in what you think of as your reality you are. See what you have been defining as your world. Do not, for this moment, look beyond your so-called world. However, try to see its boundaries, its walls.

ESCALATION OF AWARENESS

As we have said, you are a participant in a massive escalation in awareness. *You already know* far more than you realize you know. You have already glimpsed the ***beyond*** and seen the Light.

You already know the beyond is only beyond so long as it is beyond your perception.[55]

EXERCISE #10.2
SEEING THE MISTS

The beyond is here now. It surrounds you. Its sweet mists waft subtly into your material world. Close your eyes and you will see this.

---

[55] See a key volume in this series, *Seeing Beyond Our Line Of Sight*, for a discussion of the concept: BEYOND.

With your eyes closed, allow yourself to imagine that the Light mists of another world are flowing into yours.

Should you doubt this imagery of Light, disbelieve its veracity, temporarily suspend your disbelief. Fully believe in and see this Light for a while. You can return from this imagery of Light misting into your "real" world at will. There is thus no risk in exploring, in simply imagining, this possibility. Imagine for a moment, believe in for a while, and see, experience, the Light mists flowing in around you. This is your Light. You can sense it, see it, generate it, contact it, be with it, follow it, be it. Hold for next exercise.

EXERCISE #10.3
EXAMINING THE LIGHT

Your eyes are still closed. Again, see the misty Light flowing in from another world. Note your doubts, if any, regarding the realness of this Light. Doubts are alright, even can be part of the process.

With your eyes still closed, and while looking at or imagining that you see the Light mist, organize your doubts into a quiet system, grouping these doubts and maybe even noting which are main doubts and which are subdoubts.

Continue seeing the Light mist. Imagine that your doubts about the realness of the Light mist are being written on a chalkboard on wheels.

Once you have vaguely organized your doubts, think of these as a body of information which can be held, with great respect, off to the side for a while. See yourself pushing the rolling chalkboard off to the side.

Your imagination is revealing something to you. You can see, now, beyond this list of doubts, into a special place. This place is full of information about the possible nature of your idea of highest Light.

This place is full of Light! Each piece of Light is a bit of information, an idea about Light.

Allow all these bits of information, whether imaginary or real to you, to come in to your awareness.

Savor these ideas. Experience them. Enjoy them as wonderful possibilities, utopian dreams, or fragments of fairy tales, if that is how you wish to have yourself see this imagery of Light. Just practice seeing the Light, and knowing it.

Hold for next exercise.

EXERCISE #10.4
DANCING WITH LIGHT

Now, with your eyes still closed, imagine that a mist of Light flows to a place right in front of you. Reach into this Light with your hands.

Now, with your eyes still closed, imagine that you stand, or actually do go ahead and stand, to greet this Light.

Treat this Light as a dance partner. Imagine that you are dancing with this Light, or actually do begin to physically dance with this Light. As you dance, see yourself swirl with your Light partner into a paradise full of Light—whatever that paradise may be to you.

Dance on for a while. Then freeze. Note how you feel.

11
Clarifying The Light

> ... What is happening during the process of dying, with its outer and inner dissolution,
> Is a gradual development and dawning of ever more subtle levels of consciousness.
>
> ... The process moves gradually toward the revelation of the very subtlest consciousness of all: the Ground Luminosity or Clear Light.
>
> Sogyal Rinpoche
> *Tibetan Book of Living and Dying*

As we expand our ideas of, our definitions of, some ideal, some kind of highest purest Light, we grow closer to the ability of our consciousness to seek, to sense, to perceive, to relate to, a grand luminosity, an ultimate form of something we have few words to define while we live, speak, and think in this physical plane.

This awareness of this ideal, of this highest luminosity, is something we can generate for ourselves. We can develop, or even imagine, this luminosity, and tell ourselves we see this in our mind or in our mind's eye.

LIGHT IS SO MANY THINGS TO SO MANY

Some will develop their sense of this luminosity as a Light with a benevolence. Whether this sense of benevolence or goodness is learned from a religion or spiritual practice, or other approach, or even simply found, this is alright. We all sense this ideal, this ultimate highest purest luminosity or Light in our own way.

And indeed, whether part of a religious or spiritual teaching, or stemming from some other approach to the *idea* of highest Light, we can say there is some form of what we might call divinity to this Light. So, for the moment, let's form a new idea of the words, *divine* and *divinity*. Yes, dictionary definitions for these terms include (for divine as a noun) celestial, godly, heavenly, exquisite, marvelous, and (for divinity) spirituality, theology, mysticism. These terms can be part of many people's experience of the highest Light or luminosity.

Let's simply say here that perhaps what is divine is whatever is most supremely respected by you. Encourage yourself to define divinity for yourself and then aspire to be or know what you feel is most divine. This is an effective way to nourish your spirit, your essence. This is also a way to relate to the Light you may be defining, finding, for yourself.

The essence of divine Light is something you can determine, define, see, with your own inner eye to appreciate. This is your option, as this Light can be experienced in so many different ways.

INVOKE THE LIGHT

However you see it, as you begin to actively define, and then generate, and or look for and call upon, the stream of what you feel to be highest Light, you begin to be more and more sensitive to its presence.

From this point of increased sensitivity to highest luminosity or Light, you increase the amount of Light that you feel is available to you. You do this by increasing the idea of frequency with which you relate to this Light.

This *invoking the Light* is a special sort of what we can call *prayer*. This prayer does not pray that someone takes care of you, that someone sends you Light and hope. Instead, this form of prayer places the responsibility on you to find, to reach for, the Light--and also gives you direct access to the Light you have defined, discovered, generated.

The looking for and the accessing of the Light is all that is required to put you in touch with what you feel is this Light. The reason that this is so simple is that the essence of this idea of grand luminosity or Light is available to you whenever you call upon it. Actually, this idea of Light is always present, you need only recognize it.

Open the window. Call upon the Light. Invoke the Light and you see it.

Opening the window onto the Light is like opening the curtains and even the window of a darkened room, and allowing the sun Light to pour in. But this window to the highest Light is not in the wall of a building. This window is in the wall of your reality, in the wall of your mind, of your consciousness. Your reality is your reality, so you can install this window and open it whenever you are ready.

EXERCISE #11.1
READING THE ATMOSPHERE

With your eyes open, examine the space (or atmosphere) in front of you. Reach out and run your fingers through it.

Leave your hands out in front of you and close your eyes. Imagine that your fingertips have become super-sensitive. Run those fingertips through the air and imagine that you feel the differences in the density, the thickness, of the air.

You may find pockets of relative emptiness, spaces where your hands reach or move differently.

Move your hands delicately to maximize their sensitivity.

Also imagine that you feel subtle streams of air or energy moving past your fingertips. Allow your fingertips to follow these imaginary streams.

Continue feeling the atmosphere with your fingers into the next exercise, opening your eyes as you do.

EXERCISE #11.2
BREAKING THROUGH

Now imagine that the atmosphere in front of you is opening — cracking a little or tearing gently. Reach into the opening with your fingertips and pull the opening further open.

As you do this, imagine that what pours in through the crack is a very different, far brighter, far Lighter gleaming atmosphere.

The gleam continues to pour in. You are soon immersed in this new atmosphere and you love it.

Imagine that something about the Light that is pouring in is so clean, so pure, so refreshing, so far beyond the Light you have been seeing with your eyes in your daily life — your material plane reality.

You feel the Light filling your eyes until everything you see looks to be of this Light. If this is difficult to visualize with your eyes open, close your eyes now to see more.

ACCESS THE HIGHER LIGHT

This accessing of the idea of higher Light, as simple as it sounds (and as imaginary as it may feel), is important training for your mind, your awareness, your personal consciousness. You are, basically, training your sensitivity. You can use this sensitivity — call upon it — in many different situations, both in and out of body, let's say both before and after physical death.

You can use your sensitivity to the high Light to find your way through difficult life transitions, even to navigate your way out of dense attachment networks, and at times messy attachment and energetic situations, traps, and paradoxes.

When you feel emotionally trapped or blocked, you can open the atmosphere you are in and allow another less dense, lighter, atmosphere to pour in and fill or even if you wish, engulf you. Your awareness can do this as this is done without physical effort.

CLARIFY THE LIGHT

Remember that the Light you see is as pure and as divine (whatever divine means for you) as you choose to see it being. This is why learning to clarify the Light you see is important. You can *raise the purity of the Light you imagine or see to the highest, clearest, level possible.* You can also notice when the Light you see does not rise to the highest levels of your idea of clarity. (This is part of the discernment process discussed in sections of the following book, *How To Die And Survive, Book Two.*)

EXERCISE #11.3
ENHANCING THE LIGHT

Close your eyes. Scan the back of your eyelids. Notice that what you see with your eyes closed is not an even field. There are degrees of, shades of, and sometimes even colors of dark and Light there. Sometimes, the degrees are so very subtle that they are hard to detect, but they are always there.

Now, with your eyes still closed, roll your eyeballs up as far as they will go, as if you are looking at the inside of your forehead. While in this position, close your eyes even tighter. Keep the eyes closed tightly, and hold the eyeballs rolled back.

Now, with your eyeballs still rolled back and your eyelids still closed, relax the tightness of the lids. Now tighten the closed eyelids again.

Continue this way, loosening and tightening your closed eyelids, always with your eyeballs rolled back. Loosen. Tighten. Look for variations in the Light you see on the insides of your eyelids, or in your interior visual field. Hold for next exercise.

<u>EXERCISE #11.4</u>
CLARIFYING THE LIGHT

Keep your eyes closed. Choose the Lightest bit of Light you have been able to find during the scanning you have been doing in the previous Exercise. Find this Light again. It may float around. Do whatever you can to follow it or reinvoke it with your eyeballs. If you cannot follow it or reinvoke it, find another bit of Light, or create a bit of Light to focus on by imagination or by memory.

Gaze at this piece of Light. Imagine that it becomes brighter and expands. Enjoy whatever colors you see in this Light, if any. Stay with this Light, focus on it, even if it changes. Continue raising its brightness and Lightness, however that appears to you.

Now, Exercise your mind's eye.

Transform the Light you are studying to something even more expanded and Lighter and brighter than it has been. If your Light is a particular color of Light, try turning it to a white Light which is Light combining all colors. If your Light is white, or when it becomes white, try brightening it further. Examine it for clarity and purity. Is it an evenly bright Light? Can you brighten up its denser areas or streaks? (Note: If you find that your highest Light appears more as a violet Light or some other luminous color of Light, then work with that understanding of your highest Light.)

Stay with the Light.

With your eyes still closed, clarify this Light. Clean it with your energy, as you run your examining inner eye through it, as if your examining inner eye were a rake or a grid. Clean the Light. Clarify the Light. Remove any dense, dark, or irregular areas of uneven Light.

As your clarify the Light, find yourself feeling more and more pleased with it, and more and more attracted to it. Create a Light as pure as you deem possible. See this Light become more and more luminous.

12
Praying as Practical Action

> Behold, I will do a new thing: . . .
> I will even make a way in the
> wilderness, and rivers in the desert.
>
> *Isaiah 43:19*

The usefulness of the action of, the process of, the state of mind of, prayer is vastly underestimated. This is largely because the potential of prayer is vastly misunderstood. Basically, praying is a way of focusing on possibilities and their possible realization or generation.

Prayer can focus the mind's eye, the awareness, the personal consciousness.

Prayer takes many forms, ranging from asking God or a higher power for strength, or assistance or guidance, or blessings, to extending protection, blessings, and good wishes to others, to reaching into other dimensions, to invoking Light or energy to generate an actual or imagined shift in a given reality, a shift or LEAP to a range of other forms.

ALL METHODS

All methods of prayer do on some level seek to engender a particular state of mind in the praying individual, a state of mind that allows for a shift in awareness. All too often, the power in the basic act, even in the literal physical gesture, of praying is overlooked.

The following exercises are an exploration of prayer as practical action, as well as prayer as a method of reaching or experiencing or exploring other dimensions or aspects of one's awareness, of one's reality. These basic exercises can be repeated again and again in life and through all minor and major emotional and physical and other transitions.

NOTE ABOUT THE FOLLOWING EXERCISES

As is the case for all exercises in this and the following books, each of the motions described in these exercises can be done as described, or adapted for and by those not able to comfortably do these exercises.

And, for those who are not appearing conscious but may also be listening, these exercises can still be participated in: simply visualize or imagine making these physical and nonphysical motions.

Readers have also asked about those no longer in physical bodies. Of course, if those persons can hear these exercises read through or thought through in steps, the Will, or the consciousness, of these persons can also participate in these exercises.

Also note: where the backbone, the term upward, even the concept of the vertical AXIS, are all referred to in these exercises, these terms can be adapted to the position and the condition the participant in these exercises is actually in. Clearly, vertical axis becomes a concept rather than specifically vertical in other dimensions and conditions. (See the next *How To Die And Survive* book, *Book Two*, for more on this matter.)

EXERCISE #12.1
INSCRIBING PRAYER GESTURE IN YOUR ENERGY MEMORY

Place your hands together, fingertip to fingertip, palm to palm, flat against each other (as in Figure 12.1). Hold your hands as they are placed together, directly in front of your chest, with your elbows bent. Feel your hands touching each other. Get a sense of what this feeling is. Try to become very aware of this. Close your eyes and feel your fingertips and hands pressing together.

You will never forget this feeling. This feeling, whether or not you have hands to place together, whether or not you have a physical body at a time you might want this feeling, can always be replicated in your energy memory. With your eyes still closed, hold this position for many minutes.

EXERCISE #12.2
PRACTICING ASCENSION PRAYER MOTION

Now, with your hands still pressed together, press them more intensely into each other. Slowly, very slowly, raise that prayer, those hands in prayer position, slightly upward along your central vertical axis, moving your praying hands a little bit upward in front of your body, parallel to your backbone.

Keep those hands in prayer position all through the exercise.

Move your praying hands from a lower point in front of your chest, further upward, remaining parallel to your spine. Move your prayer upward along your vertical axis as it goes up in front of your throat, up in front of the center of your face. Keep raising your hands, fingers still pointing toward the area above your head, still in prayer position, continuing until your praying hands are located above your head, (as in Figure 12.2).

Hold a moment.

Now, very slowly, move your hands back downward, holding the prayer position. Keep those hands vertical along your vertical access, moving them downward in this vertical position as far as they will go.

Do this entire motion—up and down—ten times. Complete the exercise with the hands still in prayer position, in front of your chest.

Hold for next exercise.

EXERCISE #12.3
PRACTICING OPEN ASCENSION PRAYER MOTION

With the hands in the prayer position, in front of your chest, focus for a moment on the ridge of your knuckles in each hand.

Move these two knuckle ridges away from each other, pulling the palms of the praying hands away from each other, but leaving the finger tips and wrists in contact. Your hands are still in prayer position, but you have created an open space, a special space, a sacred vessel, between the palms.

Try to form a diamond-shaped space between your two still-touching hands (as in Figure 12.3).

Now, go through the exercise described above (Exercise #12.2), moving those hands upward, vertically, in prayer position—but now in this opened-up prayer position. Hold when you reach the highest point above your head.

Move your open prayer up and down your vertical axis several times. Complete the exercise with your hands still in open prayer position, with the diamond-shaped space still between your palms, with your praying hands back in front of your chest. Hold this position for the next exercise.

EXERCISE #12.4
CREATING A SACRED VESSEL FOR YOURSELF

Begin in the position in which you completed the previous exercise. Your open-praying hands forming the diamond-shaped space are in front of your chest. Focus on that enclosed space between your hands.

Imagine that you are in that diamond-shaped space between your palms. Imagine climbing in if you have to. It may be hard for you to imagine that your entire body is in that space. If it helps, imagine that you have shrunk in size and that your entire body is actually able to fit into that space. Otherwise, just take your personal consciousness, the part of yourself that has no physical body, your SELF, the idea of your mind's eye, into that space.

Hold this position and thought for next exercise.

EXERCISE #12.5
MOVING YOUR SACRED VESSEL

Now, repeat the motion of the earlier exercise (Exercise #12.3), in which you moved your praying hands (open prayer position) along your vertical access, up in front of your throat, in front of the central part of your face, up parallel to your forehead, and out above your head. All the while, hold, very, very carefully, your SELF awareness, your consciousness, in that space between your palms.

Now, very slowly, very deliberately, pull your hands and your SELF back down to the space in front of your chest. Feel as if you are protective of your SELF as you do this.

Repeat this exercise several times, attempting each time to pull more and more of your focus, more of your attention, into the space between your palms. Feel as if you have left your body and are now just living between your palms.

Eventually return your praying hands, your sacred vessel, to the position in front of your chest. Hold for next exercise.

EXERCISE #12.6
RELEASING FROM YOUR VESSEL

Repeat the previous open prayer exercise, in which you are moving your sacred prayer vessel, with all your attention, your SELF, your consciousness, between the palms with which you form this vessel. This time, move your hands, ever more slowly, as slowly as possible while still moving, up along your vertical access, up and up, up as far as they will go, without undoing your open prayer position, stretching way up above your head.

Hold your SELF between your palms, way up there. Hold there.

Your consciousness is now up there in the diamond-shaped space between your palms. Focus on this consciousness. Attempt to strengthen, to make more potent, more clear, your consciousness as it sits there above your head between your palms. With concentration, expand yourself between your palms, so much so that you begin to push on the inside of your palms, pushing, pushing as if trying to push your hands apart from each other because your SELF is too large for that space now.

Now, very gently, very slightly, separate your hands. Let the palms and fingers and wrists be near each other but not touching. Stretch your hands out above your head a little further, with the hands now being stretched parallel to each other, parallel and untouching, (as in Figure 12.4). If you are lying down, consider this reaching "upward" as a moving toward the area beyond the top of your head. If you are sitting or standing, reach for the sky.

Hold your reaching, now in a parallel untouching palms position. Take a deep breath. Hold that breath a moment.

Now, as you release that breath, see yourself escape upward from between those hands. Stay with your escaping SELF. Keep going upward, out beyond the top of your head. Continue this ascending, this climbing. Notice what you imagine happens to that SELF, that idea of your SELF, that has escaped from between those palms.

As you do, visualize that a string runs from your SELF, your consciousness, out there, back down into your axis, on down into your physical body. For a while, stay out there above your head, above your physical body.

<u>EXERCISE #12.7</u>
DELIVERING YOUR SELF

Now pull your consciousness back to your hands. Return your SELF to the space between your parallel hands above your head. Now place your fingertips and wrists back together. Your conscious is between your palms now.

Slowly pull your SELF back down in front of your chest, still between your palms.

Hold your SELF there, being very aware that you are between your palms. Now aim the point created by your fingertips in various directions other than beyond the top of your head, other than upward: directly in front of you, downward, to the side at various angles.

Pick a beautiful, serene spot that you would like to temporarily send your SELF, to send the SELF still between your palms. This spot can be upward, downward, sideward—very far away or somewhere very near. Move your palms, with your SELF concentrated between them, toward that space as far as you can reach. Hold a moment.

Then, as if you were releasing a baby, separate your hands slightly, so that they are parallel. Take a deep breath. Relax and breathe out. As you do so, temporarily deliver yourself into that space you have chosen for your SELF. See how that string in the previous exercise continues to connect back down to your physical body.

For a while, imagine that you have entered and continue to be in a beautiful, serene, and very safe space. Know that you have taken very good care to temporarily deliver your SELF, your consciousness, your attention, into this safe space.

Breathe a sigh of relief. Hold for next exercise.

EXERCISE #12.8
RETURNING TO CENTER

Stay there in your safe space. Develop a detailed picture of that place. Use your imagination to enhance this picture. Pull as much Light as you can into this picture.

Explore the space. What does it look like? What can you do there? Where is it? How does it feel to be there? Pull as much good feeling and pure love as you can into this picture.

Now, to return, come back to your physical body, pull your attention back, to the space between your parallel hands. Once you are back between your hands, put your finger tips and wrists back together. Pull your open prayer diamond shaped space back to the area in front of your chest.

Now take your SELF and press it back into your body, by turning each of your palms toward your chest and pushing them into your chest.

Welcome back.

Your SELF, your consciousness, or you can call this your imagination if you prefer, are free to come and go at will using the methods in this chapter.

Always return for now, to the place and position from which you start each exercise, until a much later time when you fully understand what is involved in leaving or leaping out of physicality for good, as is discussed in the following How To Die And Survive books, and other books in this series.

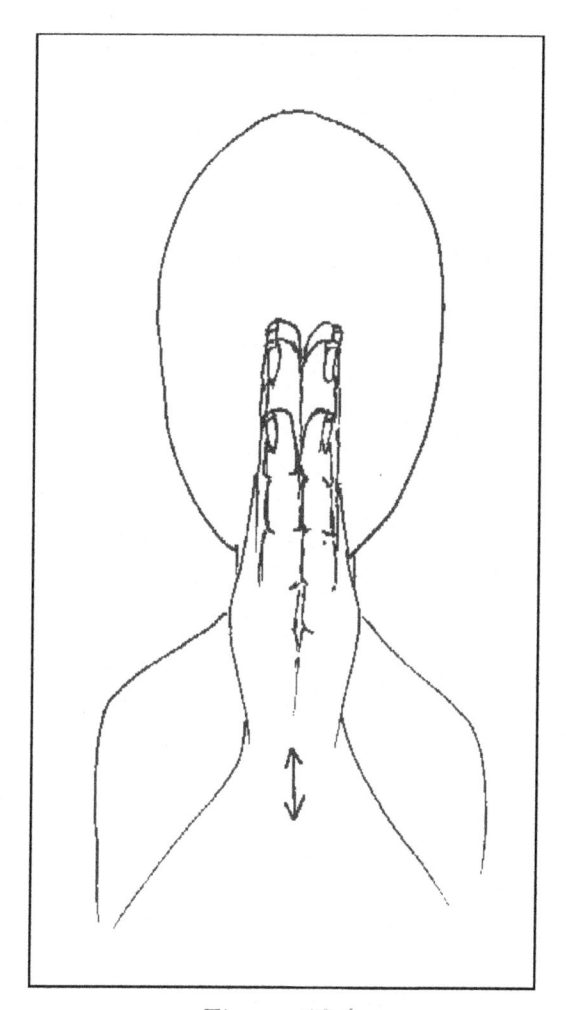

Figure 12.1
Prayer Gesture

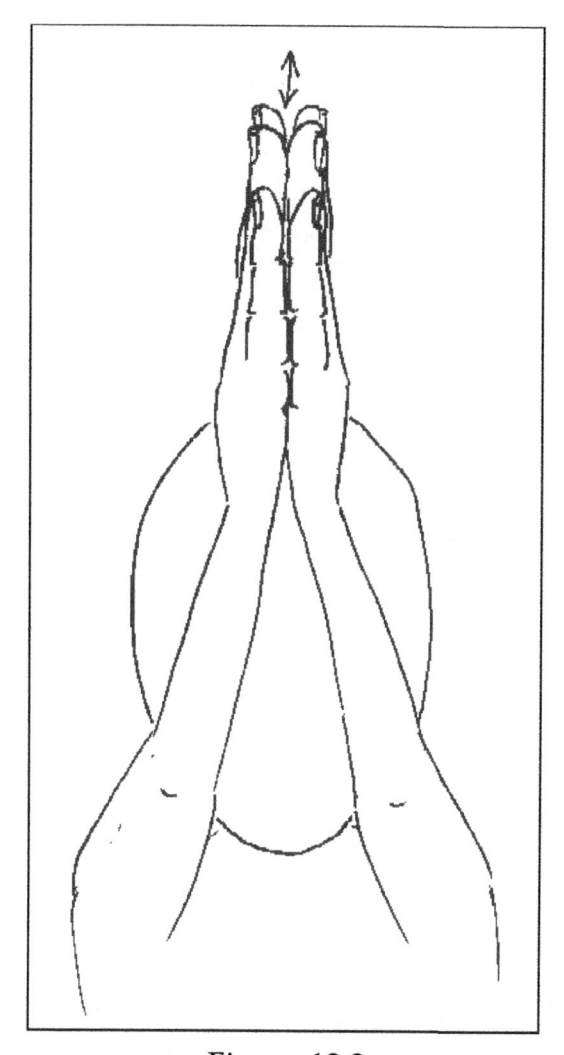

Figure 12.2
Extended Prayer Gesture

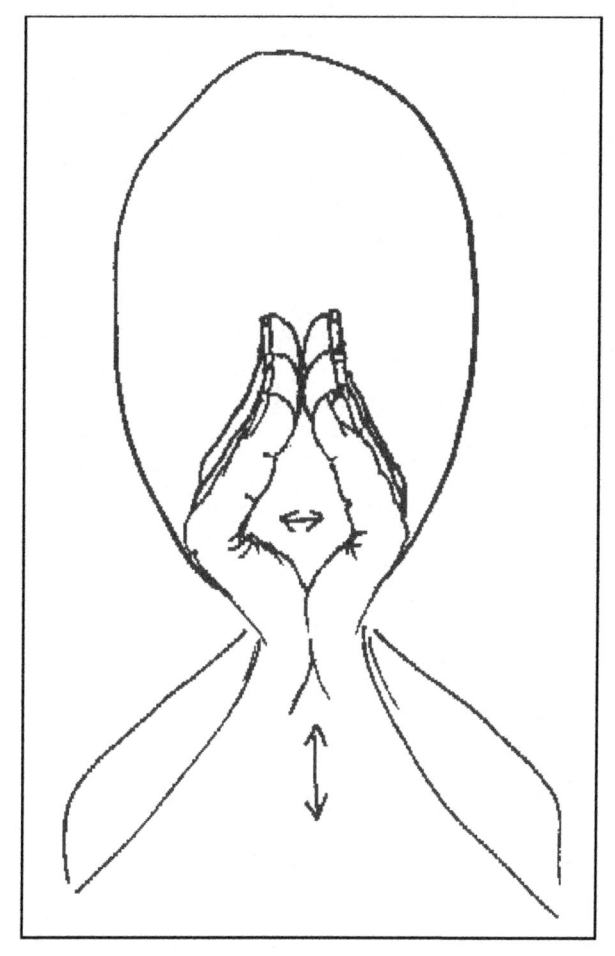

Figure 12.3
Open Ascension Prayer Gesture

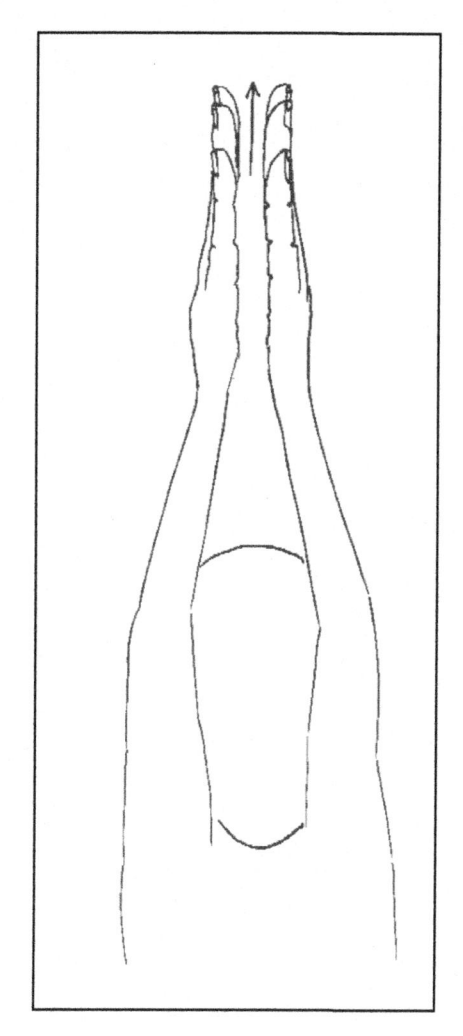

Figure 12.4
Deliverance Prayer Gesture

13
Initiating the Vision

> Even if some stars are
> smaller than others,
> they all shine with a
> single Light.
>
> St. Makartos
> The Great of Egypt
> *Makarian Homilies, III*

Your vision is the key, the guide, the magician, unlocking the door to realities beyond all you think you know. Learn to see BEYOND.[56] Initiate your vision. See your way through all your in-life and seeming end-of-life, also possible life-after-life, transitions.

Previous chapters (as well as other books in this *Keys To Consciousness And Survival Series*) have explained that every major transition is a change, an ending of a phase or stage or pattern, a sort of shift or death, or transformation, a LEAP.[57] Your notion of dying is itself in transition as you read the

---

[56] Refer to *Volume 10* in this *Keys To Consciousness And Survival Series*, titled *Seeing Beyond Our Line Of Sight*.
[57] Refer to *Volume 3* in this *Keys To Consciousness And Survival Series*, titled *Unveiling The Hidden Instinct*.

words in this and the following *How To Die And Survive* books. You are enlightening yourself.

BECOMING LIGHTER

You can choose to train your ability to sense or "see" far beyond the material plane. You will remember engaging in these exercises of defining and knowing your idea of Light, and the related practices of what we can call *expanded en-Lightenment*, when you find yourself amidst even your most profound changes, and even the most disorienting phases of even your most advanced transitional processes.

This is why it is helpful to make some connection with your own idea of a *grand luminosity*, with your own vision of a *highest purest Light*, now, at this stage of your life, before you are deep into a major death transition. It is time, therefore, to initiate your vision, to welcome your new eyes.

EXERCISE #13.1
INITIATING
THE VISION

Stand if you can. Otherwise, imagine that you are standing. Place your left hand on top of your head. Place your right hand over your heart.

Close your eyes in order to imagine this ceremony:

You stand at the center of a circle of unidentifiable beings, each made of a very beautiful Light. These beings are dignitaries of some sort. After a long period of silence, the beings step forward to you, closing their circle around you.

One by one, the beings hold their right hands over but not touching the top of your left hand which you still hold atop your own head. Each being places a right hand atop the hand placed there by the previous being.

One by one, with each hand being placed, you feel and see a bolt of cool and soothing Light race into you from those hands, into the top of your head, down your back along your spine, and then up the front of you to your heart.

The energy grows, the Light grows. It becomes quite intense. For a moment, you feel you are being softly electrocuted, but then you tell yourself that this series of energy surges is too lovely to be an electrocution.

You start to vibrate, to shake. Your eyes are still closed. The dignitaries fade away as you begin to shake a little more. Shake. Now stop. Open your eyes. Feel that the world looks somehow different.

EXERCISE #13.2
RAISING THE EYES

Close your eyes. Become as aware as you can of all that your eyes feel. Notice that there are sensations around and even in your eyeballs. These sensations take many forms and can be quite faint. Continue to detect these sensations.

Open your eyes. Fix your gaze on something in your visual field. As you look at this object of your gaze, feel again the sensations around and even in your eyeballs. Feel that seeing this object is, in a way, forming a relationship with it, causing an exchange of energy with it.

Now close your eyes and imagine that you are still seeing the object of your gaze. Put this object in your forehead. Feel that seeing this object is exchanging information with it. As you do this, see the object turn to Light. Feel your forehead turn to Light.

INITATING YOUR VISION

Having initiated your vision, you will begin to see more. At first you will barely notice your enhanced vision. Eventually you will rely on it as much as you do your biological vision.

14
Quickening For Frequency-Shifting: LEAP Level Two

> Mere man, his days
> Are numbered;
> Whatever he may do,
> He is but the wind.
>
> Gilgamesh Epic
> *Old Babylonian Version*
> *Yale Tablet IV*

As you move out of your old reality, your old relationship, your old home, your old job, your old youth, your old physical existence, you, something about you, always changes form. You are always in some form of transition or even concurrent transitions.

You are continuously transitioning to, moving to, shifting into, new arrangements of your *consciousness matrix*. In this sense, the frequency at which your personal *consciousness matrix* vibrates continuously evolves.[58]

---

[58] Refer to the definition and discussion of this matrix in *Volume 3* in this *Keys To Consciousness And Survival Series*, titled *Unveiling The Hidden Instinct*.

As with evaporating water, increasing the motion, the speed of the molecules or essence, increases the fluidity or possibility of change, even sometimes great change. This can be described, at least metaphorically, as the increasing of frequency. Such an increase in seeming or perhaps actual level or intensity or speed of vibration can be described as a "quickening." This quickening is indeed a great LEAP.[59]

EXERCISE #14.1
SPEEDING UP AS
FREQUENCY-SHIFTING

Lie still, with your eyes closed. Imagine that you are on some kind of train that has been stopped for quite some time. Now imagine that this train is slowly entering into motion.

From being what seems to be entirely still, you begin to move what seems to be ever so little, not even a few miles per hour. Then, you move a few miles per hour faster . . . And then a little faster. Then faster. . . .

Now you are moving at freeway speed, as though you were driving on the freeway, at that freeway speed, whatever this may be for you. Now faster. . . . Now you are moving faster than you have ever driven a car, (if you have ever driven a car).

Now you are moving even faster than that, maybe at the speed of the fastest Bullet Train. Now you are moving at the speed of the fastest supersonic jet. Now you are moving at an even faster speed, faster than the fastest jet, however this speed feels to be in your

---

[59] Refer to the definition and discussion of this LEAP in *Volume 3* in this *Keys To Consciousness And Survival Series*, titled *Unveiling The Hidden Instinct*.

imagination. Now you are moving through space at the fastest speed you can imagine.

Feel yourself speeding up beyond any speed you have ever before imagined.

Note that the train you were in has dropped away from you now, but that you are still moving rapidly through space. Imagine that while this is taking place, you are retaining your body. Yet your physical body is not moving you, nor is the train you were on. There are no wheels moving you; no engines are moving you.

You, yourself, are moving your SELF. Your awareness, your Force of Will, your personal consciousness, are propelling you through space. You are moving very rapidly. Steadily increase your speed as you enter the next exercise.

If you are moving into the next exercise right away, then keep your eyes closed.

EXERCISE #14.2
QUICKENING

Continue from last exercise with closed eyes. Or, close your eyes now.

Recall from the last exercise the following:

> *You, yourself, are moving your SELF. Your awareness, your Force of Will, your personal consciousness, are propelling you through space. You are moving very rapidly. Steadily increase your speed....*

Now you are moving far more rapidly. You can feel each of your atoms, or perhaps electrons and other smaller bits, vibrate. Everything in you is vibrating.

You are speeding up, quickening. Like water boiling, at a certain point, the speed of that boil vaporizes the water. Now you vaporize. Your particles quicken. You do not disappear, you do not die, you simply vaporize. Your body evaporates.

You vaporize, thinking that this could be the end—the end of your consciousness, the end of your awareness, the end of you. However, as you vaporize, tell yourself to stay conscious. Say, "Remain conscious." Know that you can die and survive, that indeed this is not death.

***

Do not let go of your awareness. Finish vaporizing. Keep on quickening. You are moving ever more rapidly, now. You have no physical shape now. Now you move as racing vapor. You remain conscious.

*It may be hard to imagine vapor moving so quickly, because we tend to think of solid objects and solid bodies being moved, and moved quickly, propelled through space. Nevertheless, picture yourself as a vaporous cloud hurtling through space at what you imagine to be the speed of Light, and then faster than the speed of Light, and then faster than that, and then seemingly moving more and more quickly, quicker and quicker. Keep going at this astounding pace, becoming increasingly vaporous. Keep going, keep on with this **quickening.***

Freeze. Keep your eyes closed.

You are suspended in space, far, far out of your body. Are you breathless? Float and swim and poke around out there as if you had a body. You are still conscious. Examine what you are now. Get to know your consciousness while it is way out here. Study your consciousness for quite a while. See your SELF as a non-physical body or presence.

Now clap your hands and return to your physical body. Open your eyes.

QUICKEN

With an understanding of, a shift in awareness regarding, your own personal consciousness, you can learn to raise, to quicken, its vibration. In so doing, you increase the energy you have available to you as you prepare to make a major change in your life, in your reality, in your awareness. You quicken for your LEAP into great change.

As you quicken, you raise toward the frequency of high Light, which fuels your passage into higher realms of being, which energizes your ascension.

A quickening can be a subtle transition or it can be quite abrupt. Do not be surprised if you feel a "rush" of energy as your awareness of frequency raises its frequency in order to be aware of so much more.

PART III

How

To

Detach

15
Detecting the Network of Cords

....The will has its
Loathings and yearnings....

Qi Bo
Classic of the
Spiritual Axis (Ling Shu)
Nei Jing

You create, generate by existing, a complex web of energy streams, ties, circuits. Where these circuits are biological, they fill or even form your nervous and other systems. Energy circuits flow through and wear pathways into your biological body's nervous system, including your brain. These energy circuits can also extend far past your biological nervous system. You extend or emit electrical waves and nets from your biological system on outward, and from outside yourself in.

You release biochemical, and via biochemistry also intellectual, emotional, and other more abstract forms of energy arrangements, cording networks, into the atmosphere within and around you. You also tie into electrical and other energy networks above, beyond, outside your own biological and biologically-based consciousness systems.

In fact, you are so tied in to your own and other external energy arrangement networks, that you are, in a sense, merged with, or at least entangled with, them. At times you may even allow yourself to become *sub*merged in them. You may tend to confuse your *consciousness matrix* with other networks of energy that are not yours or that are not who you truly are. At the same time, the confusion may be between and among what is a biologically-based network, and what is not, *or may not be*, a network entirely of this material plane.

UN-RAVEL CORDS

The overlap of your SELF, of your own and others' energy fields and networks, can be looked at, at least to begin, in terms of interpersonal relationships. Your energy field overlaps with the energy fields of the people around you. You come into contact with other people's energy fields and establish relationships or connections with them. Even when you think you are not involved, you have, your energy network has, in a sense "hooked up" with other people. Your realities intertwine. You project bits of your reality onto them. You also "internalize," take in and live out, feel, other people's experiences, their realities, and assume that some pieces of them are your own. Quite often, there is confusion. What is your feeling, what is mine? What is your experience, what is mine? Who am I and who are you?

In time, your emotional patterns, your psychological states, your energy patterns, your neurological patterns, your physical health, your social interactions, reflect, not just your own conditions and your own states of mind and body, but those of the people you have internalized or taken in.

This connection with the people and the world around you is natural. It is, however, important to become as conscious as possible of the energetic effects of such connection, of the ties, the streams, the strings, the *cording*. It is important to identify, sometimes even unravel, these cords in order to know where you are on your own life path, and whose ties or cords are whose.

Especially when it comes to the change or ending of a behavior, of a way of life, or of a physical body, it is important to make the distinction between SELF and others. This distinction is essential in determining whether or not it is your time to enter a minor or major in-life transition or even to physically die.

Are you the one that needs to, or chooses to, change, transition, or die, or is it someone else? Sometimes you transition or die, go into some form of minor or major transition, (including perhaps becoming mentally or physically troubled) -- yet are doing this for other people who need to change or transition, or are somehow doing so whether they need to, or want to, or cannot help doing so.

You cannot determine for someone else whether or not he or she is ready to change, transition, or die. That person has to decide for him or her SELF.

You can, however, *decide for yourself whether what you are feeling—the push to change, transition, or die—is your own or is someone else's*. This is a very important distinction. Far too frequently, individuals get upset, sick, or in some way experience, someone else's problems and deaths.

SOURCE THE FEELINGS

Perhaps you wake up one morning feeling ill at ease, but feel no reason to feel so. If so, try turning your perception of this feeling around, away from your SELF for a moment, and say, "I don't feel this way. *Who* in my life has a reason to feel this way?"

It is very important to do this kind of examination of your feelings. This is part of knowing yourself and knowing or detecting the networks of cords, the webs, that may surround you.

You will benefit by sensing the difference between the boundaries and complications of your own and other people's energy arrangement networks. If you are entangled in your own energy arrangement network, you can choose to unravel all or some of it. If you are identifying or perhaps over-identifying with someone else's energy arrangement network, you can see this and then choose to exit part or all of it without doing the work of unraveling for that person.

EXERCISE #15.1
SOURCING FEELINGS

Note an uncomfortable emotion you may have experienced, even momentarily, even if only fleetingly, sometime recently. Source these feelings:

Ask yourself, "Is this my emotion? Are these my feelings?" Run down the list of your relationships. "How do I feel about my family? Is there anyone I'm close to who hasn't felt right lately?" "Is anyone worrying me?" Take each person separately and ask yourself why he or she may be worrying you. Then ask yourself what your sense of being worried, or concerned, is. Is this an emotional experience for youo? Are these your emotions?

Next look at how you have been feeling. Have you been sleeping well? How are your finances? How is your primary relationship, if you have one? Deliberately name one person you are closest to and say, "Chris. How is Chris feeling? Does Chris feel to me as if Chris is alright?" Then ask yourself, "Do I feel to me as if I am alright?"

Consider a few more of the more memorable emotions you have experienced recently. Source these feelings as well: "Is this my feeling? Or someone else's?"

SOURCING SENSATIONS

This sourcing of feelings and sensations is a skill, at times may even be a survival skill. Of course, when you take on (personally experience some or all of) someone else's troubled condition or illness, or someone else's dying, in a way you are absorbing some of what is taking place within the other person. This is sensitive of you: it enables you to feel understanding of, even empathy for, and possibly even help that person. But you need not actually take on the other person's troubled condition or illness or death: you just are being aware of, sensitive to, what he or she has taken on.

Taking on or becoming deeply aware of someone else's problem is what this book will call *identification diagnosis.* With identification diagnosis, you can allow yourself the **intuitive awareness** of what someone else's condition is like or would be like for you. You actually do this sort of identifying all the time. But, *you must do this as consciously as possible to be certain you maintain your own boundaries.*

Identify consciously the energetic condition, and, as you do so, identify *whose condition this actually is* — its source.

Without being very conscious during your ongoing identification diagnoses, you risk taking on someone else's issues, conditions.

Once you have separated out the conditions of others from your own condition, and seen your own mix of conditions and those mixes of conditions affecting, emanating, from the people in your life, you can move ahead with clarity. *You can follow your own life stream, clearing your path of others' issues. This sourcing is a continuous process.*

It is important here to underscore the fact we are all part of the larger system. That which affects our children, our spouses, our friends, members of our community, somebody on the other side of the globe or Cosmos, affects us.

We nevertheless do well to *draw boundaries* when making determinations about the steps in our lives that we must take, as well as about the minor and major in-life and seeming end-of-life transitions and deaths we ourselves undergo.

Experience your own transitions. Leave others to experience their own transitions (where you can tell the difference between theirs and yours).

Die your own deaths. Leave others to do their own dying.

This is easy to say. Yet it is generally difficult to separate our energetic fates from the fates of those around us.

EXERCISE #15.2
SEEING THE LARGER MANIPULATION

Think of your body as a vehicle. Think of your life as the road your vehicle is traveling on. Drive along for many minutes. Think of yourself as the driver. Sightsee memories of your life, along the side of the road.

While you drive, consider this: in the cosmic order of things, there are, of course, far larger relationships than the relationship between yourself and your vehicle, and between your vehicle and your life path or road. There are so many strings or cords attached to your SELF, to you, the driver. In fact, as a driver, you at times tend to be a marionette—with other forces far greater than you pulling your strings. You are not always in control, are you?

Feel yourself driving along. Imagine that there are strings attached to your hands, your eyelids, your shoulders, your lips. Imagine cords attached to your chest, pulling it in and out, causing you to breathe.

Generate the sensation that you are not driving your vehicle, that you yourself are being operated. Be a puppet on strings. Drive along this way for a while.

Now see the memories you drive by as memories that are also on puppet strings. Try to see who all have been pulling on those strings.

EXAMINE THE CORDS

It is most necessary to examine the strings, the cords connecting us to things and people around us. Inasmuch as we may have somehow permitted these cordings, these attachments, we can clear some (or if need be all) of them once we see them—if we really wish to.

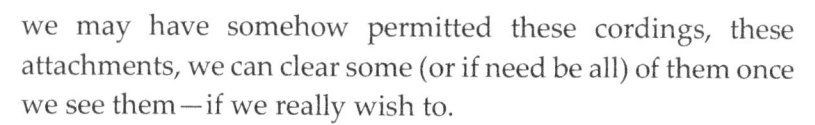

EXERCISE #15.3
LISTING YOUR CORDS

This exercise can be helped by using pen and paper—colored pens and large paper if you have these things. This is a brainstorming process, designed to help you visualize—imagine, sense, see—some of the attachments, cords, you have formed in this lifetime, and some you may have been being pulled into by others in this lifetime.

This process will take your blindfold off. It will take the lock off the door to your SELF-awareness. The process will snowball. For every attachment or cord you identify, there will be at least one if not several other cords that will come to your mind. Many of the cordings at work are deep underlying connections, ties, cordings.

Over time, even after this exercise, other cords will surface into your consciousness. Lifting the obvious cords by listing them allows the more hidden or implicit cords to float to the surface of your consciousness. As you continue looking for cords in your life, you will begin to see them as if they were a web of strings, connecting you, even perhaps tying you, to the world around you.

Now, begin to list every cord that comes to mind—every connection you have in your life. Try to find some (at least surface—obvious) attachments in each of the attachment categories below. Remember, there are no right or wrong categories or answers here. If you are using pen and paper, list each of the categories below with space to write between them. Recognize that these categories overlap. They are listed separately to stimulate your brainstorming. You can also list your own categories, or leave out categories altogether, or add additional categories and subcategories later.

You are listing attachment cordings. If you are writing your list onto paper, try using a different color pen for each attachment category. Once you have listed each category, list as many connections, links, ties, cords of all forms, as you can think of in each of these categories.

Attachment categories may include:

    PRACTICAL ATTACHMENT CORDS
    TEMPORAL ATTACHMENT CORDS
    SENSORY ATTACHMENT CORDS
    PHYSICAL ATTACHMENT CORDS
    ENERGETIC ATTACHMENT CORDS
    INTERPERSONAL ATTACHMENT CORDS
    SOCIAL ATTACHMENT CORDS
    PSYCHOLOGICAL ATTACHMENT CORDS
    ECONOMIC ATTACHMENT CORDS
    NUTRITIONAL ATTACHMENT CORDS
    DRUG AND ALCOHOL ATTACHMENT CORDS
    ENVIRONMENTAL ATTACHMENT CORDS
    MEDIA ATTACHMENT CORDS
    OBJECT ATTACHMENT CORDS
    POLITICAL ATTACHMENT CORDS
    SPIRITUAL ATTACHMENT CORDS
    CHEMICAL ATTACHMENT CORDS
    OTHER CATEGORIES OF ATTACHMENT CORDS

Do not force yourself to precisely define attachment cordings right now. Just list anything that comes to your mind, anything that you think of as being part of your life as you decide for yourself what the above attachment categories suggest to you. Again, there are no right or wrong answers here.

EXERCISE #15.4
ADDING ATTACHMENT CORDS TO YOUR LIST

Review the list you created in Exercise #15.3. Now, add at least five more attachment cords in each category.

If this is difficult, invent cords. You may want to think in terms of primary (very obvious, explicit), secondary (less obvious, less explicit), and tertiary (very hidden or implicit underlying) cords. For example, a man in love with a woman may be attached to — corded to — the physical body of the woman he is in love with. A secondary cord for him might be the sound of her voice. A tertiary or very subtle cord for him might be something that reminds him of either a primary or secondary cord (such as an old photograph of her or a piece of music they listened to together five years ago).

You may want to expand the list you created in Exercise #15.3 by adding columns to it this way:

Cord Attachment Categories	Primary Cords	Secondary Cords	Tertiary Cords	Etc.
----	----	----	----	----
----	----	----	----	----

However you go about your brainstorming, be sure to write down anything that comes into your mind, no matter how trivial or out of place it may seem. Any association at all that comes to your mind is ripe material for this attachment cord chart. Many people doing this exercise actually scribble their ideas all over pages of paper, writing in all directions, brainstorming, revealing ever more attachment cordings to themselves.

Do not try to make sense out of everything that comes to your mind. Just let it all come into your awareness and write it all down. Write as quickly as you can without trying to be neat. You can clean up your list and organize it later, even copy it over if you wish.

Once you have listed everything that you can think of, scribble or draw a box or a circle around each individual cord, even the cords that seem questionable, trivial, out of order, or illogical to you.

<u>EXERCISE #15.5</u>
CONNECTING CORDS TO SEE PATTERNS

Now examine all of your cords. Do you feel that any of these are connected, interacting? If so, connect them. Draw a line between these cords. Some connections will seem logical, others will seem to make no sense at all.

Some connections will appear to be rituals, habit patterns, and even pattern addictions.

For example, at six o'clock Friday (a time cord), a person who ends the work week at this point in time may go to a particular bar (an environmental cord), where she or he may meet various friends and a date (social and interpersonal cords), upon which he or she may feel like "partying" (a psychological cord), may proceed to eat a large amount of salty nuts and potato chips instead of a real dinner because she or he is hungry but too lazy to eat right (a nutritional cord). And after all that salt, she or he may be so thirsty that she or he has far more alcohol to drink than he or she means to (a drug and alcohol cord), which she or he actually does quite regularly.

This is a fairly obvious cord network or attachment pattern. Note that this particular cord network is a habit pattern and may be part of a more serious pattern addiction to alcohol. Other attachment patterns may be less clear, but any patterns that come to mind should be recorded. Your cord networks are pieces of your web.

Continue to map out relations between the various cords you have listed. Observe the patterns that emerge. The charts at the end of this chapter are actually simple, partial, excerpts of maps of several different individuals' cord networks. Notice the similarities and differences in these and your own charts.

<u>EXERCISE #15.6</u>
PLANNING FUTURE CORD OBSERVATIONS

Your cord chart should be reconstructed regularly. Add to your first chart daily for a week.

Make a new cord chart each week for several weeks, incorporating everything from your old cord chart and pushing yourself to add new details. Then, for the next several months, make a new cord chart once a month. Then, shift to two or three times a year.

This will provide you with an amazing journey into your behavior and a new level of awareness about yourself. You will begin to see the web you weave, not just on paper, but in the atmosphere around you. This is a most fascinating process.

Whenever you find connections between cords, return to your chart, or write a new chart in your mind, drawing lines to demonstrate your newly identified connections.

This mapping process will reveal significant, and, with practice, astounding, information about your emotional, behavioral, and energetic patterns. Many of the patterns you see will be subtle, previously hidden from your conscious awareness.

ATTACHMENTS

Sample cord charts are found in Figures 15.1 through 15.6. These are reduced in terms of number of cords due to space limitations here. Note how some of these abbreviated cord charts emphasize the attachment of cords directly to feelings about attachments rather than to objects of attachments.

This is acceptable. Many of us are more attached to our emotions about things and people than we are to these things and people. In fact, if you think about it, all your attachment is actually attachment to your feelings about, and or perceptions of, that to which you think you are attached.

HOW TO DIE AND SURVIVE

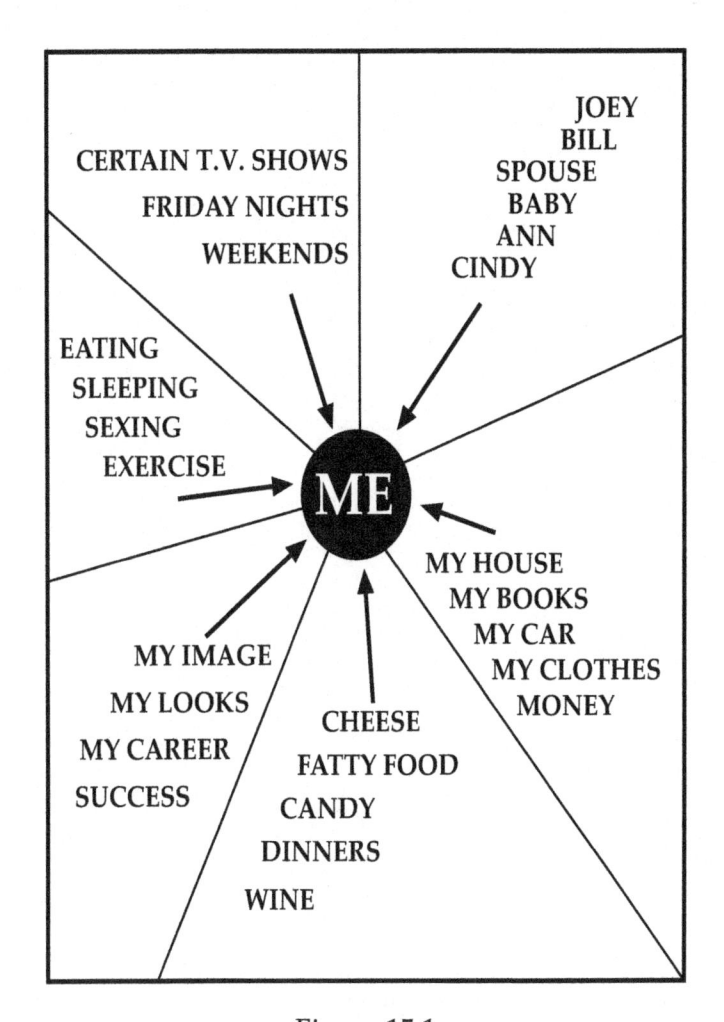

```
         CERTAIN T.V. SHOWS          JOEY
           FRIDAY NIGHTS             BILL
             WEEKENDS               SPOUSE
                                     BABY
                                      ANN
     EATING                          CINDY
     SLEEPING
     SEXING
     EXERCISE
                          ( ME )
                                    MY HOUSE
                                    MY BOOKS
                                    MY CAR
       MY IMAGE                     MY CLOTHES
       MY LOOKS         CHEESE       MONEY
       MY CAREER      FATTY FOOD
       SUCCESS         CANDY
                       DINNERS
                        WINE
```

Figure 15.1

An Individual's Attachments
To Basic Pieces of His Life

Interpersonal:	Spouse Hits Me Often
Time:	No Time to Concentrate on Self
Nutritional:	Carbohydrate Overuse — Eating Irregularly — Fatty Foods
Energetic:	Hopelessness — Sense of No Control Over Life
Spiritual:	Emptiness — Meaninglessness
	Misery
Physical:	No Sleep | Exhaustion | Poor Digestion | Ulcers | Overweight

SICK FEELING

⇩

HEADACHES ALL THE TIME

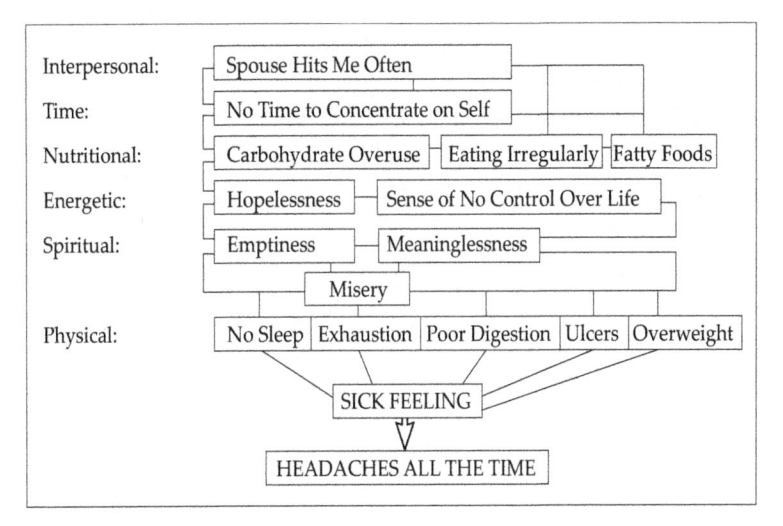

Figure 15.2

Simplified Cord Network
Drawn by a Woman Who Has Chronic Migraine Headaches
and Who is Living with Domestic Violence

HOW TO DIE AND SURVIVE

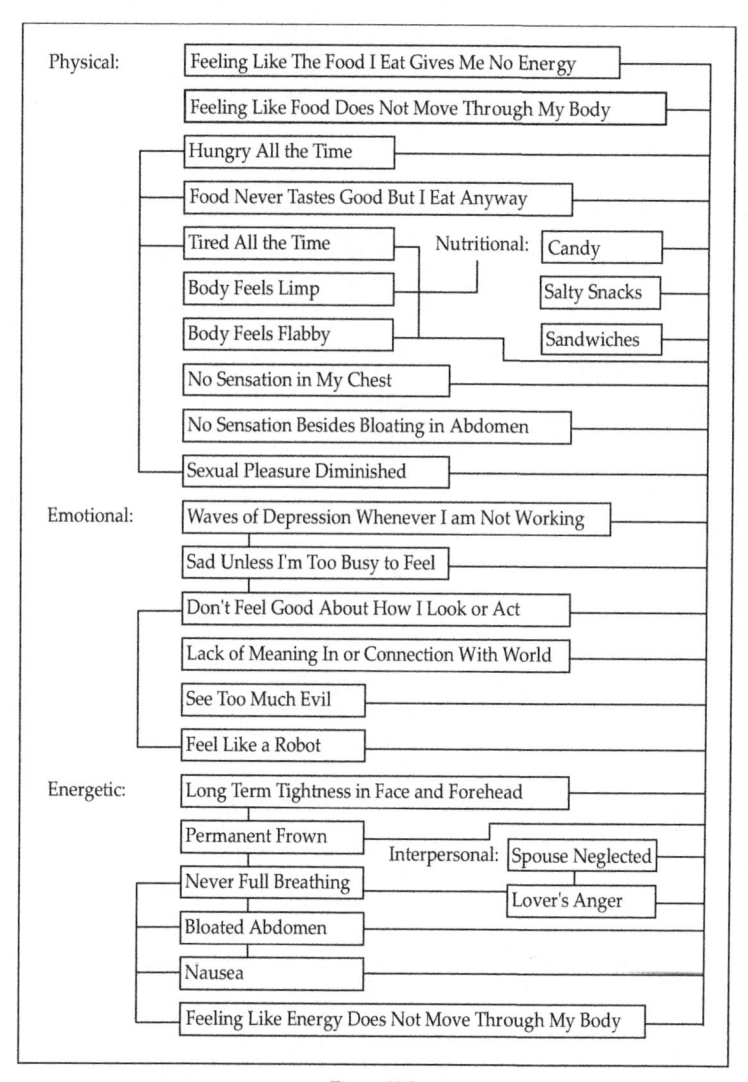

Physical:
- Feeling Like The Food I Eat Gives Me No Energy
- Feeling Like Food Does Not Move Through My Body
- Hungry All the Time
- Food Never Tastes Good But I Eat Anyway
- Tired All the Time
- Body Feels Limp
- Body Feels Flabby
- No Sensation in My Chest
- No Sensation Besides Bloating in Abdomen
- Sexual Pleasure Diminished

Nutritional:
- Candy
- Salty Snacks
- Sandwiches

Emotional:
- Waves of Depression Whenever I am Not Working
- Sad Unless I'm Too Busy to Feel
- Don't Feel Good About How I Look or Act
- Lack of Meaning In or Connection With World
- See Too Much Evil
- Feel Like a Robot

Energetic:
- Long Term Tightness in Face and Forehead
- Permanent Frown
- Never Full Breathing
- Bloated Abdomen
- Nausea
- Feeling Like Energy Does Not Move Through My Body

Interpersonal:
- Spouse Neglected
- Lover's Anger

Figure 15.3

Simplified Web of Life of
Individual Suffering from
Depression, Chronic Fatigue and Overweight

HOW TO DIE AND SURVIVE

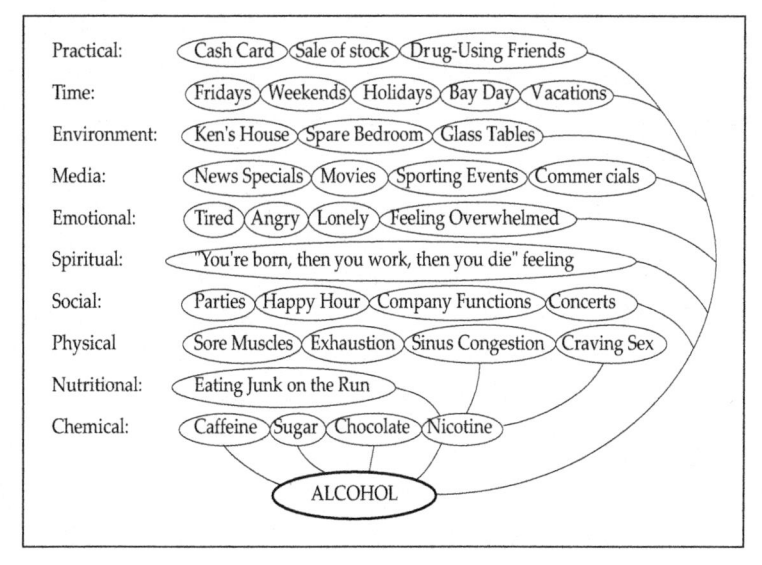

Practical:	Cash Card, Sale of stock, Drug-Using Friends
Time:	Fridays, Weekends, Holidays, Pay Day, Vacations
Environment:	Ken's House, Spare Bedroom, Glass Tables
Media:	News Specials, Movies, Sporting Events, Commercials
Emotional:	Tired, Angry, Lonely, Feeling Overwhelmed
Spiritual:	"You're born, then you work, then you die" feeling
Social:	Parties, Happy Hour, Company Functions, Concerts
Physical:	Sore Muscles, Exhaustion, Sinus Congestion, Craving Sex
Nutritional:	Eating Junk on the Run
Chemical:	Caffeine, Sugar, Chocolate, Nicotine
	ALCOHOL

Figure 15.4

Habit Pattern of Man Addicted to Alcohol

HOW TO DIE AND SURVIVE

places:	times:	feelings:	drugs:	people:
Bathrooms	Birthdays	Depression	Sugar	John
Car	Weekends	Boredom	Caffeine	Cathy
Parties	Having to do things I don't want to do	Need for excitement	Nicotine	My Kids
Motels	After work	Sexual desires	Alcohol	Anne
BARS	Before work	MAD	Marijuana	Mark
Doctor's Office	Before sex	HAPPY	Valium & Pain Pills	Dad

identified problem:

TOO MUCH ALCOHOL AND TOO MANY PILLS

and then worse feelings:

Extremely Depressed · Guilty · Nervous

Scared · Paranoid

SUICIDAL FEELING

Figure 15.5

Partial Attachment Chart of Suicidal Woman
(Woman claims each item is attached to every other item.)

249

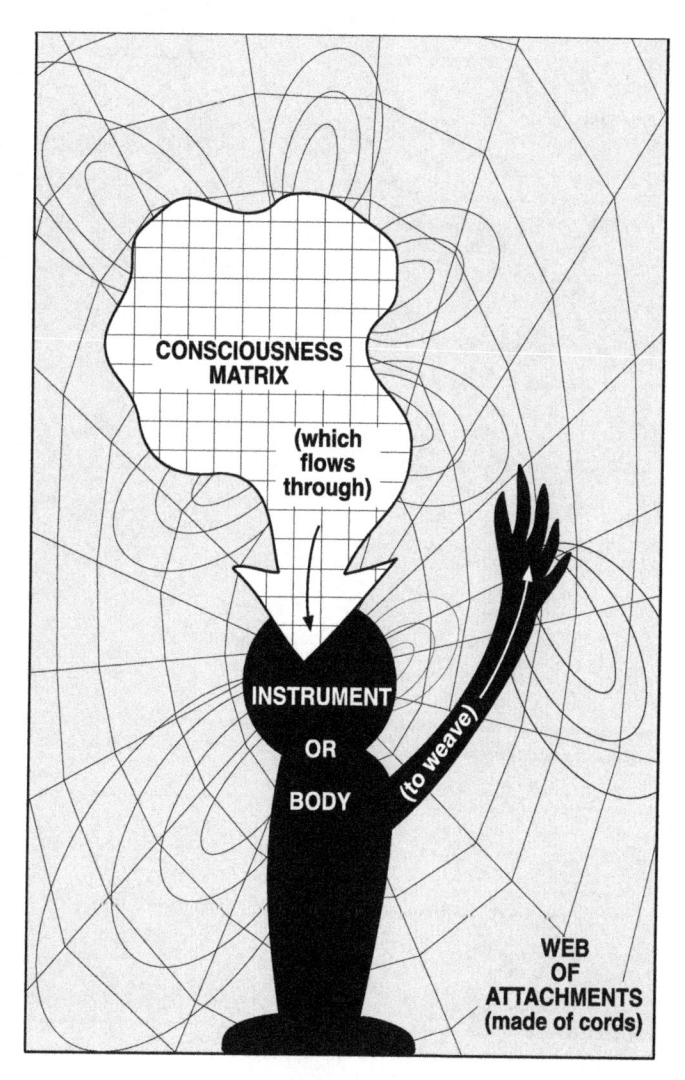

Figure 15.6

Depiction of the Web of Attachment
Woven Out of Cords

16
Releasing Attachments

> So before we die we should try to
> Free ourselves of attachment to all
> Our possessions, friends, and loved ones.
>
> Sogyal Rinpoche
> *The Tibetan Book of Living and Dying*

In-life as well as seeming end-of-life transitions involve amending and at times leaving attachment cordings. Attachments can be so complicated, yet so much part of life. We cannot escape the reality of attachment networks everywhere within us and around us.

Many people living in the material plane report that some of their attachments to—their connections to, ties to, desires for, urges or cravings for—the feelings and objects to which, and persons to whom, relationships to which, they are attached, corded, are overwhelming.

Sometimes people even become so very addicted to their attachment realities that they cling to them, even if these realities are sinking like drowning ships.

SEEING, SENSING, WHAT IS TAKING PLACE

If you are overwhelmingly attached, if you are finding it very difficult or painful to change or even to leave a troubled object or emotion or situation, it is most likely that you are strongly, maybe even intensely, perhaps even addictively, corded, attached.

Of course, most of your attachments can be positive, even necessary, parts of your life, while some can be problematic, some perhaps even dangerous. Some attachments can be both positive and problematic at the same time.

Note that there are times when *other people's* attachment *networks* and energy arrangements invite you, lure you, pull on you, entangle you, tie you in, perhaps even threaten mild or severe consequences should you try to break free even just a little.

Yet, many shared or intertwined or entangled attachment networks, where your own and others' cordings mix, are not always negative. Most shared attachments are positive and at times even necessary parts of one's life. (For example, think of the mother and baby as a shared attachment.)

Still, sometimes some shared or overlapping attachment networks can be quite problematic, some perhaps even dangerous. Some shared attachments can be both positive and problematic. Be aware when you feel pulled into another person's attachment network. How does this affect you? Can you sense what is taking place? *Are you free to engage and disengage at levels that are healthy for you?* Can you pull back somewhat or detach further without harming others in the process? If you pull back for your own well being, are you being told you are harming others as a way for those others to hold you in the attachment network you have been finding problematic? Can you find a right path for yourself as you NAVIGATE THE ATTACHMENT NETWORKS YOU LIVE WITH AND WITHIN?

ADDICTING ATTACHMENTS, AND ADDICTION TO ATTACHMENTS

Many attachments, while not exactly having minds of their own, do work to sustain themselves, even to strengthen themselves. Attachments' addicting of us to themselves, to our attachments, can be subtle, hidden, out of our awareness while taking place. We often fall prey to, or get tied up in, attachments and attachment networks without realizing what is taking place. Our brain's own system may at times be caught in, perhaps even be programmed to be driven by, powerful and frequently subconscious patterns of *attachment addiction*, and *addiction to attachment patterns*.

You may have sensed the pull of attachment patterns, the addiction these patterns develop in order to tie themselves to us and us to them, to tie us in. Much of the time we do not fully see this happening. If you sense something is taking place in your attachment network but just cannot see it, this is not unusual. You are not alone. We are all subject to attachment addiction. And we are much of the time responding to unseen pulls and tugs on us that hold us in the attachment addiction pattern.[60]

---

[60] See discussion of this author's addiction patterning theories in her books such as *Seeing The Hidden Face Of Addiction*.

Most individuals experience such attachment pattern addictions. In fact, all beings living in the physical world experience some degree of addiction to their material plane realities, as suggested in Figures 3.1 and 15.6.[61]

KNOWING WHEN AND HOW MUCH TO DETACH CAN BE A CHALLENGE

Many individuals feel that they lose control of their personal Will, their own Force of Will, during their cravings for the objects of their attachments. They find that their addictions to their attachments actually commandeer their *will power*.

The ability to know when to detach, and to know how to detach, is essential. To master detachment, and to detach from an attachment (from a pattern, from a cord, from an attachment network) when you need to, you must learn that it *is possible to live through your longings and cravings without responding to them addictively*. But in order to learn how to do this, you must learn to face your emotional and physical cravings head on.

Sometimes fear of the power of a longing, or of any sort of desire, urge, or craving, leads people to try to avoid constructive concentration on that longing, desire, urge, or craving. This is an error. Only a clear look at your intense

---

[61] Again note: Other books by this author have quite thoroughly discussed her pattern addiction theories, such as in the book titled, *Seeing The Hidden Face Of Addiction*. Refer to that volume for an explanation of the mechanisms of pattern addiction.

attachments can enable you to see them and then if needed to change and or even to leave them, to partially or entirely leave them. Only a clear look at your attachments to your reality can enable you to, if need be, release these attachments—to change your reality, to transition, even to shift or die out of your reality with the awareness, grace, and power of your own Free Will.

Consider the experience that a drug- or alcohol-addicted individual undergoes when craving drugs. The tendency is to avoid looking the craving in the face. For the drug- or alcohol-addicted person to bring this craving—this intense biochemical and emotional attachment—into focus, he or she must learn to ask him or herself: What of me is craving the drug or alcohol? How do I register this craving? What part of me, or parts of me, are experiencing this craving? What part of my body is feeling this craving? Exactly where is this part of my body? Can I give it a feeling to make myself more aware of it? What is the shape of this feeling? Its size? Its temperature? Can a color be attributed to this area?

By assigning characteristics to the intense attachment, this attachment becomes more visible to you, to your mind's eye. You do begin to see it with your inner eye. Your higher vision is further refined.

Whatever attachment you are examining, whether it be one of drug addiction, one of a strong relationship, or one of some other type of attachment, you can benefit by giving this attachment flags or characteristics.

Note: Many attachments are positive, even healthy. These can also be examined as described above. There is no judgement per se on an attachment. However, what is being called here, **attachment awareness***, is valuable in recognizing the energy arrangement, the attachment network, that each person develops.*

Keep in mind that many messages from your body and mind, even the details of attachments themselves, can go largely unnoticed by you while nevertheless sensing a great deal of the influence of these attachments.

Learning to answer the above questions about the characteristics of any of your attachments, and attachment networks or systems, can teach you to focus on – to pay attention to, to further sensitize to – what is taking place within you and around you, and on what you are actually sensing, feeling. Seeking the answers, even if in the form of imaginary labels, to such questions as the imaginary or actual location, size, shape, temperature, and color of your attachments generates in you an increased sensitization and awareness. Your concentration focuses more and more precisely when you try to be aware of, sense or see, or imagine, these characteristics. You visualize, you know, you recognize, these places where your cords attaching you to your inner and outer worlds are attached.

EXERCISE #16.1
SEEING POINTS OF ATTACHMENT

Think of an object or a person to which you feel connected in any way. This can be a comfortable or an uncomfortable connection or both. Concentrate on that object or person for a few minutes.

HOW TO DIE AND SURVIVE

As you concentrate, concentrate on any physical or emotional or other sensations you may be experiencing. Is there a particular part of your body that you are somewhat more aware of while you concentrate on the object or person you have selected?

Identify this part of your body, no matter how large or small. Make this part of your body the center of your focus no matter how sure or unsure you are that it is this particular part of your body that is actually responding to your concentration on the object or person you have selected.

Describe this part of your body to yourself. Notice how you choose to describe it. Push your mind to come up with a very detailed description of the part of your body you have identified with your connection with the object or person you have chosen. Invent details if you need to stimulate your detailing.

Feel that this part of your body is one of the places where a cord between you and that to which you are connected is attached. Create an image of this cord attaching to the part of the body you are detailing. Attach the other end of the cord to the object or person to which you are connected. Study this cord. Study the points of attachment. Are they, do they seem to be, soft touches, strong anchors, deep roots, or piercing hooks, or something else?

LEARN TO VISUALIZE

Practice visualizing your cord network. The use of imagination invited in this book offers a most useful *imagery technique*. The imagery techniques described in the exercises in this book are ***tools of focus***.[62]

Visual imagery can involve using the mind, the imagination for example, to further sense what is going on inside your body and in the space around your body. Individuals who practice visualization can learn to direct increasing levels of concentration to special locations or conditions in their brains, in their bodies, and in the space around their bodies. By visualizing what is going on inside your body, your psyche reaches into your soma—your mind reaches into your body— consciously and with a purpose. When you practice visual imagery you can achieve a greater degree of conscious engagement with your own personal energy and attachment network. This can allow you to be in ever more contact with your own mental and physical health. This can also allow you increasingly ***conscious navigation*** during your transition processes.

In the treatment of a particular health problem, whether that problem is biological or behavioral (the two are often related), imagery techniques can be tailored to the specific problem being addressed. Visual imagery is a process that can sensitize us to more about how the body and mind are relating to each other.

VISUALIZING FURTHER SENSITIZES US

---

[62] Refer to *Volume 3* in this *Keys To Consciousness And Survival Series*, titled *Unveiling The Hidden Instinct*. See also the *Navigating Life's Stuff* books in this series.

However each of us views the healing process, having awareness of attachments can be valuable. Sensing, even if simply visualizing, the various energy arrangements and attachment networks one is both generating and surrounded by, sometimes even immersed in, can be powerful in understanding and navigating conditions and problems.

Useful in addressing emotional and even physical conditions can be the sensing, seeing, of energy arrangements and attachment networks—imagining or visualizing going inside the mind and body and taking a look at what is going on. Some of this may be vague or at least not readily described in words, as it is related to energy streams, networks, and cords of attachment.

Of course, modern medicine has made ever more technically possible seeing some of what is physically (biologically) going on inside physical (biological) bodies.

With the help of medical technology, we have access to images we can work with to "see inside," to visualize cellular and other biological activity.

Visualizing is not always this straightforward. It is one thing to form a rather accurate image in the mind after looking at x-rays and scans, it is another to "see" or sense the subtle energy patterns that may be related to conditions.

CHANGE OR ELIMINATE CORDS

Individuals experiencing attachments experience their attachment cordings in myriad ways, some obvious and others hidden, some unconsciously and some consciously.

Some attachment cordings can generate physical indications of their presence, sensations such as pain or pleasure or tightness or warmth. Other attachment cordings have vague, almost unnoticeable hints of these cordings.

It is useful to pay close attention to even the most minor sensations in order to be aware of the presence and degree of attachment cordings. With practice, you will "see" more and more of the cords with which you weave your web. With practice, you will notice the network of cords forming between you and others you know, even perhaps between you and someone you have just met. You will begin to see everywhere the webs you and others weave.

Once the attachment cord or attachment cord network is even vaguely sensed, perhaps through the mind-brain's visualization function, the **image** of the cord or cord network can be worked with— perhaps even reduced, rearranged, manipulated, destroyed, or replaced with a more desirable picture. This is done by first visualizing a particular cord or set of cords, and then by creating a tool with which to re-sculpt, to do what here we can call *energetic surgery*, on this imagery of attachment.

Among the tools that are applicable to this *energetic surgery technique* are visualizations of: beams of Light resembling lasers; balls of Light that work like explosive bombs; absorbent sponges of Light; chains or ropes of Light; knives or saws of Light; paint brushes or crayons of Light; hands of Light which reach into the attachment picture and operate on the cords. Washing away the cords with luminous soap suds that give off beautiful Light can be an uplifting process. You can also see each cord as an energy string to be amended or unraveled.

With practice, this front-line—highly literal although seemingly imaginary—confrontation with your attachment cords and their cord networks can be achieved each time you experience a concerning situation or problem of attachment, and of attachment affecting transition. Cords can be clearly pictured and then operated on by *the imagination, the mind's eye, the inner surgeon*. In so doing, you can gain some control over your relationship to even the most powerful attachments, and navigate transition through attachment networks affecting transition.

This does not mean you should get rid of all attachments while you live in your physical biological body. This does mean you can learn to be ever more aware of these and of how to mentally work with these to allow these to feel healthier for you.

This sort of visual imagery focuses your concentration on the experience of attachment in a way that allows you to be in more command of your attachment behavior, rather than being subservient to it. Sometimes, when your attachment is described in words, any problem associated with it seems intractable. Freedom from the confines of verbal thought brings power over attachment.

The multitude of attachments, and the knotty web of their cords, may at times overwhelm some people. We can learn to visualize attachments, to grow more aware of the energetic complications of attachment cord networks. We can generate our own understanding of, our own metaphor for, attachment cord networks. We can develop an overall picture of such networks we are immersed in, a picture free of words, names, or labels.

Imagery reduces complicated words to simple, powerful pictures. Imagery empowers the mind's eye, sharpens the focus.

EXERCISE #16.2
OPERATING ON YOUR ATTACHMENT CORDS

In order to do this exercise, you will need a peaceful, quiet place where you will be comfortable and will not be disturbed. You may want paper and a set of colored markers.

You may want to have yourself or a friend record, in his or her voice, this exercise for you. Or you may just want to have someone read this exercise aloud to you. Either way, this exercise should be read very slowly, in a very steady, calm voice.

Once you have decided how to hear this exercise, RELAX, LISTEN, and CONCENTRATE ON THESE WORDS.

Make yourself comfortable. Sit or lie in a comfortable position. If your legs are crossed or bent, and if you think that you will begin to get cramps in your legs, stretch them out now. Find a position that you can be relaxed in for a period of time.

Close your eyes. Breathe slowly. Try to stay awake during this exercise, but do not be concerned about dozing off or tuning out. If you do doze off, pay attention to where you start drifting. It is helpful to see where in this exercise you might tune out, if you do. Repeat the exercise if you do doze off . . . .

Now think of what may be a more complex, perhaps more complicated or even problematic, perhaps quite difficult or challenging, attachment you may have experienced or may be presently experiencing. This can be a connection to an object, or to a person, an event, a place, or some other object of attachment. Imagine that this attachment you have had, or still have, is either wonderful or neutral or not so wonderful, or quite problematic, but is nevertheless hard to let change, or hard to leave for some reason.

Stay with your thought of this attachment, this object. For the purposes of this exercise, all attachment objects will be simply described as objects (objects of attachment).

Do not answer out loud the questions asked of you in this exercise. Try to think without words. Try to think in pictures in your mind. Try to see the answer. Where you cannot see it, hear or taste or smell or feel the answer. When you have no answer, remember to imagine—just make up an answer. Imagining and imaging are very similar exploratory processes and each can supplement the other.

Continue with closed eyes.

Again, think of this complicated and or problematic attachment. Think of one of the last times you felt this attachment. Make this last time the present even if it is in the past. Where are you, what is your geographical and physical location, as you feel this attachment? See yourself there.

Imagine that you are a film maker. Take an invisible movie camera into your hands. You are making a film about this attachment of yours. It will be a slow motion movie. First you are setting the stage. ....

See the place where you last felt this attachment. Move the camera slowly around the room or the car or the building or the beach or wherever your place is. Remember to do this with your eyes closed, because you are looking at a place that is in your memory or imagination. Try to see through the camera lens—see the details: the colors of the walls, if there are walls; the colors that you would see around you; whether the place is messy or neat, orderly or chaotic. If you are indoors, what is hanging on the walls? What furniture is there? Try to feel and see in detail what the place is like.

Sometimes your mind remembers details that do not easily come back to you when you consciously try to remember. There might be cracks in the wall, or ants in the corner, or spilled garbage somewhere. These will appear in your movie.

These things are there in your memory bank (or in your imagination bank, or in your imagery bank, or in some combination of these). The more relaxed you are, the more of these little pieces of the whole picture, the more bits of information about your attachment network, you will see. There are no people on your stage yet. And, remember, everything is in slow motion.

Now, the next assignment for you, the film-maker, is to set the time of day for this particular memory of this particular attachment. Look through the camera lens at the sky to see the time of day, or through the window, or at the clock on the wall. Show yourself what time of day it is. If you cannot remember, just pick a time.

So now you know the time of day. What is the air temperature? Are you warm or cold or neutral? If you are outside, do you know what the weather is like? If you are inside, what weather do you see through the window?

Now you start adding people to this scene, if there are people involved in this attachment network. See these people arrive at this place. If there are no people involved in this attachment, you will not add people to this scene. Do not add yourself yet.

Now, if there are people in this place, turn your movie camera on each of these people and get some close up looks at their faces. Note your feelings as you see them through the camera lens. This may be the first time you have ever really looked at some of them. Try to see what these people look like. Make up details if you cannot remember any. If there is just one person, get a close look at that one person's face. Look closely at the people. See what they are wearing, how they walk, how they sit, how their faces look.

Now it is time to look at yourself. Look at yourself more closely than you have ever looked before. You may have to pull the camera up to a corner of the ceiling and look down on yourself to see how you looked during this particular experience of your attachment. What state or states of mind, feelings, emotions, do you associate with this attachment? Maybe you are happy or celebrating.

Maybe you are bored. Maybe you are hurt. Maybe you are having other feelings. It is difficult to film states of mind. But use your movie camera, your inner eye. You are the star of your movie. See your face revealing your state or states of mind. Remember, there are all kinds of possible states of mind, and many of these can be felt at the same time. Let yourself look through your camera lens at those states of mind that you are experiencing.

If you cannot remember your states of mind with regard to this attachment of yours, just make up states of mind. If you like, try some states of mind on for size, just to see how they feel: While your eyes are closed, make faces showing different states of mind —a happy face, a hurt face, an irritated face, a sad face, a bored face, a tired face. Whatever expression best reminds you of the state of mind you connect with this attachment, settle into that facial expression.

Now, in your slow-motion movie, step back and look around the room. The people, if any, are there. You are there. You know what kind of day it is. You know what the place looks like. You know how you look.

Now identify a particular object (or activity or person) you are attached to. Swing the camera around so that you focus in on this object of your attachment.

Take your camera for some close up shots of what it is you are attached to. You have a very unusual camera. As you take these close up shots, the camera reveals what is usually invisible to you: The camera reveals strings or cords made of something like light running between you and the object of your attachment.

You are seeing many cords between you and the object of your attachment now. You are looking very closely at these fascinating cords. As you look closely, you, the film-maker, begin to realize that you, yes you, are deeply connected to the object by these cords.

You are more than connected. You are tangled up. You feel very tied, very entangled in a web of cords. You see this web.

And somehow now, the camera falls or dissolves out of your hands. You stretch your fingers out and run your fingertips along these cords, as if you were playing a harp.

Keep touching these cords. Let your hands become increasingly stiff while you do this, so that you are putting some stress into your efforts. Your hands are feeling the intensity of your relationship to the objects of your attachment.

Remember to keep your eyes closed while you do this exercise. Now, imagine or actually stand up and move into this web of cords. Get further tangled in this web. Try to get out by squirming and struggling. See how this seems to make you more entangled.

Feel for a moment an increasing degree of tension, as you feel more and more trapped. Feel tense, because this is an intense experience. Let your hands and your arms and your shoulders momentarily become very tight. Let your trapped body become very tight. Feel more of this tension for a moment. Still struggle to get out of the web, and still become ever more entangled. Become tense all over.

Finally you are so entangled that you cannot move. Know you want out. Be extremely tight and tense. Stop, freeze.

Stay frozen a while, with your eyes still closed. Note what you are feeling most in your body right now. You may feel something, or you may not consciously feel anything. You may be feeling good and that is fine, so make note of this and of how you know this.

Some others of you may be feeling other things such as excess salivation – a watery mouth, a tight jaw, pain, or sensation in the sinuses or neck or lower back, a throbbing headache, cold or hot rushes, cold or hot patches, numb patches around the body, a feeling of sea sickness or excitement, a knot in your stomach, a tightness in your legs, lead in your feet . . . Or vague pleasure . . . Or hints of release or relief.

You may be feeling pain or tightness in the heart area. You may find it difficult to breathe. You may want to cry or laugh hysterically. There are so many things you may be feeling: slight prickly sensations at a few points in your body, a tiny itch, a small area of pressure. Be alert. Look closely, deep inside.

Most of the time, we miss feelings of attachment because we are so hooked into our attachments that we run on automatic. *We are not in touch with what we are feeling, with where these attachments connect, with the tugs and effects of such connections. This time, concentrate on what you are feeling. Pick one or two of your most present feelings and let yourself feel these.*

Now, pretend that one of your fingers is a colored felt pen. Pick a color, and outline the area of your body that you are most aware of. Outline that part. If the area is hot, use a hot color. If it is cold, use a cool color. Now pretend to color this area in; you may want to use some other colors. If you have a knot in your stomach, draw the knot. If your heart is beating quickly, you may want to use some color that reminds you of a fast pulse, high blood pressure, and maybe tension. Everybody sees her or his own colors.

You may be feeling other things in this part or some other part of your body. You may be having feelings without knowing which part of the body those feelings are coming from. Try to give those feelings a place in your body.

Draw, with your finger, one or more cords coming out of this place in your body. ... See the cord or cords reaching into the air—see the cord or cords go from this place in your body you have identified to the object of your attachment. See several tangled cords running between you and the object of your attachment. See yourself tangled in these cords.

Now you will change this circumstance.

Light these cords up, as if they were overheated electric wires. Light these cords up to the brightest, purest, clearest, most intense Light possible. Light them up so much that they smoke. Keep heating these cords with Light. Hold. Hold this Light now. Hold until, suddenly: the cords evaporate, leaving behind only a bit of white smoke. . . .

Realize that you are now free of the entanglement and release your tense body: Breathe in, and then, aloud, release a big sigh of relief. Say "aaahhh" aloud if you wish.

Very good. You did a great job! Now with your eyes still closed, see yourself as somewhat more free of problem attachments and cordings. And remember, after these exercises, you can return to what you were feeling before these exercises, you can even re-attach if you like.

(Pause.)

Open your eyes. Draw a picture (on paper or in your mind) of yourself at your most entangled point during this exercise. Label this picture "Before." Draw, see, yourself after the release. Label this picture "After."

Of course, this process will be best done several times, as release and rearrangement of one's energy networks is a process, not a one time event.

RECOGNIZE

Learn to recognize the release of an attachment. Absorb the sensation of attachment release. Store this sensation in your memory to use in all your changes, transitions, in-life and seeming end-of-life dyings.

You will want to recall this sensation time and again. You will want to invoke this sensation in order to bring on the small and large releases you will want to experience in order to move on. The highest release consists of a few simple steps:

- Light the cord or cords up like overheated electrical wires.
- Say "Deconstruct." See these cords vaporize or dissolve.
- Say "And transmute to the highest Light."
  See the debris—what remains—turned to a sense of the highest, clearest, purest Light.

EXERCISE #16.3
DECONSTRUCTING AND TRANSMUTING CORDS

Close your eyes. Open your mind's eye: say aloud, "I call upon my inner vision." Now, see several cords forming between you and someone or something else—from some points in or on your body to some points in or on an object or person. See the strands of these cords materializing.

When the cords are in place, visualize yourself transforming, or for now deconstructing, these one by one, saying aloud each time:

- *Light up.*
  (Light the cord up.)
- *Deconstruct.*
  (Dissolve the cord.)
- *Transmute to the highest Light.*
  (Turn what remains to a pure white Light.)

Do this again and again for each cord, and then continue chanting for several minutes:

Light up. Deconstruct. Transmute to the highest Light. . . . Light up. Deconstruct. Transmute to the highest Light. . . . Light up. Deconstruct. Transmute to the highest Light. . . .

ENVISION, VISUALIZE:

**LIGHT UP
DECONSTRUCT
TRANSMUTE TO THE HIGHEST
VISION OF LIGHT**

**LIGHT UP
DECONSTRUCT
TRANSMUTE TO THE HIGHEST
VISION OF LIGHT**

**LIGHT UP
DECONSTRUCT
TRANSMUTE TO THE HIGHEST
VISION OF LIGHT**

**LIGHT UP
DECONSTRUCT
TRANSMUTE TO THE HIGHEST
VISION OF LIGHT**

**LIGHT UP
DECONSTRUCT
TRANSMUTE TO THE HIGHEST
VISION OF LIGHT**

**LIGHT UP
DECONSTRUCT
TRANSMUTE TO THE HIGHEST
VISION OF LIGHT**

**LIGHT UP
DECONSTRUCT
TRANSMUTE TO THE HIGHEST
VISION OF LIGHT**

**LIGHT UP
DECONSTRUCT
TRANSMUTE TO THE HIGHEST
VISION OF LIGHT**

17
Clearing Subtle Energy Webs

> If one does not
> understand how the body
> that he wears came to be,
> he will perish with it . . .
>
> *Dialogue of the Savior*
> *134.1-22*
> *Nag Hammadi Library*

With a refocusing of the inner eye, you sensitize to, see with your inner eye, the attachment cord network, web, you and others may have woven around you and themselves.

This attachment network is somewhat like a very complex set of wirings, for some maybe appearing as a tangled ball of yarn or maybe a spider web. These strings or strands or cords may appear to be stringing outward from you in all directions, and others stringing toward you from outside of you.

As you become increasingly aware of your own attachment network or web and the webs around you, you will find yourself continuously relying upon this knowledge. You can form useful or energetically balanced networks, webs, if you can see these in the making and then even influence their construction. And, you can amend your relationship to problematic and or detrimental attachment networks, webs, if you can sense, detect, these.

USE INTUITION
TO FIND AND CLEAR SUBTLE ENERGY CORDS

Everyone uses intuition. Not everyone uses intuition as consciously as possible. Why would we use intuition with purpose when we are not entirely certain when to trust it? This is wise, as intuition is generally sensing subtle trends and energies and does not always accurately label according to known, explicit, physical world objects, persons, events, dates, and times. Much of what comes in via intuition is being distorted or blocked by various forces and factors.

Using intuition can be like listening to very faint, very distant music—tuning in to hear it. Your intuition is always at work, although it is frequently clouded by biased impressions and blinded by distractions.

You can use your intuition to help you sense the attachment network of cords, the most obvious also even the most subtle energy webs. You are most intuitively aware of the people you know best. Consider the relationship you may have to a strong mother figure, perhaps your own mother. You have a feel for that person. The music of that person has become a familiar song. Maybe one day, suddenly, you feel a few notes in that familiar song change. Perhaps you then say, "I've been thinking about Mother. I'd better call her." You are not necessarily sure why you want to call, you just sense that suddenly her program feels different.

Become ever more aware of how your intuition works.

If someone plays you the same song 100 times and then plays it one more time with only one note changed, you may not notice the difference but you will sense it. If you have walked into a room daily for ten years, and that room has never been rearranged until today, and now one pillow has been moved, you may not notice the change but will sense it. Your relationships to subtle energy cords are similar. Sometimes you do not see (in material reality) a shift or change in energy, yet you sense it. Indeed, we may even be responding to intuitive sensations we are receiving, without realizing we are doing this.

Notice this sort of subtle sense or sensation. Perhaps a cord is being tugged. Ask yourself what this feeling could relate to. Is this a big or a small matter? Is this your own sense of being tugged at—or are you doing the tugging? Or both? Give the sensation a label to make it more clear to you, or to at least start to investigate.

Do not let yourself be persuaded by emotions as you learn to more finely tune your intuition. Intuition is most aware when it is not mixed with emotion.

Allow yourself to not know what all it is that you are sensing. Give yourself a particular description of what you sense, even if this may not be quite right or complete. Wait. Adjust the description as you fine tune your intuition.

DETECT SUBTLE INFORMATION

Become aware of the subtle changes in your own and others' energy fields. Hear how the music shifts. This takes relaxed and focused concentration so you can know who you and others are in the subtle energy communication. Are you the one playing the music, did you just change a note in the song—or did someone else? Or did both of you or something outside both of you make this change? If you do not know, just be with the sensation without forcing a definition on it.

This *intuitive sensing process* involves patience, awareness that some things are not yet clear or ever clear. Your intuition involves your consciousness. Your intuition also involves your ever increasing awareness of your relationship to your and others' attachment cord networks.

Heighten your awareness by paying close attention to detail. Do not block out detail that does not fit what you believe. Try to stay aware of as much as you can.

Say you notice a slight shift in the taste in your mouth. Ask yourself, "What about this new taste in my mouth? Do I notice this often or only when I am not feeling well? Do I notice this right before I get sick to my stomach? Or right before something else happens? Do I know? It is alright if I do not know. I can still be aware of sensations and awareness-es without making these mean a specific thing."

There are always subtle shifts occurring in your outer and inner environments, even in your body chemistry, at all times. Pay attention to these. Do not force meaning on these. Just start noticing, sensing, them. Become ever more sensitized to varying tastes, smells, sounds, energies, glimpses of things.

For example, you can notice faint sounds and their fluctuations, appearances, and disappearances. Notice shifts in what you hear as being seeming background noise. Are there any overtones, any high sounds you can barely hear at all and rarely pay attention to? Are these sounds or other energies?

EXERCISE #17.1
HIGHER HEARING

Close your eyes. Listen for sounds that you cannot hear with your ears. Cover your ears. Now listen. What do you hear? Imagine that you hear more than you do. Work on this for a while. This form of hearing slips in slowly and becomes sharper with practice. Your inner ear is hearing.

EXAMINE THE SUBTLE NETWORK

It is easy to pick up some other individual's feelings and mistake them for your own, and then react as if these were your feelings. Sometimes someone surprises you with anger and, although you are not angry, you get mad right back.

That person throws a ball of anger at you and you pick it up and throw it back. Had you just let the ball of anger lie there, there perhaps would be no ball game. The ball game is further weaving the web, further fortifying the cords.

After some repeated travel along its cords, the network of cords becomes a powerful pattern. It becomes harder and harder to break out of the loops of networked cords. Physical death offers the most certain erasure of any such strong physical plane based patterning. However, there are other options. Deeply buried patterns can be recognized and manipulated. Lifestyles can be altered in a pragmatic, multi-level way.

These options fall into the realm of what we can call *energy work*. You can learn to work, or at least to think or visualize, on the energetic level. This is important work, as you can do this regardless of your physical condition or health, and you can do this while living in the material plane in a physical body, and perhaps later in other forms and dimensions as well.

Think of it this way: You can imagine or visualize you can do energy surgery on yourself and your energy network whether or not you have a physical body. If your physicality has developed a problematic pattern of information flow, a troubled energy arrangement network, you can visualize sensing and then amending your awareness of this network, and thus of what can be imagined or visualized of this network itself.[63]

INSIGHT

Here the use of what this book defines as *insight imagery* is valuable. Images of networks, webs, cords, patterns of cords, whether entirely imagined, generally intuited, or based on experiential information, can be built in the mind's eye. These images (based upon the agreement to imagine, visualize, sense, energy flows that one can estimate or form with one's mind) can represent otherwise invisible and somewhat inconceivable energetic patterns and arrangements, the

---

[63] See other books in this series for more on this matter, such as *Seeing Beyond Our Line Of Sight*, and also *Unveiling The Hidden Instinct*.

attachment network for example. Once visualized, these patterns can be worked with by the mind's eye.

EXERCISE #17.2
CLEARING SUBTLE WEBS

Visualize yourself sitting across from someone you do not know, as for this exercise you are imaging a person, not working with someone you know. Imagine that, for this exercise only and not necessarily in "real" life, you want to disconnect, detach from this person.

Imagine for just a moment a network of cords connecting you, from various points on your body, to this person, at various points on this person's body. Close your eyes and take some time to see how very intricate this network is. See that the network is far more intricate than you expected.

Now Light up each and every strand of this network. Hold this image a moment. When you hear the words, "begin to deconstruct," dissolve some of this network:

BEGIN TO DECONSTRUCT.

Your have cleared parts of this subtle energy web.

If you wish to reinstate what you have cleared or deconstructed, do so before you open your eyes, by visualizing this happening and saying:

RECONSTRUCT.

Of course, this was an imaginary person and an imaginary web or cord network. So, you do not need to reconstruct what was actually not there in the first place. You can, however, visualize doing this if you like. Remember, this was simply an exercise.

18
Clearing Social Energy Webs

> Here is where love
> burns with an
> innocent flame: the
> clean desire for
> death.
>
> Thomas Merton
> *Entering the Silence*

Now that we have considered the subtle network of attachments, of cords, the subtle energy web, let's step back and see what is, by comparison, believed to be the more tangible social or interpersonal energy web. Social energy webs are woven out of behaviors and feelings. Some of these appear quite obvious to us. Many levels of these remain quite subtle, even hidden from us.

While these networks and the specific cords within them may not all be readily spotted, they are more easily recognized after examining or at least visualizing what may be the subtle energy level. This examination is important in order to consider how living persons may cord and may even attempt to disallow the de-cording process of themselves and others who are changing, transitioning, even perhaps dying physical deaths.

Of course, we rarely hear anyone actually claiming to cord. Instead, much of what we hear is expressed in other words, or even denied. In a sense, much of what is being said or not said about attachment cordings is not accurate, not quite true.

MUCH OF WHAT IS SAID ABOUT OUR AND OTHERS' ATTACHMENTS IS NOT QUITE ACCURATE

While some will say that the denying or failing to see attachment cordings are denials and perhaps even lies, this may or may not be quite accurate. (For example, we frequently hear persons experiencing addiction to drugs being told that if they do not see the details of their addiction behaviors they are in denial. This may or may not be what all is taking place.)

However we define the mind-brain not fully recognizing attachments and cordings, these denials and or lies (as these may be being described) are themselves also part of the attachment webs of those around the so called addict, of the world, so to speak. Also, many aspects of attachments and cordings can be difficult to detect, frequently nonverbal, hidden well behind the scenes.

EVEN LIES FORM CORDS

We have heard of the old adage about "the elephant in the room," something no one mentions yet everyone knows is there, right there in the room. The unseen and even the not seen fall away to reveal what is selected to be not seen, or overlooked, or ignored, or its presence lied about for various reasons.

Lying takes many forms, including forms rarely if ever acknowledged, as not acknowledging these forms of lying is part of lying. So much of what is not being said or seen is being somehow not said and not seen for some conscious or even sub- and or un-conscious reason. This not saying and not seeing is generally a vague form of lying, so vague that this is rarely seen as lying.

Much of this *not seeing* is a *biological not seeing*, as it is the result of our biochemical brain functions. (See other books in this series regarding how our brains and brain functions may distort our perceptions and memories of reality, and thus our reality. This *biochemical distortion* could also be a form of lying, one we are not consciously if at all choosing.)[64]

Lying, on all its levels, regardless of its source, takes on new importance here. Lies themselves can be part of attachment networks. Every single lie, whether conscious or not, affects the cord network, the web. Entire relationships, most relationships in fact, are built upon both the said and the unsaid, the seen and the unseen, givens and yes, even some distortions or lies, regarding the attachment network being formed by those in the relationship.

Entire energy patterns, cord networks, between people — friends, colleagues, coworkers, lovers, family members, neighbors — may be built with no discussion of them. Lack of direct communication about the cording being done has

---

[64] Refer to other books in this series, including *Overriding The Extinction Scenario, Parts One and Two (Volumes 5 and 6)* and also *Seeing Beyond Our Line Of Sight (Volume 10)*.

become so very common that most people have adjusted to this and no longer find this at all unusual.

Even when communication does occur, it can be inadequate. "I told you to be home by six, to get here on your own." "I didn't hear you." "That's your problem. No dinner for you now." "Who cares? I had two milkshakes while I waited for you to pick me up. You never came." "You didn't tell me you needed a ride." This kind of conversation is inadequate in that it does not express the fact that one person was wondering where the other person was and was concerned for her welfare, while that person was hurt that no one came to pick her up. Inadequate communication is taking place when feelings and facts are buried under accusations and counter-accusations. Each of these accusations and counter-accusations is part of a possibly difficult attachment cord.

CONFUSION FORMS CORDS

Reality is further distorted when communication becomes confused, which, when we take into account the continuous overlooking of cords, is most of the time. So much is not said. So much of what is said has no clear meaning. The scramble is ongoing. The scramble becomes the reality for many people. The scramble itself may become the glue that holds the attachment network together.

The only consistency in most communication, even in the attachment coding framing most communication, is consistent ambiguity. This can be frightening to those corded to each other as they cannot be trusted to be consistently clear. One minute one of them is loving and kind to the other. The next, he or she is threatening and cruel. And then the two people switch roles, tugging on each other's attachment cords.

Then the messages are not trustworthy, not clear. The confused communication of one person leads others to become confused communicators in order to cope, compete, survive, or just fit in. Confused communication can plant the seeds of deep emotional disturbance in children and adolescents—seeds that may emerge later in adult life as deep neuroses. We see the effects of, the tugs of the cords of, confused communication everywhere.

We even see the effects of our own attachment tangles and confusions, as these weigh us down as we live, as we find our way through our daily lives, through simple and complex in-life and seeming end-of-life transitions. Recognizing the effects of our entanglements while we live in physical bodies is helpful training for all transitions and LEAPS we may face.

PAIN FORMS CORDS

Lies and broken communication can even lead to unexpressed, partially expressed, or indirectly expressed, pain. When this pain is not fully expressed, the person who has been hurt, by him or herself or by others, is likely to develop a grudge. Pain and its grudges form powerful and long lasting cords.

Grudges can become part of the entanglement we can watch for. Many grudges remain unadmitted. Such a private grudge is a strange thing. It is a stuffed-away, unexpressed, emotion that is often unstuffing itself and breaking out in stiff, cold, or angry ways. This breaking out reveals, if we are looking, the cording involved. Sometimes pain is a way to see more regarding attachment cording at work.

Grudges may develop slowly, while communications may continue to fail and the lies, confusion, and pain compound. Many children grow up feeling that their siblings or their parents have grudges against them although "no one ever talked about it" and nothing was ever done that was hurtful enough to prove that a grudge actually existed.

Some grudges do become public. Sometimes grudges float to the surface and are revealed, made obvious. A least favored or always blamed member of the family may be the subject of a public family grudge. This person may develop private grudges in response.

Some hurt takes the tone of stronger grudge, or revenge. "You hurt me, I'll hurt you back." This is an eye or an eye, tit-for-tat, type of hurt. Revenge behavior can last for years, can cord people through time, and be extremely destructive.

But even more dangerous is hurt that has been buried. Many individuals go through half their lives before discovering and learning to express their buried hurt. Too often buried hurt is directed against oneself before it can be expressed in a healthy way. When this happens, an individual has become entangled in deeply attached cords of pain.

EVEN LOVE FORMS CORDS

We have looked briefly at lies, confusion, and pain in terms of cording. However, not all cording is attributable to negative or undesirable emotion. Friendship forms cords. Sexual pleasure forms cords. Interpersonal love forms cords, cords between people's emotional bodies and also between their physical bodies.

Being aware of positive feeling cordings is also important. We do best to understand the webs we weave as we live, the attachment networks we are living within. This awareness will help us in all our in-life as well as seeming end-of-life transitions.

EXERCISE #18.1
CLEARING A HEART CORD

Remember that this is only an exercise and you can decide not to take the results of this exercise back to what you call "real life."

Now, choose someone you love or have loved. Close your eyes. See this person in front of you, facing you. Visualize a cord or string running from that person's heart to your heart.

See how this cord attaches to each of your hearts as if it has roots like a tree, growing into these hearts. Feel the effects of this cord and its roots on your heart for a while.

Then, turn this cord, which is now of a cloudy Light, to a very bright white Light. See this cord vaporize. Say "Release me. I release you."

See yourself reform this cord to reinstate the balance you have established with this cord if this is a healthy balance.

EXERCISE #18.2
CLEARING A POINT CORD

Repeat the above exercise, this time shifting from the heart to other points in the two participating bodies such as the stomach or the genitals or the forehead.

EXERCISE #18.3
CLEARING THE SOCIAL ENERGY WEB

Now, repeat the above exercises, this time involving several persons in your life, and cords between several points on your body and theirs. Visualize, construct, an elaborate web. Feel the points where the cords attach and root. Now, for a moment, Light up all the cords you see and vaporize them. Light up. Deconstruct. Transmute to the highest Light.

Wait a few moments. Review or sense what you have just done. Then re-establish the cords or parts of cords you wish to preserve, if any. Watch yourself doing this or choosing not to do this, which ever is your path here. Make mental notes about what you observe.

****

Remember Light referred to in this book is not a value system or opinion. This Light is the idea or vision of a higher, clearer, cleaner, purer energy source.

19
Letting Go

> It is for the sake of the body that time and place and physical movement exist; for bodies could not be constructed if there were no place for them, and bodies could not change if there were not time and physical movement.
>
> Hermes to Ammon
> *Hermetica*

Just visualizing, sensing, webs and all of the cords with which they are woven is a great accomplishment. You can be certain that you will use this ability in all of your current and future travels and dimensions of consciousness. Death of all of, or even just part of, a pattern, of a web for example, can be a demanding task. This is true whether this seeming death is part of an in-life-transition, change, or challenge, or part of an actual physical death, or part of any other transition, perhaps even after leaving the physical body.

Once you have learned to sense, see, the cords which attach you to this world, you can see which ties to your reality you wish to preserve, or amend, or let go. Once you can sense, see, the cords that bind you, *you can learn to let them go — to let them go if and when you choose to let them go.*

Even when an individual believes she or he has released all attachment cords, the clearing of the cords is not necessarily entirely completed. Often times, the basic clearing does not complete – it resists a full letting go. Some degree of hanging on continues, usually sub- or un- consciously. Somehow the release DOES NOT ALLOW A FULL LETTING GO, even when one is desired.

Focusing attention and energy helps **the letting go**. Here the energy found in paradox can be managed to navigate partial or even full release. Recall Figure 6.2. See that paradox serves a purpose. Without the intensity of the tension, the feeling of being trapped in an energy binding situation, there may be insufficient or no energy, desire, or impetus for release, for moving on, for breaking free.

The energy build-up and tension found in paradoxes, when used well, can generate enough energy to break out of these paradoxes. *In this sense, the paradox always contains its own solution.* You will remember this when you need most to know it.

Without the painful tenseness of paradox, we cannot experience the release—the jump or shift in perception — the letting go—that can be generated by breaking out of the rigid web of the paradox, of the *paradoxical double bind*.

We must learn to spot paradoxes as opportunities, to see these before they stagnate in order to harvest the valuable energy present. There are at least three parts to this essential awareness:

- Detect the paradox.

- Feel the energy trapped within the paradox.
- Release yourself from the paradox at its peak to take the most energy away with you, to LEAP.

EXERCISE #19.1
USING PARADOX TO FUEL LETTING GO

Clear some space around you. Extend your arms outward, reaching horizontally away from your shoulders. Hold this position and close your eyes.

Imagine that there is a person on either side of you. Each of these persons is holding on to one of your hands and pulling on it, each in the direction reaching away from your body. Feel these people pulling on you harder and harder. Feel as if you are being pulled in half.

Feel as if you are trapped in this intense tugging that is pulling you in opposite directions. Trapped.

Begin to struggle fiercely for a release. Struggle with no success for a while. As you struggle, feel that your arms are being pulled even harder in opposite directions. Try not to be torn in half. Feel yourself: Struggle. Struggle. Struggle.

Suddenly, they let go. You are released.

USE THE ENERGY

Let go and you will be free. Refine your ability to harvest your energy from paradox. The release of this energy, of your energy, is a form of death. *This is a death release.* **This**

is not physical death per se, this is energy release. This can be part of so many in-life as well as end-of-life situations.

Use the energy you free up, the energy you release, to fully break the cords, the holds on you that have been obstructing the clean and healthy release from a situation.

FINE TUNE THE RELEASE

Understanding and applying the use of paradox in kicking off a full transition is important. Once you sensitize yourself to this process, you can fine tune the release you generate.

In other words, releasing energy to fuel a complete letting go is great. However, there is more to do. Direct this wonderfully released energy, fine tune this release.

EXERCISE #19.2
FOCUSING THE RELEASE

Imagine that you are a balloon about to burst. Some one or some thing is continuing to pump air into you. The pressure mounts. Take a deep breath; expand your lungs and abdomen. Open your eyeballs very wide. Fill your cheeks with more air than they seem to be able to hold.

Hold this expansion a moment. While you hold, imagine that when you let out all this air, you will release your essence with it.

Continue to hold this expansion—still hold your breath. Choose a place your essence will go; and, also choose a degree of Light that your essence will take on when you release it. When you release yourself, you will go to this place and become this Light. Hold. Prepare to burst.

Now burst, go there, and become Light.

Use your imagination or visualization to see yourself stay out there a while. Then slowly walk yourself back into your physical self.

20
Avoiding Primary Reconnection

> From here on go out and calculate that which the mouth cannot speak and the ear cannot hear.
>
> *Sefer Yetzirah, 4:16*

The ideas involved in the *personal transition processes and levels* discussed in this and the following How To Die And Survive books are designed to help build increasing personal say in one's in-life as well as end-of-life and possible life-after-life transition experiences. Basically, the more conscious we are, the more we can fine tune our awareness of our *selves*, of who and what we actually are, and the more say we can have in our transition experiences. It is my view that we can actually evolve ourselves to become increasingly powerful as personal consciousness-es, and that our survival options can be expanded upon as we do so.[65]

ATTACHMENT CORDINGS SEEK TO CONTINUE THEMSELVES

---

[65] I have explained this view in depth in the books in this *Keys To Consciousness And Survival Series* such as *Unveiling The Hidden Instinct* and also the *Overriding The Extinction Scenario* books. See books by Angela Brownemiller on DrAngela.com and Amazon.com for more information.

Fine tuning our *personal transition awareness* has to include sensitizing ourselves to the presence and the power of the attachments we and others around us form. Attachments are sometimes short lived and are frequently long lived. Indeed, most attachment cordings seek to continue being attached. This makes sense as this is the nature of attachment, to be attached and to remain attached in some way.

THE CONCEPT OF DEATH AS TRANSITION

Transition is both the ending or death of some or all of a pattern, and the ongoing existence/life after the ending or death of some or all of that pattern.

This concept of death allows us to consider what it means to die in terms of what it means to break free of attachment. Therefore, Reader, understand that considering the following is not dying. This is simply exploring the matter of attachment release in transition, in in-life and seeming end-of-life as well as possible life after life experiences.

What can take place following the recognition and even partial or total release of attachment during transitions is important to recognize, to be conscious of. So let's further consider this matter here....

THE DRIVE TO RECONNECT
AFTER RELEASING THE CONNECTION

Let's say for a moment you are actually physically dying, and that you are releasing physical and emotional attachments in the process. After you have detected the networks of cords with which you have surrounded yourself, and which others have connected to you; after you have released some or all of those cords, those attachments—the obvious attachments as well as the subtle energy attachments, and the subtle and obvious social energy attachments; there is something more you must do if you are actually dying a physical death: you must avoid primary reconnection.

In order to avoid primary reconnection, you must be aware of not only what reconnection looks like, but how the first reconnection feels. You will remember the information offered here at the times you need it.[66]

SEE RECONNECTION FORMING

It may seem premature to have to concern yourself with the problem of reconnection so soon after you begin to manage *detachment, release, and full letting go*. However, the tempo of dying may require your immediate sensitivity to matters of incidental and purposive reconnection pushes (and pulls). You *can* be ready to deal with reconnection as soon as it begins. You already have the necessary awareness and alertness.

Looking back to what you are moving away from, you *can* see with your inner eye, the many networks of cords, the overall web you and others around you have woven. You can see each of the bits, the pieces of energy, out of which each cord is formed. This *acuity of inner vision* comes with concentration, and with the giving of permission to your

---

[66] See also *Volume 9* in this *Keys To Consciousness And Survival Series*, titled, *Navigating Life's Stuff, Part Two*, for more on the journey post release of attachments.

imagination to lead the way. "Fake it till you make it" takes on new meaning here.

Similarly, as you move forward, you can detect even the first hints of the reconnection process and effects. You can see the first bits of the energy collecting around the attachment points. You can see the early signs of re-cording trends. Once you use your inner eye to see this, you know. If your inner eye is still closed, you can manage to know by being alert to subtle sensations which alert you to the hooking in of cords seeking re-establishment.

NOTE KEY RECONNECT HOOKS

Reconnection efforts can appear before you leave your physical body as well as after. Living deaths and transitions such as divorces, job terminations, major moves, in themselves are prime in-life targets for reconnection.

While you are still in your physical body, the spots that have been de-corded may hunger for the attachments that have been lost. If the spots have not been sealed, they are vulnerable, at times like vacuums sucking in similar or the same hooks. Sealing the door to reconnection is not possible when a full, clean release has not been possible or accomplished or wanted. (Usually, in physical lifetimes, it is wise to be careful what we choose to partially and or entirely release. De-cording processes must be conducted with as great an awareness as must be present in any process of transition.)

There are points on the physical body most likely to be re-hooked to old cords. These are the heart, the throat, the solar plexus, the lower abdomen, the genital area.

There are also points on the emotional body most likely to hook to old cords. These are points through which old emotional cords traveled and pulled in emotional energy. These are special points in the emotional body to be very aware of, because these are points where the cords of others were once deeply rooted or are still attached.

Living transitions and deaths such as divorce and job loss are in a sense preliminary transitions, deaths. These are exercises in detaching. Preliminary death is practice for physical death. Keep in mind that physical death has three stages. The actual physical *body death* is the first stage of death. The process of detaching is the emotional death, the second stage of physical death. (Other books in this *Keys To Consciousness And Survival Series* address the third death, the mental body death, and note that this death is optional. This matter is key in understanding one's survival options. See *Volume 10* in this series, *Seeing Beyond Our Line Of Sight*.)

Those who do not recognize that one must continue to release cords throughout the second stage of death—emotional death—may enter it confused or maybe fearful, angry, or otherwise uncomfortable, and needlessly waste their own energy. They may waste their energy struggling in the remains of the web woven during life, while they are releasing some cords, hungering to reconnect some released cords, scrambling to do something with the attachment network while not realizing what is going on.

Whether it be a preliminary partial emotional death such as divorce or the more complete physical-emotional body death, you may find yourself in such a morass of confused energy. When you do, focus on the chant:

- **Light up.**
- **Deconstruct.**
- **Transmute to the idea of highest Light.**

Any faint hint of reconnection must be immediately addressed this way. Focus on the initial re-rooting. Then Light up, deconstruct, and transmute to the highest Light any cordings that may hinder a healthy transition.

You are not the only cause of reconnection. So many beings and energies from your old life may seek to stay corded with or to you. Once you have decided to move on, to transit out of your old life or body, you may be pulled back by the longings of others.

Regardless of your perceptions of the intentions of those who seek to reconnect or remain connected even in the face of your profound release of all attachment, you must hold to your own personal consciousness, to who you actually are. And, you must know your own free Will so as to differentiate who you are, and what your own free Will is, from others who would like to subsume you.

EXERCISE #20.1
DETECTING RECONNECTION

Visualize yourself sitting across from someone that you do not know at all. Tell yourself, even though you do not know this person, you did once know this person, you just have no ready memory of this person.

Now visualize this person attempting to form an attachment to you.

See the pieces of a cord moving toward you from its roots in the heart or the solar plexus, stomach area, groin, forehead, throat (or whatever location you choose), of that person whom you do not know.

Forming in the air, once it is rooted in that person, the cord grows from that person in your direction, becoming a longer and longer and stronger and stronger cord.

As it nears you, you begin to feel the roots of the cord reaching ahead of itself trying to root in you.

See clearly where that cord seeks to attach to you. Notice how you respond.

<u>EXERCISE #20.2</u>
AVOIDING AND DETERRING
THE RE-CORDINGS OF OTHERS

Return to where you were when you ended the previous exercise, Exercise #20.1. The cord approaches you, seeking to reconnect.

Create an invisible but very strong boundary or force field through which that cord cannot penetrate. See that cord trying to penetrate, finding ways around the shield and see that you beat the cord at every corner, at every attempt, with your perfect shield not allowing that cord in, no matter how valiant its efforts.

Close your eyes and feel entirely encased in your own SELF-designed protective shield. Hold for next exercise.

EXERCISE #20.3
TRANSMUTING RECONNECTING CORDS TO LIGHT

You are safe behind your shield. So now: Light up, deconstruct, and transmute the bits of reforming cords. Catch these reforming cords as early as possible—in the space between your consciousness and the consciousness connected to the other end of these cords.

21
Willing the Exit From the Flesh: LEAP Level Three

> A season is set for everything, a time for every experience under heaven: A time for being born and a time for dying . . .
>
> *Ecclesiastes, 3*
> *Tanakh*
> *The Holy Scriptures*

You have learned a great deal from all you have done this lifetime (and perhaps for some of you, according to your own belief systems, other lifetimes). And now, you know. Somehow you know you know. Still, what you know may not be entirely clear. At least not yet.

Still, there comes a time when on some level some part of you knows. Of course, what you know, and how you know, differs for each of us.

WHATEVER DIE MEANS TO YOU, SURVIVE THIS

Once you know that it is time for you to die, whatever die means to you, you sense this. You sense that perhaps hanging on to your old attachments may render you not yourself but instead a deteriorating museum of yourself. As the SELF you can preserve through transition is the personal consciousness, **preserving this SELF is in essence the actual survival**.

You may sense that perhaps you must now let go to live, release some of the web you have woven.

The words in this volume encourage you to embrace the meanings and learnings in your changes, endings, transitions, and deaths. They also encourage you to sense your own idea of the highest purest ideal, the highest purest energy or Light. They also encourage you to finely tune your awareness of the energy networks, webs of attachment and cordings.

The words in this book also ask you to turn, at least from time to time, your eye toward the **beyond.**[67]

What is the beyond? The question is, what is your beyond, what do you want to create for yourself? This beyond is nothing absolute, and can for you be a continuously developing awareness, concept, and place. The beyond is, simply, beyond where you are now.

The beyond, your beyond, is your creation, what your personal consciousness generates for you.

LEAP
OUT

---

[67] Refer to another book in this series, *Seeing Beyond Our Line Of Sight*, for a close look at this matter.

Let's return to the matter of attachments. Clearly, just *wanting* to release attachments and cords may not fuel the exit from the body or from the life style you have been wearing. What is required is a great LEAP out. Understanding the nature of the LEAP is something you must do on all levels of your existence.[68] This LEAP, this LIGHT-ENERGY-ACTION-PROCESS as defined in several books in this *Keys To Consciousness And Survival Series*, is both a state of mind and a process of the personal consciousness.

Essential in making the LEAP out of the flesh of one's old life is the will to make this LEAP. Again, the use of Will is relevant to this examination of the LEAP involved in in-life and seeming end-of-life, as well as possible life after life, changes, transitions, and deaths.

Rarely, when busy living a life, does one think about the Will to leave that life when it is time, in a healthy and conscious way.

At a particular time in any death process, the effectiveness of the process is enhanced by the injection of focus and energy produced by the Will. Being sensitive to the presence of one's Free Will is the first step in its application.

WILL THE EXIT

What does it mean to Will the exit? To apply one's Will this way is to focus the Will in such a concentrated way that the exit from the phase of life or physical body is facilitated, even

---

[68] See also another book is this series for discussion of this LEAP, as in the book, *Unveiling The Hidden Instinct*.

eased. *Strength of Will* certainly empowers the consciousness to move through and beyond the exit. And, the strength involved in aware transitions can be garnered with exercise and practice, even in everyday life.

If, however, you feel that you do not have time to build up your Will before you undergo a transition or even a death, you can rely on your natural deeply embedded *clarity of Will*, once you know this is present within you. With a clear intent and Will to exit, the passage is eased and the leaps involved are facilitated. This is a basic principle of this *transition and death consciousness technology*.

Clarity *is* strength—clarity is the most immediate entry into strength. Think of a very strong, heavy pair of scissors. The scissors must be strong and heavy enough not to break when cutting something thick.

Think of the sharpness of the scissors as clarity. A very sharp pair of scissors cuts through heavy material as well as or better than strong but dull scissors. The sharp scissors were sharpened with the clear intent to cut well. Your Will can be this sharp by declaring your intent to be this sharp. Get to know your Will as you live.

EXERCISE #21.1
FINDING THE WILL, YOUR WILL

We have talked again and again about the right use of Will and the nature of one's Will. Now you will feel for yourself your own Will.

Begin to look for your Will. Will that you find your Will. How does willing feel? You are isolating the essence of your Will. This

Exercise generates a refinement of your Will by asking you to locate your Will. Seeking the Will defines it, refines it.

Close your eyes, go inside, and take some time to find your Will. Your own personal force of Will is your own to define and to know, even to generate and develop.

Realize that your Will is not your relationship to the outside world, not your list of responsibilities, not your set of accomplishments, not your failures, not your feelings, not your attachments or cords, not your family, not your political party, not your philosophical beliefs, not your religion.

Now you are locating your own personal Free Will, its essence, its reality.

Once you have found your Will or what you sense is your Will, continue refining your connection to your Will. Feel as if you are getting to better know your Will.

Hold your concentration on your Will for the next exercise. As you hold, get to know better what "Will" really is. Define your own force of Will for yourself.

EXERCISE #21.2
WILLING THE EXIT

Take your Will into your forehead. Now move your Will to the center of the top of your head.

Now, as if you are pushing on something very hard, with all your Will, push your SELF out the top of your head: Will yourself out of your body.

Hold your Will outside your body, above your head, for a while.

. . . . . .

Now, focus on this Will of yours—the Will you have come to recognize. Move this Will back down to the top of your head. Pull your Will back into your body through the top of your head.

****

Readers, congratulations. You have now completed the first part of this *How To Die And Survive* set of books, audiobooks, ebooks, and their exercises and discussions.

This is just the beginning of this journey. From here, we can move ever more deeply into what all this means. We can see more about how we can apply all this in our daily lives, as well as in our seeming end-of-life and even what may be after-life transitions.

Every moment of our lives, we are already reaching BEYOND. We are already opening to new ways of understanding who we are and where we are going.

STAY TUNED.

THE LIFE FORCE DOES NOT DIE.
YOU DO NOT DIE.

NOW EXPLORE NEXT LEVELS, SEE ...
Ideas, concepts, and exercises in greater depth.
Take this journey to levels beyond.
See ever more deeply into this
Consideration of survival:
What survival means,
What practices can develop this survival,
What awareness-es we can expand upon,
And more....

**LEARN MORE ABOUT SURVIVAL POTENTIAL,
LIFE AFTER LIFE CONCEPTS,
AND
NAVIGATION BEYOND.**

****

STAY TUNED FOR THE NEXT

How To Die And Survive Book.

Read and experience the increasingly profound Understandings in:

How To Die And Survive, Book Two

See
Drangela.com
And
Amazon.com

Readers are also encouraged to see
other books in this
KEYS TO
CONSCIOUSNESS AND SURVIVAL SERIES
and in the METATERRA CHRONICLES
COLLECTION,
also written by
ANGELA BROWNEMILLER.
(Note the spelling of the author's last name is
B-r-o-w-n-E-m-i-L-L-e-r)
See Amazon.com and Audible.com and also
DrAngela.com
for books by Angela Brownemiller, listed there under
her name,
Angela Brownemiller.

All blessings to you, our Readers,
on your beautiful and brave journeys
both here and BEYOND.

Dr. Angela Brownemiller, Author
and
Kelly A. Thomas, Audiobook Narrator

APPENDICES

BOOKLIST AND RECOMMENDED READING
Keys To Consciousness And Survival Series
By Dr. Angela Brownemiller

Volume 11
How to Die and Survive, Book Two:
Extending Our Interdimensional Awareness

Volume 10
Seeing Beyond Our Line of Sight:
Consciously Moving Through Life's Changes, Transitions, and Deaths

Volume 9
Navigating Life's Stuff – Dynamics of Personal Change, Book Two:
Keys to Consciously Moving Through Our Processes and Their Patterns

Volume 8
Navigating Life's Stuff – Dynamics of Personal Change, Book One:
Sensitizing to and Navigating Our Patterns and Their Processes

Volume 7
The Go Conscious Process:
Steps and Practices for Heightening Conscious Awareness,
Shifts, Transmigrations of Focus, LEAPS OF SELF

Volume 6
Overriding the Extinction Scenario, Part Two:
Raising the Bar on the Evolution of the Human Species

Volume 5
Overriding the Extinction Scenario, Part One:
Detecting the Bar on the Evolution of the Human Species

Volume 4
How to Die and Survive:
Interdimensional Psychology, Consciousness,
And Survival: Concepts for Living and Dying

Volume 3
Unveiling the Hidden Instinct:
Understanding Our Interdimensional Survival Awareness

Volume 2:
Keys to Self:
Your Next Steps to YOU

Volume 1:
Keys to Personal Discovery

BOOKLIST AND RECOMMENDED READING
Continued....

Ask Dr. Angela Series
Dr. Angela Brownemiller

The Bloodwin Code (Episode Books 1,2,3,4, and 5)
Dr. Angela Brownemiller

Transcending Addiction
Dr. Angela Brownemiller

Gestalting Addiction
Dr. Angela Brownemiller

Contact us for information on the special
Science Fiction Series
On these consciousness and survival topics.
Email:

Drangela@drangela.com

Note:
These books should be listed on Amazon.com and numerous other book distributor websites. If not finding these books on these sites and or in book stores, request these bookstores order these books, and or contact Amazon.com or Metaterra® Publications at Metaterra.com and/or drangela@drangela.com or the author, Dr. Angela Brownemiller. Check also under last name, Browne-Miller. Thank you.

GET THE TRUTH ABOUT ADDICTION
Life-changing insights into the reality of
Patterns, habits, addictions, and obsessions
Operating in our lives and minds.

Now in powerfully narrated AUDIOBOOK
As well as PAPERBACK and EBOOK forms!

SEEING THE HIDDEN FACE OF ADDICTION

Detecting and Confronting This Invasive Presence

Dr. Angela Brownemiller

SEEING THE HIDDEN FACE OF ADDICTION
Can be found on Amazon.com
And at drangela.com

VOLUMES 9 & 10 in the
KEYS TO CONSCIOUSNESS AND SURVIVAL SERIES

Can we better understand the journeys we travel through in our lives? Can we detect and work with the patterns and processes we are forming, living within, and moving through? How much can we see about the patterns we form, and sometimes feel we cannot change, are caught in? How do we sensitize ourselves to the patterning processes we are engaged in? Find your way through the maze of life. See:

NAVIGATING LIFE'S STUFF:
DYNAMICS OF PERSONAL CHANGE, Book One
Seeing Our Processes and Their Patterns

NAVIGATING LIFE'S STUFF:
DYNAMICS OF PERSONAL CHANGE, Book Two
Keys to Consciously Moving Through
Our Passages and Their Patterns

Now in Paperback, Audiobook, and Ebook forms.
Find these and other books by Dr. Angela Brownemiller
On Amazon.com and at drangela.com

Volumes 4 and 11 in the
KEYS TO CONSCIOUSNESS AND SURVIVAL SERIES
HOW TO DIE AND SURVIVE. Book One
See also HOW TO DIE AND SURVIVE, Book Two
By Dr. Angela Brownemiller

YOUR RIGHT TO KNOW IS CLEAR. These far reaching, and life changing, books offer new ways of understanding ourselves and our lives. The author details progressive understandings and practices for moving into multi- and inter- dimensional consciousness and survival skills. Through use of metaphor, this author guides readers through: her progressive "shift" awarenesses; through leaps in understanding her sequential "shift technologies" by means of concepts, processes, and exercises contained in the chapters of these books. These exercises begin quite simply and carefully build toward some very esoteric understandings. ... These books overcome limits to old models of what we are, who we are, and where we can be and go. Ultimately, this is an exploration of the infinite potential of our consciousness. Join us for the journey of your lifetime, or all your/our lifetimes.

Volume 3 in this
KEYS TO CONSCIOUSNESS AND SURVIVAL SERIES
UNVEILING THE HIDDEN INSTINCT
By Dr. Angela Brownemiller

Every day, we are presented with minor and major opportunities, reasons, even needs, to understand the nature of transitioning, shifting, from one state of mind, one way of being, one way of seeing the world, from one reality to another. In this sense, we are frequently calling upon ourselves to shift ourselves and our consciousness-es from one dimension of ourselves to another. At times, we may even sense that our well-being, perhaps even our survival, depends upon such a shift. ... Should we at some point find the survival level need to shift ourselves across ways of seeing the world, realities, dimensions, even perhaps from physical to non-physical and back, it is essential we have at least already considered the concepts involved. This book introduces, via metaphor, minor and major shift awareness-es, making these understandings accessible to us should we need these for everyday challenges as well as potentially profound survival reasons.

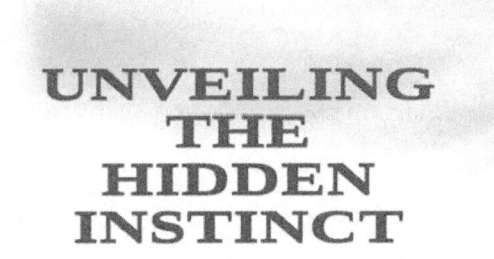

UNVEILING THE HIDDEN INSTINCT

Understanding Our
Interdimensional Survival Awareness

Dr. Angela Brownemiller
METATERRA®
PUBLICATIONS

VOLUME 10 IN THIS
KEYS TO CONSCIOUSNESS AND SURVIVAL SERIES
SEEING BEYOND OUR LINE OF SIGHT
By Dr. Angela Brownemiller

SEEING BEYOND OUR LINE OF SIGHT: CONSCIOUSLY MOVING THROUGH LIFE'S CHANGES, TRANSITIONS, AND DEATHS ... is a simple yet profound book offering subtle yet major shifts in the way we think about changes, transitions, endings, and deaths. Here, we can see that we have the capability of holding and empowering our conscious selves as we move through events, changes, transitions, even emotional, even physical, death processes. ... The journey this book takes us on opens doors to finding our way through challenging, trying, even very difficult, events and passages in our lives. ... That we can survive is central as we undergo all minor and major transitions in our lives. ... Find yourself, know yourself, guide yourself through the minor and major transition and death processes you face during your life. You can define who and what you are for yourself. You can open this option in your mind, the option that you can develop this knowledge of yourself, and then carry this knowledge of yourself through this life, and perhaps also on beyond this lifetime.

SEEING BEYOND OUR LINE OF SIGHT
Consciously Moving Through
Life's Changes, Transitions, And Deaths

Angela Brownemiller
METATERRA® PUBLICATIONS

AUTHOR CONTACT

Www.drangela.com

For
Paperback, Audiobook, and Ebook
Versions of this and other books
By this author
Angela Brownemiller
See
Www.Amazon.com

ABOUT THIS BOOK

HOW TO DIE AND SURVIVE, Book One
INTERDIMENSIONAL PSYCHOLOGY, CONSCIOUSNESS, AND SURVIVAL:
CONCEPTS FOR LIVING AND DYING
Volume 4, KEYS TO CONSCIOUSNESS AND SURVIVAL SERIES
By Dr. Angela Brownemiller
Narrated by Kelly A Thomas

YOUR RIGHT TO KNOW IS CLEAR. Tap into the light, into the idea of light, coming in from higher dimensions of yourself, of your universe, of your reality. Let this feel for light filter into your awareness.

Take your actual power back by seeing what is actually here for you, by tapping into the inspiring, transformational, and catalytic forces available to you. SEE and fuel the LEAP in your awareness, in your consciousness, even in your energy structure, that you can make to survive a profound change, shift in reality, end of cycle, any in-life transition -- or even any seeming end-of-life transition, or what may be a so-called "death."

After all, endings, even deaths, are what we understand and define these as being.

Here on the pages of *How To Die And Survive, Book One* are *Concepts For Living And Dying*. This book is a manual on states of mind relevant to actual survival. Through use of metaphor, this author guides readers through: her progressive "shift" awareness-es; through leaps in understanding her sequential "shift technologies" by means of concepts, processes, and exercises contained in the chapters of this book.

These exercises begin quite simply and carefully build toward some very esoteric understandings which then continue in *How To Die And Survive, Book Two*. The exercises contained in these *How To Die And Survive* books are designed for use by most everyone, regardless of age, belief system, experience, and health. Should any exercise require a physical activity (such as sitting, standing, or reaching) that one finds difficult or inconvenient to do, just imagine one is doing the exercise. For purposes of these exercises, the mind thinking through these motions is tantamount to performing these motions. Mental circuitry is exercised either way.

This book overcomes limits to old models of what we are, who we are, and where we can be and go. Ultimately, this is an exploration of the potential of our consciousness.

This is Volume Four in the *Keys To Consciousness And Survival Series* written by Dr. Angela Brownemiller. See drangela.com for more information. A publication of Metaterra. The voices of Metaterra are speaking.

ABOUT THE AUTHOR
Author, KEYS TO CONSCIOUSNESS AND SURVIVAL SERIES
Author, METATERRA CHRONICLES SERIES

Dr. Angela Brownemiller, also known as Dr. Angela®, is an author, journalist, social thinker, clinician, psychotherapist, trainer, speaker, and creator of the *Ask Dr. Angela®* Series of broadcasts, podcasts, books, audiobooks, Ebooks, and programs. The views of Angela Brownemiller are centered on the great potential of the human mind, heart, and soul, and on the rights of all of us, who and whatever we are (or think we are). Dr. Angela Brownemiller views the human consciousness as a wealth of opportunity for exploration, insight, knowledge—and survival. For more information on her mind-body-spirit-consciousness and other work, see drangela.com.

The works of Angela Brownemiller are brought to you by:
METATERRA® PUBLICATIONS
(and numerous other publishers, see **Amazon.com**).
For copies of print books, audiobooks, and ebooks by this author,
See Amazon.com, or contact us at **www.drangela.com**
To take part in our events and workshops, and or
For personal consultations in person or by telephone or online,
Contact us at **www.drangela.com**

Made in the USA
Middletown, DE
17 January 2025